The Kitchen We Keep

Stephanie Nelson

Threefold Ink

For the two "T"s in my life.

Author's note

I've opted to use a version of Sicilian dialect throughout this book to stay true to the characters' heritage with translations when necessary. Please be aware that it looks and reads differently from traditional Italian. Guditillu! *Enjoy!*

Chapter 1

Summer 1960

Heat from the stoves hovered in the air like a dense fog. Sweat dripped down my spine, pooling at the edge of my apron, but I didn't stop. I couldn't. The dining room still buzzed with clinking glasses and demands for more bread from hungry customers waiting for their pasta.

"Joe!" I shouted, turning from the row of ovens with the last pan of bubbling lasagna. "Your tortellini are exploding. Dump them out and get another pot on fast!"

Startled, he whipped his head down to the large pot of boiling water in front of him, lips forming an "O" as the cheese floated among broken tortellini shells.

The line cooks had entered what I liked to call "the twilight zone" of the evening, when they either ran on muscle memory or flamed out. But tonight, flaming out wasn't an option. I demanded focus. I didn't care if it came from muscle memory or pure brute strength.

Rounding the counter to slice the hot lasagna, I gave Joe an encouraging pat on the back. As our newest member of the team, he deserved some slack after working five evenings in a row, plus a few lunch shifts. That's where my generosity and encouragement ended, though. I might have been the only woman in the kitchen, but I refused to mother them.

"Go easy on him," my father whispered in my ear as he walked past, pushing open the swinging doors into the dining room to greet the latest wave of customers.

My father, Marco, lived for Friday and Saturday nights, for the hustle, the chaos, the full dining room. It was where he came most alive and most himself. Of course, it was a family affair, running this restaurant. My mother, my two sisters, and I spent most of our time here when we weren't at school or doing house chores. We'd greet, seat, and cook for the cast of regulars who frequented this place, which my father opened over twenty years ago.

It wasn't only us, though. As Cucina Bella gained popularity, my father had to hire a small staff to accommodate the steady growth that came with being one of the few authentic Sicilian restaurants on the west side of Chicago. Sure, there were many *Italian* places. More opened each year. But Cucina Bella was the oldest and only place to get a true *Sicilian* meal outside of Little Sicily.

From my post in the kitchen, I heard my father greet the DeLano family with a hearty, "Bon vinutu!" *Welcome.* I imagined him grabbing Mr. DeLano around the shoulder while pecking a quick kiss on Mrs. DeLano's cheek before placing the customary breadbasket on their table, the one nearest the kitchen, which my mother reserved for them each Friday.

"Someone needs to bus the four-tops in the back!" My father yelled as he barreled up to the pass to collect the next round of plates to be served.

"Not me!" shouted Jessy from the sink, covered in soap from his elbows down as he scrubbed the tomato sauce from the endless pile of dirty dishes.

I rolled my eyes.

It had only been a week since my father tentatively turned over the kitchen operations to me, and the last thing I wanted to do was leave my post as chef. In the *kitchen*. Not as front-of-house staff, where most people, my mother included, thought I "should" be.

If you asked any Italian woman over the age of thirty living on the west side of Chicago, women didn't belong in a restaurant kitchen. Sure, they cooked meals fit for the aristocracy in the privacy of their own homes, as most good Italian women did, but not for money. Oh no, the shame! That was a man's job.

My mother didn't bother hiding her feelings about my ambitions to cook professionally, either. I often caught her tsk-ing and shaking her head when she saw me in my work apron, hair pulled back, yet somehow still a mess. I might have been one of the only nineteen-year-old female chefs this side of the Mississippi, but it was 1960. Times were supposed to be changing. And one day, if everything went according to *my* plan, I would be the one running this place and possibly even others. Other girls had chosen to attend college or to get married right after graduation, but neither of those options appealed to me. Despite bringing home decent grades, I'd never been very studious. My mind and heart had always been in the kitchen.

I wiped my hands on my splattered apron, untied it and smoothed my unruly dark brown curls back into a tight bun before heading out to clear the tables. A blessed blast of chilled air hit me as I stepped out of the kitchen, cooling the sweat beads that still dripped down my back.

I scanned the room. No sign of *him*. I let myself relax too soon, but I needed a moment. With a deep inhale, the familiar scent of fresh bread and our signature sauce filled my nostrils.

"When are we getting a new busboy?" I murmured to my father as we brushed shoulders in the crowded dining room.

"Too good to clean a few tables now, huh?" he said, face cracking into his famous toothy grin.

We went through busboys like paper towels, often and unceremoniously. In truth, I loved witnessing people connect over the food we cooked, and I didn't get to see it often since I'd been promoted, so spending a few minutes in the dining room wasn't all bad.

Most people wouldn't think much of Cucina Bella if they came in off the street. It had that well-worn look of a place that had stayed the same even in the face of massive, mostly unwelcome, change in the city.

Red-and-white checkered tablecloths draped over every table, and the wood-paneled walls were full of photos from around the tight-knit community and various famous people who had visited, all in mismatched frames. But what newcomers couldn't see was the neighborhood that gathered here throughout the week. The families who had brought their children who had grown alongside me and my siblings, some starting families of their own.

Tonight was no different—except it was getting late, which meant the customers would either leave soon or get rowdy.

Out of the corner of my eye, I noticed the Buccatti brothers sitting in the corner booth with three empty wine bottles scattered on the table. "Sitting" wasn't the right word, because all four of them were talking over one another while gesturing so intensely that their behinds weren't even touching the padded benches. While I took this as a sign we were in for a full night, a sense of comfort swept over me as I stacked the dirty plates on top of one another, balancing them on my arm.

This place had been home to me. Here, I understood who I was and who I wanted to be.

Navigating between the tables to take the dishes back to Jessy was tricky since a few of the tables' candles had gone out. I'd liked to have said the dining room was intentionally dark, with only the handful of small gas chandeliers original to the building flickering above giving it an intimate glow, but in truth, my father had never gotten around to updating them.

It was almost last call for food, so I gave myself permission to relax a little. No more large orders to fire up tonight. Before reaching the kitchen, I spotted Anthony Russo at the host stand, standing tall and clean-cut in his blue and white striped button-down shirt tucked into his brown trousers, hair combed and gelled to one side.

I let out a heavy sigh. No one could say he wasn't conventionally handsome.

I ducked through the swinging doors, out of sight, but not far enough that I couldn't overhear my mother greet him with an upturned falsetto in her voice.

"Bonasera," *good evening*, my mother greeted him. "Great to see you. Would you like a table?" she asked.

"Good evening, Mrs. Bianchi. If it's not too late. Rosa working tonight?"

I rolled my eyes. Of course, he was looking for me. I'd been dodging him for two days.

"Sure is, dear. I'll let her know you're here." I could tell by the tone of her voice she was giving him her brightest smile, the one rarely bestowed upon her children.

My mother wanted nothing more than for me to marry Anthony and pop out two small children in quick succession. It had been her goal since I graduated high school that summer. Get me out of the house and squash my dreams all in one blow. Very convenient for her. Very depressing for me.

I saw Anthony's appeal. He was the most eligible bachelor in our small Italian community, descending from a decent Catholic, church-going family that owned a large wine distribution company. I'd never have to work another day in my life. But that was the problem: I wanted to work. I wanted to cook. Nothing else mattered.

Not to mention, Anthony was a notorious ladies' man. He had broken more than a few hearts over the years, moving from one girl to the next in a quick succession. Although for men, that wasn't a bad thing. Not so much the other way around.

Anthony and I had grown up playing hopscotch and climbing trees together in the city park. Our mothers had been good friends since they were young girls, and I wouldn't have doubted it if they'd had our union planned from birth—a much-used punchline between our families.

Anthony and I used to brush it off, laughing at the ridiculousness of it, but that had changed. It went from being a playful joke to being a real possibility almost overnight.

And a few days ago, while taking one of our usual strolls through the neighborhood park behind my house after the restaurant closed, Ant had stopped and laced his fingers through mine. I let out a small giggle at the gesture.

"I've been meaning to talk to you about this for some time now," he said, looking at me. I straightened my back. "We're not kids anymore, Rosa. You mean a lot to me. And I know it drives you crazy when our families tease us about being together. But maybe…" he said, looking at his feet. "Maybe they're on to something?"

I blinked at him, not comprehending his words.

"You don't really think that's a good idea, Ant. Do you?" Ant was the nickname I had given him back when we were in kindergarten.

"I'm serious, Rosa. We make sense together. Lord knows I've dated enough girls to know."

I slapped his shoulder. "That's the truth."

"Well, what do you say, then? Should we give it a go?"

I must have looked like a deer in headlights because he took a small step back before regaining his composure.

A bubble of laughter escaped from me. He had to be joking.

Ant let go of my hand, and a shadow crossed his features as he looked off into the trees lining the sidewalk. I took a small step toward him.

"I'm sorry. You caught me off guard. I thought you were kidding."

"I'm serious, Rosa. Will you think about it?"

I nodded and turned away to walk home, determined to end the conversation before it got more awkward. Until then, I'd given no serious thought to us being more than friends. It had been nothing more than an inside joke between our families. Or so I thought.

Somehow, I'd avoided him for days afterwards. But tonight, he'd caught up with me. Even after losing sleep over our conversation, I still didn't have a confident answer for him. Before I even set down the tray of dirty plates and cups, my sister Camille grabbed my arm and pulled me into the walk-in refrigerator.

"Why is Ant here looking for you? You haven't talked to him yet?" she asked, face so close to mine I could smell her lilac perfume.

"No. I haven't had the time. Plus, I don't know what to say yet."

"Tell him, 'Yes, I'll marry you and have your gorgeous babies.'"

"I can't say that! It's Ant. How do I even look at him as anything other than the boy who chased me around the park with a dead frog when we were eight?"

"Are you blind? Open your eyes. Any girl on this side of the city would faint on the spot if Anthony Russo asked them to go steady."

"Yes, and I'll end up like every one of them: brokenhearted," I argued.

"Ant won't do that to you. He's been in love with you since you both were kids. You're just too oblivious to see it." She threw a dish rag over my head.

I love my sister. I do. But she was every bit the love-struck cliché of a teenage girl. The hopeless romantic in her had been rooting for me and Anthony to get together ever since it was appropriate to talk about. Plus, Camille had been pining for Anthony's best friend, Jackson, for years. This would be one step closer in her master plan to marry him.

"I'll talk to him tonight, after we close," I said.

"Don't make him wait too long. You might lose your chance."

"I thought you said he was in love with me?" I narrowed my eyes at her.

"Ugh. I can't see why," she joked, tossing her hands in the air.

To my surprise, Ant wasn't anywhere to be seen once I finished closing the kitchen for the evening. I expected to find him waiting for me in one of the front booths, as he'd done many times, but only Camille sat in the now dim dining room, writing in her journal under candlelight.

"Everyone go home?" I asked.

Camille glanced up from her notebook, squinting her eyes through the dark to find me. "Looks like it. Pa told me to wait for you. Anthony left a few minutes ago. He looked exhausted."

A twinge of guilt fluttered in my stomach. If I had lost sleep since our last conversation, Ant likely had, too. I owed him a conversation.

"Guess I'll have to catch him tomorrow. Ready to go?"

"Sure. I'll walk you back home."

"You'll walk me home? You're not coming with?" I asked with a hint of suspicion. Friday nights often ended with Camille sneaking out of the house to meet up with friends.

"Oh, come on, Rosa. Please cover for me. The girls are going to a dance tonight, and rumor has it, Jackson's going to be there!"

"Ma will have your backside if she finds out."

"Well, it's a good thing she won't find out! I'll be back in bed by midnight, promise." She extended her pinky finger as I placed my hands on the worn table between us.

I couldn't say no to her. Only a year younger, but always my baby sister, I would have done anything for Camille. I often worried that one day she'd take her rebellious side too far.

"Fine. But please be careful. And no drinking. I smelled it on you last time. You're lucky Ma didn't catch you before you showered in the morning."

"I'm already eighteen. If the law says it's okay, so should Ma and Pa."

"When Ma and Pa care about what the city of Chicago says is okay, you'll see pigs flying," I said, smoothing my hair again. "If you stay home, I'll sneak a bottle of wine from the cellar into our room," I tried as a last attempt to keep her out of trouble.

She returned a long, sideways glance. We both knew I'd get two sips in and fall asleep, like last time.

After locking up and heading out for the night, we spotted Anthony sitting on a bench under the lamppost on the opposite side of the street. Camille gave my hand a small squeeze.

"Midnight, I promise," she said before darting off into the dark.

I drew in a steadying breath as I made my way to the bench where he sat, all shadows and highlights from the bright fluorescence. Even here in this harsh lighting, he looked handsome. As I settled next to him, his knee bumped against mine, but neither of us bothered to move.

"Hi," I said, the sound feeling rough on my throat.

The hum of the lamppost vibrated above us, where dozens of small bugs hovered near the light.

"Are you avoiding me?" he asked.

"Yes and no," I answered, tilting my head to the side. "I planned to talk to you tonight after closing, but you left."

"I felt silly waiting around."

"Ahh, yes. The ladies' man isn't used to having to wait."

"That's not fair," he said, jerking his head toward me.

I didn't correct him, but it was in fact fair. Anthony Russo had never had to wait for a girl.

That's how I knew he was serious about what he had said to me a few days ago. I wanted to respect that, but I was feeling like a fish out of water. I'd never gone steady with a boy. Of the two dates I'd been on, my mother had arranged both in the company of an adult chaperone. Ironically, the only boy I'd ever been alone with was Ant.

"Okay. I'm not sure what to say, though," I said, staring down at my tired work shoes.

"Tell me what you're thinking. Be honest."

"Are you sure this isn't just our parents talking? Have they finally worn you down?" I realized it had been a large part of my fear all along.

We locked eyes for a long moment, and my heart rate sped up, hammering in my chest. I prayed he couldn't see the flush creeping up my neck. No one had ever looked at me the way he did in that moment, and it was nearly impossible to endure the intensity. When I glanced down at our feet, Ant drew his hand up to my chin, gently guiding my head back to him.

For a long moment, we stayed that way. Ant holding my face in his hand until he leaned forward, resting his forehead against mine. The fragrance of his distinctive cologne, allspice and pine, swirled, making me lightheaded. It was either that or the unfamiliar sensations coursing through my body. I had a clear path to my future, one that included cooking and running Cucina Bella. Was there room for a relationship with Ant, too?

Before I could work it out, his warm lips closed over mine in a tentative, soft movement, sending a shiver down the back of my neck. My breath caught in my throat, but I didn't want him to stop. On instinct, I leaned in. Ant brought his other hand up to caress the side of my face, letting a low noise slip from his throat as our bodies pushed together on the bench.

If this was what kissing always felt like, I finally understood why girls went boy-crazy. Being that close to Ant awakened every part of my body, sending sparks all the way through my fingertips when I laid my hands on his chest. As the kiss deepened, I melted into the comfort and familiarity of my best friend.

Little did I know it would tip my entire world off balance.

Chapter 2

June 1961, a year later

"Let's go, Camille. We're going to be late, again," I huffed as I watched my sister swipe another coat of stain over her already candy-apple red lips.

"Okay, okay! They're not even here yet. Calm down."

"Yes, but Ma and Pa might get back any second. They'll have my head for taking you out when you're supposed to be with your study group."

"They know full well I will not be studying tonight," she said to me in the mirror with a tilt of her head.

"I'm sure they do, but we don't need to give them a reason to punish either of us by reminding them. I'll meet you downstairs. If you're not ready when the boys arrive, we're leaving without you."

I'd wait for her. No matter how long it took. And she knew it too. We showed up for each other. No excuses. It had been like that since we were little girls. Over the years, we leaned into the comfort of having a built-in best friend and confidante. Although in small ways, things between us had changed since last summer. We saw each other less. I worried more. Camille became more reckless with her schemes and even more love-struck by the day. The latter of which could be said about me, too, now that Ant and I were going steady.

He'd worn me down quickly after that kiss on the bench outside the park, and I realized my resistance was futile. I wanted his lips on mine again.

You could say things moved fast after that, and you wouldn't be wrong. We fell into an easy routine, one that seemed preordained from the beginning. When Ant didn't have class at DePaul University, he'd walk me to work or wait for me after closing to walk me home. On our days off, we ate dinner at each other's houses with our families, went to the beach downtown, and sometimes went to jazz and dance halls when I could slip away without Ma noticing too much. Camille often tagged along, now seeing Jackson on and off, to her utter delight. All the pieces were falling into place, according to some plan I'd only started to make sense of. But in my naïve head, we were only having fun.

I heard a low rumble and peeked out the lace curtains on the front door to see Ant's black-and-white T-bird pull up to our little brick two-flat that looked nearly identical to the nine others on the block.

"They're here!" I shouted up the stairs as I grabbed my shawl from the antique wall table in the foyer and pulled open the heavy front door. My youngest sister and my parents were at Cucina Bella, giving me and Camille our first night off in over a week. When Jackson found out we had the night off, he promised to get us into the new dance hall downtown.

Ant had to honk the horn twice before Camille skipped down the front steps and hopped into the back seat next to Jackson.

We'd both dressed for a night out on the town, me in a black satin A-line dress with a skinny gold belt that accentuated my waist. I'd saved up a month's worth of wages to purchase it from Marshall Field's after seeing it in their display window on Michigan Avenue and had been dying for a reason to wear it. Camille stunned in a tan silk dress with white polka dots and a white pillbox hat affixed to her perfect updo.

"Don't you both look ravishing," Jackson said. Camille squealed with delight. She'd always been a sucker for compliments.

"I can't wait to get you out on that dance floor," Ant whispered to me as the car pulled away from the curb, and something fluttered in my chest.

I hadn't quite gotten used to being his girlfriend in public. At first, the sneers and glares from other girls made me uncomfortable. I wasn't used to being looked at, especially not with jealousy. But the more we ventured outside of our tight community, farther into the city where almost no one recognized us at all, the more I relaxed.

Thankfully, Ant had left the top on his car, knowing that we'd both throw a fit if we ruined our hairdos on the ride over. Even with the top on, you could see the clear, beautiful night sky as we zipped down the quiet neighborhood streets. The warm air floated in through the windows, and I could identify which neighborhood we were in by the aromas of the food coming from the passing restaurants—Greek, Mexican, and Polish.

Being from the west side of Chicago, it only took a few minutes to get into downtown, almost a straight shot. I'd walked it more times than I could count, but at night, the air tingled on my skin, charged with energy and possibility that both excited and terrified me. Ant was used to going to clubs and staying out late, as were most college-aged boys. For me, the experience was still novel.

Until Ant and I became a couple, I only went downtown during the daytime to shop, and rarely ever left my block after dark, except to walk home from the restaurant. With him, my world had opened, and I had to remind myself often to stay focused on my goal: cooking and one day running Cucina Bella. Distractions be damned.

My mother still had other ideas and my sisters started taking bets on how long it would take for Ma to work Ant into the conversation every morning. She was pushier than ever about our relationship taking the next "step." I tried as best I could to brush off the implication.

Meanwhile, the more time I spent away from the kitchen, the more I doubted myself and my relationship. Things had been fun with Ant over the past year, but as time went on, the conflict between him and the restaurant took up residence in my thoughts more than I'd care to admit.

Pa never mentioned it, but we both knew that I'd been cooking less than I should have been if I wanted to learn the ropes and grow my skills. Still, he stayed silent, knowing my mother's desire to see her eldest child married to a man like Ant took precedence. He'd be more comfortable letting the feud play on its own, even if he did want me to fill his shoes one day.

With the music from Ant's car stereo blaring, we pulled into a packed parking lot on the corner of a busy downtown intersection and paid the attendant. We all rolled out of the car, toppling over each other and buzzing with electric energy. In the dim shadows of the parking lot, Jackson pulled out a silver flask from his jacket pocket and took a long swig before passing it to Camille, who flashed me a quick look of hesitation. I shrugged my shoulders, knowing she was going to do what she wanted, anyway. We were safe with Ant and Jackson, after all.

When it was my turn, I politely declined, waving it away.

"Oh, Rosa. Take a sip or two to loosen you up for the dance floor!" Camille cried.

"It's okay, baby. You don't have to drink anything if you don't want to," Ant reassured me, pulling me into him by the waist.

"More for us, then!" Jackson sneered, chugging back another long gulp before capping it and stowing it safely back in his linen jacket.

It's not that I was against drinking, but I had never developed a taste for liquor. A few years ago, I'd tried whiskey with our older cousins on Christmas Eve and made a complete fool out of myself as a coughing fit seized my throat after one sip.

"I'll order a glass of wine when we get there," I said to make up for my lack of enthusiasm. In Chicago, women could legally drink at eighteen, but men had to wait until they turned twenty-one. Seemed like a fair enough rule to me, but it forced boys to smuggle in flasks wherever they went.

Rounding the corner, we heard the whoops and hollers of young people gearing up for a full night as the line for the new dance hall wrapped around the block.

"It'll be midnight before we get in…" said Camille, face contorted in dismay.

Jackson grabbed her hand and said, "Nah. Don't worry. I know the bouncer." He led us to the front of the line, and I could feel dozens of eyes boring into our backs as we cut in line ahead of them.

"Teddy, how's it going tonight, man?" Jackson asked, shaking the large man's hand. At the entrance to the club, the bouncer sat on a rickety metal stool that looked like it wanted to collapse under his weight. His loose-fitting leather jacket hung off his shoulders in a casual but intentional way that signaled, "I'm cool but don't mess with me."

"Jack-y, my boy. So good to see you. This your lady?" he asked, eyes scanning up and down Camille's body.

"You know it. This is Camille."

"Good for you. This your sister, Camille?" he asked, finally turning his gaze to me and Ant.

Ant answered for her. "This is my girl, Rosa." His grip around my waist tightened.

Teddy's eyebrows raised in amusement. "Well, we can use all the pretty ladies we can get in there. Go on in." He unclipped the velvet rope across the small entrance and pointed through the tinted door. A chorus of groans echoed behind us from the growing line.

At first, I couldn't see a thing. The hallway leading from the door was dark and smelled of stale beer. We shuffled unsteadily in single file until our eyes adjusted. From the right alcove, a young woman in a tight teal dress greeted us.

"Welcome to Mister Kelly's. Let me show you to a table," she said.

Impressed, I bumped Camille's shoulder. Most of the places Jackson brought us to were cheesy dance halls. That this place had a hostess and tables boded well.

As we filed down the narrow corridor, the music became louder until we came to a stop at the top of a grand staircase. The stairs led down to a sunken room lined with plush velvet booths framing a dance floor lit by a row of spotlights. Long, heavy, dark drapes hung from the ceiling along the walls. A large, ornate stage stretched across the back of the room, where a three-piece ensemble played as a woman dressed in a tight, glittering gown belted out a popular swing song. Dozens of couples filled the dance floor.

The hostess led us to a booth near the stage lit by a gold lamp and a collection of small votive candles. It curved around in a U-shape that made it feel intimate, yet sophisticated. A small vase of lilacs sat in the middle, and I could smell their pleasant fragrance as we slid in. Not even two minutes later, a waitress appeared, ready to serve us drinks. I ordered a glass of Chardonnay along with Camille, while the boys poured brown liquor from their flasks into empty cups. Drinks in hand, we toasted.

"To Jackson's connections. May they never end," Ant said, already loosening up from Jackson's flask.

"Here, here. And to the merriment ahead," Camille added as we clinked glasses over the table.

Not long after we emptied our first round, Ant grabbed my wrist and led me to the dance floor. I'd never had much natural rhythm, preferring the precise and almost surgical movements needed to navigate a busy kitchen, but tonight I tried my best to let the music take over.

It had been two weeks since I last saw Ant, who'd been traveling in Italy with his father to meet their wine suppliers. Now that his father had officially told him he'd be taking over the family business after graduation, Ant only had two more summers to make the necessary introductions and learn the ropes.

"You look stunning tonight. I love the new dress," he murmured into my neck, hugging my hips close to his as we swayed with the beat. My cheeks warmed at his compliment, grateful to be another blur among the dancing couples.

I'd been bewitched by Ant in the year we'd been together. He unlocked some carnal need I hadn't known existed. Even so, doubt creeped in when we weren't together. Something about us didn't feel as easy as it should have. I kept waiting for it to "click," for my heart to catch up to my brain, but I still caught myself jerking away from him, forgetting he could now touch me tenderly. We never spoke my hesitation into existence, but I knew he noticed, both hoping it would fade, become normal with time.

After a few songs on the dance floor, we flopped into the booth with heavy breaths, reaching for the tall glasses of ice water on the table. Out of the corner of my eye, I caught the lighting shift on the dance floor. In unison, we all looked around when the band switched to a low, slow jazz number. In the center of the floor, a man knelt on one knee in front of a woman with the biggest smile I'd ever seen. It lit up her entire face.

We couldn't hear them, but a moment later he swung her around in an embrace, and the large, sparkly diamond on her left hand glinted in the light. She looked positively glowing with happiness. As if she could float off into oblivion now and everything would be fine. Someone had picked her. She was chosen.

Cheers and claps erupted from around the club, and the band started playing a more upbeat number. A bottle of champagne for every table, compliments of the owner.

"You better not propose to my sister in a club," Camille said across the table, pointing a finger at Ant.

"I'd never dream of it. I have something better in mind," he said, squeezing my arm under the table.

My throat went dry, and I almost choked.

"Well, don't wait too long. Lord knows, you've already wasted enough time being *friends*. Time to get a move on."

Camille was drunk. Clearly. A proposal, marriage? No, it was too soon. Sure, someday in the fuzzy, distant future, I could see myself married. But I had so much to do before then. Namely, more cooking and learning. It had only been a year since Pa named me head chef, and it'd be more than a few until he handed over the restaurant which would only happen if I could hold off Ma for long enough. I couldn't be a chef, a restaurateur, and a new wife, right?

Wide, expectant smiles glared back at me from around the table.

"Excuse me. I need to use the ladies' room."

I slid out of the booth, not looking back. Pushing open the heavy wooden door, I beelined to the sink, turning the cold side of the tap as far as it would go. Years ago, a veteran line cook had taught me to run my wrists under cool water when I overheated or became overwhelmed. It worked most of the time. As my heartbeat slowed, the door swung open, and Camille sidled up next to me.

"You okay?"

I looked at her in the mirror. "Yeah. Just too warm, that's all."

"Do you wanna get out of here? I can tell the boys we're ready to go—"

"I don't want to get married." I turned to face her. "Not yet. I need more time. Please, you'd tell me if Ant was planning something, wouldn't you?"

She wrapped her arm around my shoulder but avoided looking me in the eye.

"Oh, Camille, no. Talk him out of it. It's not time."

"Rosa, it's been over a year. Haven't you made him wait long enough? Don't you love him?"

Love? I loved the kitchen. I loved the restaurant. Did I love Ant?

"Do you think he'd still let me cook? Run the restaurant?"

"I don't know. Does it really matter? You'd be his wife; he'd take care of you."

There it was. The assumption that all women wanted the same thing: love and a family of their own. I couldn't possibly want a career, too. How selfish of me.

"I don't want to be taken care of if it means I have to give up the restaurant. I want to run it. I want to be a chef." I threw my hands in the air. No one seemed to get it.

"No one is saying you'd have to leave. But you might want to once you're married. Ant loves you."

I groaned. No amount of wedding bliss would convince me to give up on my dream. Every time I attempted to explain this to my sister or mother, I was met with resistance. As if only they knew what was best for me. In Camille's case, it always came from a place of love and naiveté. My mother, on the other hand, was certain that the only path started with an engagement and ended as a housewife and mother.

"Once you have children, your world changes. You'll be needed at home," she'd argue. As if she didn't help Pa run the restaurant while also raising three daughters. When I'd point that out, though, she'd tut and wave it away, saying that she didn't have a choice.

I fixed my lipstick in the mirror and told Camille I'd meet her at our table. Gripping the sides of the counter, my reflection stared back at me. I needed to get a hold of myself. Ma always told us that selfishness was an unattractive trait in a young woman.

Was I being selfish, though? I knew deep down in my heart that my loyalty to my family ran deeper than any of my dreams. And in my mind, ensuring the survival of our family restaurant was protecting the family, too.

We danced a few more rounds, but the evening's earlier glow dimmed to a watery haze before we called it and headed back out into the balmy summer air to Ant's car. When we got close to home, the car puttered to the curb a street over, making it look more plausible we'd only been a few blocks away at a friend's house instead of out dancing on the town. Camille had even stowed her book bag in Ant's car, which she now slung over her shoulder.

Before we turned onto the street where our house took up the corner lot, proud in its angular brick facade, we both wiped our faces and lips with tissues to remove the makeup we'd caked on earlier. Although I was twenty and Camille eighteen, we still lived under our mother's roof, and her rules reigned. A fact she didn't let us forget.

Ma encouraged Ant's courtship, but she'd only recently come around to the idea that we could go out unchaperoned. We'd managed, and the busy restaurant made it easier. Ma and Pa spent most of their nights at Cucina Bella, leaving me and Camille at least one night a week without them when we had off, though rarely together. Poor Ivana, my youngest sister, was forced to tag along with my parents and spend many evenings in a back booth, reading her dime-store comic books.

Safely tucked in my twin bed pressed against the far wall in the room I'd shared with Camille since she was born, I replayed the almost flippant way Ant spoke of our future engagement, like it was already a done deal, mere details to sort. I had to admit that after the shock had worn off, a small part of me was thrilled at the thought of marrying Ant. Wasn't it every girl's dream to be chosen? To be plucked out of the sea swarming with other bright and beautiful girls? Ant and I made sense.

"You'd make a gorgeous bride, Rosa," Camille said from her identical twin bed, voice heavy with sleep. "Don't overthink it. Talk to him."

Sleep evaded me, my future teetering on an invisible edge.

Chapter 3

Loud pops and booms from outside rattled our single-paned windows in the kitchen. I'd been jittery all day, and not just because it was the Fourth of July and the second dusk rolled in, the city lit up.

"Those watermelons won't cut themselves, you know," Ma called out, and I flinched from a burst of fireworks that sounded like they'd exploded right behind us.

I turned back to the cutting board, gripping the chef's knife tighter as I pressed it through the thick green rind. Sweet red juice bled onto the speckled Formica counter, sticky and bright.

My parents had thrown the block's annual Fourth of July party since before I could remember, every year adding new friends to the head count. The preparations started weeks earlier when my mother and I spent days crushing and bottling ripe tomatoes. Each year, we'd hand-make half a dozen types of pasta for the party, all served in large tin platters on folding tables in our backyard.

The spread was notoriously grand: a buffet of pasta, antipasto dishes, and desserts, including our famous Bianchi cannoli. Always too much, but that never mattered.

That year, a record number of people stopped by, but as the evening wore on, it dwindled down to a more manageable crowd, mostly comprised of our family, Ant's family, and our immediate neighbors. Still, I couldn't relax.

"Come on, Rosa. The table is out of watermelon," Ma said over her shoulder as she went back outside.

I picked up the heavy platter of melon and carefully navigated my way through the backyard, placing it on the overcrowded table and taking a quick inventory of the other food.

As I scanned the table, I noticed the radio had stopped, so I started weaving my way around the buffet tables to tune it back to a local station, but halfway there, I realized it wasn't only the music. Everything had fallen silent. A prickling sense of unease crawled up my neck as I met a dozen pairs of eyes all fixed on me. My heart rate kicked up. Heat rushed to my cheeks.

I glanced down, checking for watermelon juice on my shirt, then my skirt, brushing at invisible stains. I ran a hand over my hair. Still intact.

"Rosa, will you join me?" My head jerked up to where Ant stood on the stairs leading from the back door. My eyes locked on him, and I slowly crossed the yard. Everyone smiled as I passed by.

I stopped before the set of stairs and looked up at him without saying a word, the lump in my throat growing. Ant's fingers found mine and pulled me up to a small landing near the door.

As the music suddenly stopped, I realized what was happening. Ant kneeled on one knee, looking up with the expectant face of a child on Christmas morning. My world suddenly narrowed to a single point on the back steps of my childhood home.

"Rosa, I've waited for twenty years to ask you this," he started, eyes crinkling at the corners from a wide smile.

No, no, no. Not yet.

I coughed. "Oh dear, I need a minute, please. Come inside?"

Trying to play it off as embarrassment, I hid my reddening face from the crowd on the lawn.

Ant jerked his head back in surprise, rushing to stand. With my hand still in his, he led us through the kitchen and then into the living room.

"What's wrong?" he asked, eyes wide with fear, or maybe humiliation. It was hard to tell.

"I'm s-sorry," I stuttered. The words I knew I needed to say evaded me as my entire body clenched. Last night, I'd prepared what I'd say to him after the party. Explain to him I couldn't give up on my dreams to marry him, if that's what he expected.

"I, um, planned to talk to you tonight in private. I'm so sorry for doing it like this," I mumbled, heat rising in my face. "You caught me off guard. That's all."

"Sorry for doing what?"

"For ruining... whatever you were just doing." I waved my hand in the air. "But I need to ask you something."

"Can we do it quickly? Everyone is waiting." His eyes scanned back out the kitchen door, anxious energy pouring off him in waves. I'd ruined his moment. He had every right to be annoyed.

"Will you still let me work? I mean, at the restaurant. You don't expect me to be a housewife, do you?" I shifted my weight from one foot to the other, not daring to meet his eyes.

"What? That's what you're worried about?" he almost snapped out. "It'll all work out. We'll be happy together, and our families want this for us. This is right, Rosa." He grabbed my hand and rubbed his thumb across the top. "I promise to take care of you if you'll let me." His tone softened to a near whisper. "Now, can we go back out there? People are waiting, babe."

And that was that. His non-answer would have to do for now. There was no way I could have turned him down in front of our families and friends. I would just have to hope he meant it when he said it would all work out.

Ant spun on his heels and led me back out to the steps before my voice could even catch up with my thoughts. *How did I get here?* My throat constricted as panic bubbled up. Taking three slow, deliberate breaths, I scanned the yard for my mother. She looked ecstatic, which calmed my nerves enough to focus on Ant.

It would all work out.

"Okay, now she's ready. And doesn't she look beautiful?" he joked before returning to one knee. The crowd laughed and nodded in agreement.

"Rosa, my dear friend and love. It's always been you. Even when we were little kids climbing trees in the park and skinning our knees, our paths were destined to be united. It's taken nearly two decades, but here we are now, with our futures in front of us. Will you do me the honor of building that future together as my wife?"

I looked around at the eager faces staring back. All familiar, yet somehow now strange, an eager hunger buzzing among them.

Off to my right, my mother clutched onto my father's arm like a life raft, nodding her head to hasten my answer. My father, eyes wide, lips pursed as if he'd been sucking on a sour candy. And my sister Camille: Bambi in the forest at night. Then everyone else came into a fuzzy focus, a chorus of wide grins waiting for my expected acceptance.

I nodded, not at all confident my voice wouldn't betray me if I'd tried to speak.

Ant stood, sliding the delicate diamond solitaire in a gold band onto my finger. I forced a smile as the guests erupted into cheers, their joy echoing louder than the doubt stirring uneasily inside me. Even the fireflies seemed to dance in approval, tiny sparks against the twilight, oblivious to the tight knot forming in my chest.

The early morning sun blinded me as it blazed through the threadbare curtains on the restaurant windows.

Not able to catch more than a few hours of restless sleep after the block party, I snuck out as the sun rose to get a few undisturbed hours in the kitchen, the only place where I felt in control. Where I could operate based on my gut and intuition, not expectations.

I'd been working on a new recipe for lasagna, one that used mushrooms in place of ground beef, for a couple of weeks, but it challenged me. The dish would be a hard sell to most of our customers and would likely never see its way onto the menu, but I couldn't get enough of the meaty, earthy flavor of mushrooms reduced in red wine and herbs.

Pulling out my tattered and sauce-splattered notebook that held hundreds of scratched recipes and notes, I reviewed the entry from the last time I attempted the dish. Apparently, I'd not reduced the wine enough or cooked the liquid sufficiently out of the mushrooms because it came out soggy. Noted.

As I tied my apron around my waist, the kitchen door swung open, making me jump, bumping into the stack of pots and pans behind me.

"Pa, what are you doing here this early?"

"Morning to you as well," he said, eyes not quite open.

It was rare to see him at the restaurant this early unless we had deliveries or pickups to make. And after last night, I'd expected him and my sisters to sleep in at least a little. Ma, of course, would never allow herself such an indulgence.

"Oh, sorry. I'm just surprised to see you, is all. Good morning."

"I want to get caught up on the bookkeeping while I have the time," he said in his thick Italian accent that never softened even after immigrating here three decades ago from Palermo.

Part of me admired this tiny act of rebellion. It said, 'You can make me an American on paper, but I'll never give up my Sicilian identity.' But truthfully, as a young girl, I'd always winced when my father spoke to non-Italians. Ma had adopted the typical Midwestern accent by listening to the radio station day and night, which she still did. The only time I ever heard her slip back into her natural dialect was when she yelled, usually in Italian.

Pa came up beside me to look over my shoulder at my notes.

"Trying again, mi piccola?" *My little one.*

"I need to figure out the right wine to mushroom ratio. Then I'll have it." I knitted my brow together.

"Reduce the wine to three-fourths of a cup, but add in half a cup of mushroom stock," he said, pointing to the space where I had jotted down the amounts from my previous attempt.

"Mushroom stock…" I mumbled. Why hadn't I thought of that?

Pa turned to head back to his small, dark office in the corner.

"Pa, wait," I called after him, desperate to talk to him about what happened last night.

He stopped and threw his head over his shoulder, eyebrow cocked.

"I'm nervous."

"About the lasagna? No need. I just told you how to fix it." A look of confusion crossed his face.

"No. About Anthony," I said, not moving. "About marrying him. Do you think he'll understand?"

Pa blew out a long breath. He knew what I meant.

"I hope so. But sometimes we must give up the things we hold most dear for the chance of something better. And your mother is rarely ever wrong."

"But what if she is this time? Ant is great and all, but you know how traditional his family is. I don't think they'd understand. This place is everything to me," I said, looking around at the mess I'd made on the counter. "Maybe I'm not ready."

The deep lines around Pa's eyes softened as he looked down at me. "That boy loves you. And you just made your mother a very happy woman. She's already called the entire church phone tree to spread the good news."

"But don't you want me to run Bella someday? Like we planned?"

He seemed to consider this before responding. "No one is saying you can't. Though, it might look different from what we'd thought. Ant's family has connections we could never dream of having. Look at your mother. She never planned to run a restaurant, and she's half the muscle behind this place, even though she'd never admit it."

He was right, of course. But Ma didn't receive any of the credit. Cucina Bella was Pa's restaurant. His name was in every article ever written about the restaurant. He was the one who received the handshakes and praise over the delicious food, not her. Everything she did faded into the background. That was just the way it was.

Before I could respond, he'd already stepped into his office and closed the door.

For the next hour, I chopped, sauteed, and reduced until the pan of lasagna bubbled in the hot oven. By then, a few of the staff had trickled in for prep work and the day officially began.

"Congratulations, amore mio!" Riccardo boomed as he burst through the doors, rushing up in a chaotic swirl to wrap his skinny arms around my shoulders. "Our Rosa is going to be a married woman!"

I brushed him off with a tight smile. Riccardo had been working at Cucina Bella for over a decade, and I had once looked up to him as a second father, but I was technically his boss now. Boundaries had to be maintained, although sometimes with this lot, that was futile.

"Oh, come on, aren't you excited?" he prodded. "It is a wonderful thing!" He then regaled us with how he met his wife, a story we'd heard thousands of times over the years. We all groaned in unison.

"Leave her alone, Ricky," Stella, our head waitress, called from the dining room. "Not everyone is as in love with love as you."

Ricky raised his hands over his head. "Mi arrendo, signorinas." *I give up, ladies.*

I looked down at the ring, still where Ant had placed it, now covered in red tomato sauce. Slipping it off, I rinsed it under soapy water and dropped it into my purse, where it'd stay safe and out of sight for the rest of my shift.

Before we knew it, the doors opened, and we were off to the races, serving lunch for dozens of tired patrons suffering from the bottle ache of last night's activities. The kitchen slung out plate after plate of pasta e fagioli, breaded eggplant sandwiches, and caponata, our lunch staples that provided comfort and hearty substance to line their sour stomachs.

Ma had taken the day off to clean up the remnants of the party, but Camille wandered in a few minutes past opening time, as usual.

"Stella's going to have your behind," I hissed as she popped in to grab her serving apron.

"Couldn't be any worse than Ma. She was tied to be fit this morning. Made me scrub the hallway toilet before I could leave. I escaped before she had me on the floor with a toothbrush and Pine Sol."

My mother kept a clean house, and by that, I meant she put all of us to work regularly, but even for her, scrubbing a toilet first thing in the morning was a little extreme.

"Well, you'd better get out there. The line at the door isn't getting any shorter," I said, elbow deep in flour and egg batter.

Before disappearing into the dining room, she called back, "Jackson rang this morning. We're going to meet him and your fiancé at the beach tomorrow!"

I took a deep inhale. *Fiancé.* I was going to have to get used to it now. On the bright side, the outing might give me and Ant a chance to finish our conversation. Plus, some sun on my almost translucent skin wouldn't be a bad thing. The other day, Camille compared me to a baby seal in a snowstorm.

All afternoon and evening, I worked without a break to push my concerns over Ant and our engagement to the back of my mind. At one point, I saw Ricky look across his workstation to Joe with wide eyes and an unamused expression. Maybe I'd been too hard on them, but how else were we going to stay on top of the order tickets that kept coming through at an unrelenting speed? The day after a holiday was notoriously busy at the restaurant. People didn't want to cook anymore, and I understood. They didn't have the time, or they got sick of their wives' five rotating dishes. But cooking was all I wanted to do. It was the only thing keeping me from stumbling into the depths of my own thoughts.

Finally, after Camille flipped the open sign to closed on the front door, I sat with the few staff who'd hung around for a quick meal of pasta alla Norma, a favorite among those who knew. Pa had whipped it up as the last table finished their plates of cannoli and settled their bill. We ate like prison inmates who'd only seen stale bread and water for years: ravenous, reckless, and past the point of manners.

Those who still had even an ounce of energy broke into a few bottles of wine, and someone turned up the radio we kept in the back of the kitchen. Some nights, I'd join them for a few rounds of shared camaraderie after a hellish shift. But not tonight.

I ached for my bed. And not a second after my head hit the pillow, my body gave in to a deep, fitful sleep.

By morning, I couldn't remember my dreams, but their echoes had left me disoriented. To shake them off, I got up and hurried downstairs to help Ma with breakfast and cleaning before Camille and I took off for the beach.

Making breakfast for the family on the weekends had been my responsibility since I could stand on a stool to reach the stove. Most people probably assumed I'd inherited my love of cooking from my father, but the truth was that my mother had lit the flame.

My fondest memories of her came from my youth and spending time together in our modest kitchen, whisking up cornetti croissants, biscotti, and fresh bread. Back then, the family consisted only of the four of us, and Ma had more time. It had been years since I had seen that soft, slow way she used to carry herself. Life had weighed her down, and although we butted heads, I felt a duty to help her. She was my mother. Even if we didn't much like each other now, my respect for her remained.

By the time I had placed the fresh fruit, jam, and bread on the table, an eerie quiet had settled over the house. Ma and Pa huddled together in his small home office, which had been our den before he converted it. And my sisters were still upstairs, probably just waking up.

I had my head in the fridge looking for a carton of milk when Ma threw the glass-paned doors of the office open and yelled for all of us to meet in the kitchen.

"Now!" she added at a volume that made several pairs of feet pad quickly down the stairs.

Four of us sat around the kitchen table as my father stood behind Ma, hand on her shoulder.

"Your father and I have some news," she started, waiting for my father to pick up where she left off. After a beat, though, she continued, sitting up straighter, "Starting tomorrow, you will see some new faces around the restaurant. Your father has taken on a partner."

Camille and I exchanged confused glances. What did she mean, a *partner*? The restaurant was ours. He'd paid it off years ago. It had been something Pa boasted about frequently, especially after a few glasses of wine.

"Are we expanding?" I asked.

"No. Your *father* is not expanding. He's run into a financial snag and needs some extra help, that's all. Everything will be fine. And hopefully, this will only be temporary."

I looked at my father for more explanation, searching for even a hint of the full story, but he kept his eyes trained down at the peeling white paint on the table.

Heat crawled up my throat. I deserved to know the truth, more than just a quick and shallow heads-up. The restaurant would be mine someday.

Before thinking, I blurted, "That's it? That's all the information we get?"

My mother whipped her head toward me. "Rosa, this isn't your business. Stay out of it."

The air had been sucked out of the small kitchen. Camille and Ivana sat motionless, looking anywhere but at me. They knew what I knew: it was certainly my business, even if Ma didn't think so. I prayed at least Pa still did.

"That's that." Ma clapped her hands together and looked at my youngest sister. "Let's get going. The church rummage sale won't run itself."

My father was the first out the door. He didn't stop to say goodbye or to pull me aside, like I'd hoped. He paraded through the house without stopping until he pulled the front door open and disappeared into the humid summer air.

Camille grabbed me by the elbow, shaking me back to life.

"Come on, we're going to miss the bus," she said, slinging her bright blue and pink beach bag over her shoulder. No one besides Ivana touched their plates.

Still too stunned by my mother's news to protest, I let her lead me to my room to change and then we sprinted down the sidewalk to the corner stop to catch the bus that only a few years ago had replaced the notorious Green Hornet streetcar to North Avenue Beach. Honestly, I preferred taking the bus downtown rather than riding in Ant's large T-bird. On the bus, I didn't need to sit properly or be concerned about my hair getting windblown.

The bus had just pulled up to the corner curb when we came running down the sidewalk. Inside, people filled the benches and aisles, holding onto the overhead handrails. If it weren't for all the oversized beach bags, umbrellas, and folding chairs, it was likely another twenty or so passengers could have comfortably sat. But it was summer and a weekend at that. Everyone wanted to be at the beach, us included.

We rode in silence for a while, focusing on not falling over every time the bus lurched forward. After our legs adjusted, Camille broke the silence.

"Where's your ring?" she asked, looking up at my left hand, holding the metal hand loop.

"Oh, shoot." I began digging around in my purse, which was conveniently at the bottom of my own absurdly large beach bag. "I took it off last night at work, and I completely forgot to put it back on," I explained.

Camille cocked her head. "You'd better not lose it."

"I didn't want it to get dirty. Or slip off into the tray of lasagna."

"That'd be just your luck."

"Don't I know it," I said, slipping the ring cautiously back in place. *Although then maybe Ant would call off the engagement,* I heard a small voice say. I looked around, surprised at my own thoughts. How ridiculous. I didn't want Ant to call it off, for goodness' sake. I only wanted him to tell me he understood. That I didn't have to give up the restaurant, which he'd do if he loved me. And I had to believe he loved me.

"What do you think is really going on with Pa and the restaurant?" Camille asked.

"I don't have the slightest idea. But whatever it is, they're not telling us the full story."

"I've never seen Pa like that before. It was like watching a kid realize Santa's not real."

I laughed out loud, because that was exactly what it looked like. No one could ever say Pa ran the roost and most of the time he played the good cop, but he could hold his own, when needed. Ma, on the other hand…

"I'll try to find out more," I said as the bus pulled up to the beach, depositing us in front of the bathhouses.

Chapter 4

"Camiiiille," squealed Maria, Ant's younger sister. She ran up to greet us as soon as we spotted the group lounging on the hot sand near the water. "I'm so happy you're here! I was starting to worry you'd missed the bus. I told Jackson to pick you up, but you know he couldn't wait to get here." She rolled her eyes as she hopped from one foot to the other, trying to keep her feet from burning.

Lying on an array of beach towels, three girls from DePaul University who were friends with Ant and Jackson chatted along with the group of neighborhood boys who'd been friends since childhood. I scanned the towels for Ant, but before I could finish, someone grabbed my shoulders from behind and placed a kiss on my cheek. I swiveled around to see Ant standing there shirtless, chest glistening in the sun. He held a football in one hand and laced his fingers of the other through mine. As a college athlete, he kept himself in good shape.

"Hey there," he said, walking me over to an open spot next to his towel. "Want something to drink? I brought a cooler with some pop. And maybe a few beers." He winked at me, and something in my stomach fluttered.

"A pop would be great." I sat my bag down, unrolled my towel next to his and hovered while he reached into the cooler. I'd never liked removing my cover-up on a public beach. Not that I minded wearing a bathing suit. That part was fine. It was only the actual act of taking *off* my clothes in front of people that made me cringe, even if I wasn't naked underneath. Thankfully, I'd found an all-black bathing suit that covered everything, while cinching my waist to accentuate the hourglass shape I'd inherited from Ma.

While Ant still had his back to me, I slipped my gauzy dress over my head and stuffed it deep in my bag.

"Well, don't you look great," he said, turning back to me, hand outstretched with a cold Coke bottle.

I ignored his comment, but could feel my cheeks burning red.

"I was just playing a quick game of touch ball with the guys. Do you mind if I finish and then we can take a dip together?"

I nodded and watched as he ran back toward his group of friends, who'd been making kissy faces at him. Ant didn't seem to mind; he had confidence in spades, something I'd always admired.

The early afternoon sun baked the throngs of beachgoers. Camille had already slathered on her baby oil and laid out on her towel like a sun goddess performing her daily worship ritual. In the water, children and young teenagers splashed each other, eliciting a few high-pitched screeches from a group of girls tiptoeing in.

I slid my sunglasses down off the top of my head to get a better look at the glittering water with its soft waves crashing ashore and took a deep breath, filling my lungs with the scent of body oil mixed with sun-warmed algae and damp wood. The tension I'd been carrying in my shoulders released slightly, but I couldn't fully relax. My mind kept wandering back to the restaurant, and what my father had gotten himself into.

Lost in my thoughts, I jerked in surprise when Ant plopped down beside me a few minutes later.

"Hey, you," he said, leaning back on his hands. "What're you thinking about so hard?"

Ant had known me since before I could even walk, so it wasn't surprising that he could read my body language, just as I could read his. Although since we'd started dating, our casual familiarity had changed, and often the space between us felt muddled, as if made of fog.

I blew out a long breath. I might as well tell him, I thought. He'd find out soon enough.

"Pa is taking on a partner at the restaurant."

"Ah, so it finally happened, then?"

I whipped my head around to look at him.

"What do you mean, 'finally happened?' Did you know about this?"

Ant lifted his hands in defense. "Woah, Rosa. Come on now. It was only a matter of time before Marco's gambling debts caught up with him. I'm honestly surprised it took this long."

I had no clue what he was talking about. Gambling debts?

"What are you talking about?" My voice rose a few octaves. "You don't know?"

"No, Anthony, I don't know. Care to fill me in on what I'm missing?" I lowered my chin and glared at him. He drew his chest back a few inches.

After a beat, he shook his head and softened his face. "Babe, your Pa's in deep with the Outfit's bookies. Can't stay away from the action."

I knew about the Chicago Outfit. I'd have to have been living under a rock not to. Or at least outside of Little Italy. Sam Giancana, the organization's top guy, had come into Cucina

Bella for dinner throughout the years, which was a big deal to the staff. But my father had always seemed uninterested in it all. I'd once overheard Pa call them "goons in suits" to Ma.

"He's borrowed money from almost every family in the neighborhood to cover his debts. Looks like his goodwill ran out," Ant said, looking at the strip of sand between our towels. "I'm sorry. I thought you knew."

"Of course I didn't." I paused, turning the new information over in my mind. "But I'm confused. So what if he has some debt? Is that why he's taking on a partner? He bought the restaurant outright years ago."

Ant stared back at me blankly, like I should already know the answer. Then it clicked.

"No, he wouldn't gamble the restaurant. He wouldn't do that. That's our livelihood. My inheritance."

"Maybe he didn't put it up, but the Outfit doesn't care. If they don't get their money, they'll take whatever they can until the debt's repaid."

My head spun. I couldn't wrap my mind around this revelation. If it were true, my entire childhood had been a farce. Every time Pa said that Cucina Bella would one day be mine was a lie. Or at the very least, a thinly held hope. My breath grew unsteady, like I needed to gulp some fresh, cool air, so instead I sipped the cold Coke still in my hand.

After a minute, Ant reached across my towel and placed his hand on my upper thigh.

"You don't need to worry about it. We're going to be fine. Better than fine, actually." He squeezed my thigh gently.

"Can we help him get the restaurant back?" I asked voice soft. Selfishly, I knew there was no chance I'd ever get another cooking job anywhere else. No one would hire a young woman as a chef, especially one without experience outside of her family's restaurant. This was my only shot.

"If they're letting him stay on, which is what it sounds like, then he still has the chance to work off his debt."

The knot in my chest unwound enough for my breathing to steady.

"Okay, that's good. I'll pick up extra shifts, and hopefully we can get this handled quickly," I said, running my fingers through my now sweaty hair. "You're right. It'll be fine."

"Rosa, what're you talking about? You can't continue to work there. Not with the Outfit taking it over. It's not safe. You could get hurt." His voice had lowered to the tone he reserved for "serious" topics.

Right then, a large beach ball landed between us, kicking up sand in my face. Camille ran after it.

"Oops, sorry!" she shouted as she grabbed my left arm to hoist me up. "Come on, let's get in the water!"

My pop bottle flew into the sand, spilling what was left. I let her lead me down the wet sand toward the busy shore. Before I could protest, we'd plunged into the cool water and waded out waist deep. It was refreshing against my warm skin, small goosebumps forming down my arms.

I wanted to ask Camille if she knew about Pa's gambling but decided against it. This wasn't the place. She should be able to enjoy the afternoon, blissfully ignorant of our father's indiscretions. Before she found out, I'd need to talk to Pa. I told myself not to jump to conclusions before he had the chance to set the record straight. It could all be a misunderstanding. Gossip, for all I knew. No sense in getting her all worked up, or myself.

Looking back toward the beach, I saw Ant propped on an elbow, chatting with one of the DePaul University girls. He must have said something funny, because she threw her head back in laughter and rested her hand on his biceps. Women fell over themselves trying to get Ant's attention. It'd been that way since middle school, when he shot up over six inches in the summer between seventh and eighth grade. He'd had his fun, too.

Would it always be like this? Me, looking in from the outside, wondering if his playboy days were behind him?

"Having a good time?" I asked Camille to distract myself.

"I don't know," she said. "Jackson hasn't even said hello yet. I feel silly."

As if on cue, we watched as Jackson brushed the sand from his shorts and made his way to the shoreline, wading into the water toward us.

"Feels good," he said to Camille, dipping his shoulders in. "What's the fresh gossip today?"

Camille looked at me with a rueful smile.

"Nothing at all," I said, splashing some water at her.

Jackson leaned back in the water, floating next to Camille. "Thanks for coming," he said, eyes locked on her.

I headed back to my towel, to Ant. To remind the DePaul girls of what wasn't theirs, even if I wasn't sure I wanted it.

The yeasty scent of baking bread wafted into my bedroom, waking me with a gentle politeness the next morning. My bed groaned as I rolled over to see the sun already well above the treetops, blazing through the sheer white curtains hanging over the one window in our shared room. Camille still slept, curled around herself, like a half-moon. The jangling of our doorknob had woken me at two in the morning as she crept back in from a late-night rendezvous with Jackson, I assumed.

Not wanting to disturb her, I tiptoed out of the room, pressing my hand against the door to buffer the sound of the old latch. By the time I made it to the kitchen, a strange awareness had settled on my shoulders. Ma was up, and breakfast had already been made.

"Bon jornu, bedda mia." *Good morning, sweet girl.*

Confused, I slid into a chair at the empty table. My eyes watched her suspiciously as she moved around the kitchen. Terms of endearment rarely crossed her lips.

"Are you hungry? Of course you are. You need to eat," she said, piling a plate with bread and fruit.

"Morning, Ma. You should have woken me up. I would have helped you make breakfast," I said, still wary of this upbeat version of the woman who looked like my mother.

"No, no," she said, waving her hand in front of her face. "I wanted you to sleep. You've been working so hard lately. Eat your food."

Sicilian women, Italian women in general, showed their affection by feeding you. Even the hardest of all Nonnas would show their love by how often and well they cooked for you. Ma was no exception.

Marissa Bianchi—Vitale before she married my father—had grown up in a small village outside of Palermo, Sicily with her mother, father, and fourteen siblings until she immigrated to Louisiana when she was twelve. She rarely talked about the trip, but from what I could gather, it had been traumatic.

My grandmother, Anna Vitale, had begun the voyage across the Atlantic with ten of her children. My grandfather, Enzo, and the five oldest boys stayed behind in Sicily to save up funds. Mama Anna, as we called her, arrived in America with only eight children, the flu taking two of her daughters as toll, one of which was my mother's twin.

In Louisiana, the growing population of Sicilian immigrants found work as farm laborers. Mama Anna was no different, putting my mother and her siblings to work on a small strawberry farm owned by a distant "friend" of the family until the wife accused my grandmother of stealing and they were forced to leave the area. I once overheard Ma explain that the wife's husband took a liking to my then-young-grandmother and hadn't much cared to have temptation lurking around.

Shortly after, they made their way north to Illinois and settled in Chicago, where they reunited with Enzo and two of my mother's brothers several years later. Ma's two eldest brothers had died back in Sicily working in the mines. In Chicago, they worked seven days a week operating produce stands inside the city.

Suffice it to say, Ma was made of tough stuff. It ran in her blood, so she rarely showed a softer side, and when she did, we walked on eggshells, afraid to break the spell. My sisters and I respected her, but we also feared her. Ma never let a day pass without reminding us of our good fortune. "Ricordati sempri du pani ca mangi," she often said. *Always remember the bread you eat.*

I ate every morsel of food she'd put on my plate as she watched me in silence. The air between us felt strange. Normally, there was a circus of people running through the house, but not that morning. Ma had let everyone sleep in, knowing I'd still wake up early.

"Where's Pa?" I asked.

"He's already at Bella. He wants you to meet him there this morning. But I wanted to talk to you first."

Ah, there it was.

"What about?" I asked.

"I know want to cook."

"You mean be a chef? Run a restaurant? I don't hide that from you."

"I know, I know. But these things are hard, Piccola. Harder now," she said, letting her Sicilian accent slip out, sliding over her words.

"Harder? How?"

"I need you to think about your future. The restaurant will never be a place for a woman to cook, but your father has always insisted it would be fine. That he would protect you. But now things are not the same. It is not safe. And you have Anthony to think about," she tried to explain, without explaining anything.

"Ma, I'm not understanding. The restaurant is not safe?" Of course, I knew she was referring to the Outfit, but I needed someone to say it, to confirm what Ant had told me the previous afternoon.

My mother squared her slight shoulders and widened her once beautiful but now tired eyes at me. The sweet façade now gone. "Rosa, please do not try to fight me on this. It does not matter whether it is safe or not. Women should not be cooking in a restaurant. It is not right. It is not how things are done, and you will have a husband soon. A husband who can take care of you. You should feel lucky, but instead, you act as if it's a sacrifice to be fortunate. Plus, you must take his reputation into consideration. What will people say about him if his wife continues to work a man's job?"

"I don't care about other people. Let them say what they want. I'm a good chef, and I love it. Also, I find it ironic of you to lecture me about working a man's job. You, your sisters, and Mama Anna worked as farmhands for years after you came to America."

Her jaw went rigid as she drew in an unsteady breath. "That was different. We didn't have a choice. You have a choice, and instead, you're acting like a naïve schoolgirl who forgets her place. It's time to let go of your childish fantasies and grow up. You are a woman now."

I sat frozen to my chair. Never had she been so direct about my future. There'd been plenty of eye rolls and scoffs in the past, but now her true feelings about my strange ambitions had been revealed, and it was as if someone had gutted my insides with one sharp swoop of a knife. The last shred of hope that she was secretly proud of me vanished.

Ma's chest fell, and she reached across the table, touching her fingertips to my forearm.

"I don't want to be harsh. But things have changed. Your father will explain it to you today. I only want what's best for you," she almost whispered the last part. Smoothing the apron on her lap, she stood and made her way to the sink.

"Now, go wake up your sisters before you leave."

Chapter 5

The bell above the door let out a playful jingle as I stepped through, expecting to find the place empty. Instead, several unfamiliar faces turned in unison to look at me. I faltered for a moment, unsure if I was in the right place, but as I turned to look back at the door, I heard my father's voice boom through the dining room.

"Rosa, you are here. Come, come," he said, motioning for me to follow him back to the office. Before I moved from my spot near the door, I slid my gaze around the restaurant. Two men I did not know stood behind the bar, busying themselves by reorganizing the liquor bottles and glassware.

"Where is Julia?" I asked, not looking away from the men as I walked by. Julia had been our bartender for more than a decade and would never let anyone else touch her work area. A few years ago, my father had ordered new barware without consulting her, and he found the new glasses boxed up, sitting by the dumpster the morning after they'd arrived.

One of the men, the younger of the two, caught my stare as he cleaned a glass with a wet rag. I looked away, confused.

"There have been some changes," Pa said as he continued straight through the dining room, not paying them any mind.

He wasn't wrong about that. One of the murals, a large Italian countryside landscape that had always hung on the wall above the bar had been removed. A painter in blue overalls stood on a ladder, working a paint roller over the faded rectangle left behind. In the back, a stack of new cream-colored linens sat on one of the dinner tables as two women I did not recognize ironed them.

The lights hummed above us as we entered the office.

"What's going on?" I asked, confused and on edge.

"Oh, that?" he waved a hand in the air. "We are getting new lighting installed above the tables."

"Okay, but I meant what is happening with the restaurant? Who are all these people?" I said in a low voice. I didn't know if they could hear us through the thin walls.

"It is the new partner. He wants to attract more customers from outside the neighborhood."

I sat down across from his desk in the squeaky old chair, careful to avoid its rusty metal arms. A blazing heat welled in the back of my throat, and I had to clench my teeth tight to swallow it. Cucina Bella belonged to my father and my family. No one had the right to barge in and demand changes. Not after it had become one of the most dependable and respectable establishments in our community. People counted on us to be there for them; to be a steady staple in their chaotic lives. We'd held our neighbors' wedding celebrations, retirement parties, and funeral receptions. We'd seen their families grow, and their relatives grow old. Now, they were trying to turn us into a flashy, hip restaurant like the ones opening down the Magnificent Mile. What would the neighborhood think?

"Pa, this isn't right. You know it."

"There is nothing to be done. We must go along for now," he said, shaking his head, his eyes pleading with me to drop it.

I'd had enough of people treating me with kid gloves. Ma was right—I was a woman. I deserved the truth, and I wouldn't leave until I had it. Not if it meant my future went up in flames.

"Are you in trouble with the Outfit? Did you gamble the restaurant?" I asked as plainly as I could.

"Shhh, Bambina. We do not speak of such things," he said, eyes darting around as if someone was listening to us.

I did not care if the new staff overheard us. They shouldn't have been here to begin with.

"So, it's true? You owe them?"

Pa didn't need to say anything. The sad, guilty look on his face said enough.

"I'm working on it. We will get it back. But we need to stay out of their way and do as they say for now," he exhaled into the stale air between us.

"How, Pa? How do we get it back? And please tell me you're done playing the numbers."

"Yes, yes. I am done for good. I have learned my lesson. These are not people to mess with, they mean business. Sal told me I can work off my debt. When the restaurant has made back in profit what I owe, plus interest, it will be ours again."

"Who's Sal?" I asked, not sure if I wanted to know.

Pa looked around as if we weren't alone in his small office. "He's the Capo for this part of Little Italy," he whispered. "His team will be taking over operations of Bella for a while. We will need to play by their rules." He eyes met mine. "That means some changes. I need you to be okay with them until we get back on our feet."

"What rules?"

He hesitated, looking everywhere but at me.

"He does not want a woman in the kitchen."

My heart sank. How can he tell my father who can and cannot work in his kitchen?

"Rosa," he paused. "This is serious. He will let you cook lunch on the weekdays, but if you want to be here, you'll need to serve during dinner. And no more coming in early alone. This is not a safe place for a woman anymore."

"It's not safe, so I've heard," I whispered, more to myself. "But where will I practice my recipes? How will I help you work off what we owe to get our restaurant back, then?" My eyes filled with tears that I refused to let spill over. "This is not right."

He walked out from behind the desk and pulled me up into one of his famous Papa Bear hugs my sisters and I loved.

"Everything will be okay. I will keep you safe, but you must let me. You will practice at home for now, until we figure something else out." He pushed back, holding my shoulders at arm's length. "Come on. Let me introduce you to the new staff."

Together we walked back into the dining room. I must have been in shock because I didn't protest as I shook the hands of the two new waitresses who'd been wrangling the linens earlier and mumbled polite, "hellos." Absently, I wondered where Stella had gone, but I knew she'd been fired.

As we turned away from the new, shockingly young waitresses, I asked Pa, "When will I meet Sal?"

He swung his head around midstride. "Never, if I can help it. Be careful who you say his name to," he warned before softening his brow at my concerned expression.

I'd never seen this side of my father. He was the man who let worry run off his back like water off a duck. In all the years he'd owned Cucina Bella, there had been a fair share of setbacks, like when the kitchen had caught on fire during dinner service and we lost half of our ovens. He could have given up when he realized how much it would cost to replace them. Instead, he didn't miss a beat connecting with an old friend who installed and repaired commercial kitchen equipment throughout the Chicago area. I don't know how he did it, but we had new ovens the next working day, and to my knowledge didn't owe a thing on them.

Before we went back to the kitchen, we made a quick stop at the long bar.

"Aldo, Lou, this is my daughter, Rosa. She will be cooking lunch some days and waitressing in the evenings. Keep an eye on her, please," Pa said as the two men looked up from their work.

"Nice to meet you, Rosa," Aldo said, nodding. He was a bit older than my father but had more gray running through his thinning hair. His skin looked like brown leather, as if he'd spent decades working outdoors before picking up bartending.

My father slapped Aldo on the back. "Aldo and I have known each other for years. We both grew up on the same street in Little Hell." Little Hell was a nickname many locals gave to the area of Chicago where most Sicilians ended up after immigrating years ago. It was not a friendly place.

Aldo gave a quick nod and went back to work unloading the boxes of new liquor. Lou, on the other hand, stood with his dirty cleaning rag thrown over his shoulder, watching us. I nodded in his direction but couldn't see his eyes through his floppy, sandy-brown hair. He was younger than Aldo by a few decades. Probably closer to my age. When I dropped my gaze down to the pint glass he was holding, I noticed his hand looked rough and calloused. When he caught me staring, he set the glass down and reached over the bar with an outstretched hand.

"It's a pleasure," he said as I folded my hand inside his, which was much larger and warmer to the touch than I expected. Our eyes met for a brief second, and I could have sworn he smirked at me. A breath caught in my throat. Nerves. I wasn't used to strange men in a place where I'd always felt safe.

"Lou is from out of town, all the way from Waukegan. Finishing up his schooling here in the city," my father explained.

I threw him a questioning look, as if to say, "Is he one of *them*, the Outfit?" and Pa shook his head almost imperceptibly. I relaxed a few degrees. At least he had that going for him.

"Been talking to Lou for a few weeks now about helping me keep Bella's books from bleeding out. He's only a few credits shy of his accounting degree, but he also knows his way around a shaker and ice, so he'll be here a lot until one of those high-rise pencil-pusher gigs snaps him up," my father continued. "I'm serious now, fellas. Don't let no one touch my girls."

My face must have reddened because Lou pursed his lips to hold in a small chuckle.

"You got it, boss," he said, already back to wiping out the rest of the pint glasses.

My father and I stepped back into the kitchen.

"Not a lot has changed in here, and I don't imagine it will. But you should know I had to let most of the kitchen staff go, including Ricky. His brother works for these people, and I cannot have anyone getting hurt on account of... everything," he said, running his fingertips along the edge of the clean steel table in the middle of the room. "Part of me is looking forward to being back here in the kitchen. I have missed it." He explained that Sal decided to replace most of the staff with people he knew and could trust.

My father had learned how to cook from his mother in Sicily. When he was a young boy, most of the men in his tiny village had gone to America to find work and sent money back to their wives and children still on the island. Pa's father had made the voyage when Pa was only seven. Being the eldest of his siblings, it fell to Pa to help his mother, Bella, with the care of their two-room house and his two younger brothers while she worked for wealthy families in Palermo as a house-cleaner. Their situation was common but also difficult for the women and mothers left behind.

When Pa was ten, things changed. A letter from his father had arrived. He'd found work for Marco in America, now that he was old enough. Pa left the island the next day and never went back. His mother died ten years later of the flu and his younger brothers eventually made their way to the States. One of them lived in Chicago with his wife and kids, and the other found work on the railroads out west and moved every few months. My grandfather, Nunzio, still lived with my uncle in Chicago.

The work Nunzio found for my father was neck-breaking and dangerous. Since Pa was small for his age, a construction company hired him to climb the tall scaffolding of brand-new skyscraper buildings and deliver supplies to the welders and other tradesmen, often crawling through tight openings around the narrow outside frame of the buildings, hundreds of feet above the ground. It paid little, but it was how he learned to speak English.

At home, Pa still cooked all the meals. It was Nunzio who suggested he go to a trade school to become a line cook when he was eighteen. The year he graduated, he opened Cucina Bella and met my mother at a local produce stand where she was peddling fruit from a few of the farms outside the city. My father, being who he was, was never content only working a line. He made Bella into the institution it became with my mother at his side.

All of this, my family history, their sacrifice, would be for nothing if we did not fight for the restaurant. We would get it back. It was my only hope.

Word must have spread fast because the normal evening rush was more like a steady trickle that came to a full stop well before closing time that night. Lunch had been much of the same, with only the regulars coming in on their breaks to eat at the bar. A few of them asked about the changes but were met with half-hearted grunts from Aldo and nothing from Lou. I worried that we'd lose even our most loyal customers if this kept up.

"When are Ma and the girls coming in today?" I asked my father as we chopped zucchini side by side for the lunch prep.

"Camille will be in to work dinner, but Ma and Ivana will stay home. No need to invite trouble."

I let out a long sigh. Part of me was relieved they wouldn't be here to see this. But the other part craved some sense of normalcy. To see them, as usual, bustling around the customers, would have put my nerves at ease and probably the neighborhood's as well. But I understood. Things would be different now, and I had to get on board. I had no other option.

Later that afternoon, I slipped off my dirty chef's apron and replaced it with a black server's uniform for the first time in over a year. In the bathroom, I took a long look at myself in the mirror, hands perched on either side of the porcelain sink. I looked a mess. My hair had puffed out from its tight bun, frizzing into a halo of small curls around my forehead and my eyes were deep dark wells staring back at me. It had only been a few hours of this new reality, but now time stretched, never ending.

"Get yourself together, Rosa," I spat at my reflection. "You want to be respected, then do the work."

Do the work. It was something my father picked up from his time at the trade school, learning the ins and outs of cooking and restaurant management. Many of his teachers dismissed immigrant students, chastising them in front of peers when they didn't understand instructions in English. In his second year, Pa took a class from a Polish man who'd immigrated as a young child. He told his students, "Do the work and the rest would follow." My father taped the saying on his desk the day he opened the restaurant two decades ago.

Camille had arrived in the time I took changing and stood in the entryway as I made my way back out. Her wide eyes said everything they needed to. When she caught sight of me in a server's uniform, her brow lifted, and she cocked her head in question. I pulled her into Pa's office.

"What in the blue devil is going on?" she demanded before the door even closed behind us. "Where's Julia, and why are you in black?" She looked me up and down.

"Oh, Camille," I said, unsure of where to begin. "Pa is in trouble with..." I scanned the small room before continuing, "...some bad people. He's in gambling debt."

Camille leaned in. "So, it's true? The rumors that he's been involved with the Outfit?" she whispered.

"You knew about this?"

"Not really, just that he likes to bet on horse races and such. It's why the radio is always tuned to the sports station. Jackson told me a few months ago that he lost a big one."

"Why didn't you say anything to me?" I felt blindsided for the second time that day.

"I thought you knew. Or maybe that you wouldn't care," she said, biting the inside of her cheek like she always did when she was nervous. "I don't know. Sorry, I should have said something. Are we losing Bella?"

"No. Pa told me he can work off his debt. But they are taking over operations until then. And the new boss isn't a fan of women working the line." I gestured to my outfit. "So, I'll be on the floor with you."

"And Stella?"

"They fired her, along with Ricky and Julia." I didn't want to go into the real reason Ricardo wasn't there anymore. Not my place.

Camille frowned, but didn't appear all too shaken up. I had always admired that about her, the way she could roll with the punches.

The next few hours crawled by as we stood near the drinks station in the back, watching the half-empty dining room. Although the usual crowd skipped dinner, the bar remained busy with unfamiliar faces popping in every few minutes to check out the place.

"At least one of the new bartenders is easy on the eyes," Camille said, nudging me with her elbow.

"You mean Quasimodo over there?" I asked, pointing my chin to Aldo.

Camille batted my shoulder. "No! The younger one. He keeps looking at you."

I had noticed it, too. Twice, I had caught Lou watching as I passed the bar to ring in my table orders. Each time, a spike of anxiety swirled in my stomach, but I ignored it, contemplating my decision not to wear my engagement ring. Taking it off while at the restaurant had become a habit, but now I wondered if it would be safer to keep it on, given the situation.

"That's Lou. Dad hired him to help him with the books. I don't think he's one of them," I explained. At least, that was what I had gathered from our brief introduction earlier.

"Smart and handsome. Introduce me later?" she asked, all doe-eyed.

I laughed, shaking my head. Camille, always on the hunt. "Sure."

Although I only had a couple of tables, the few I waited on gave me the opportunity to scope out the food the kitchen sent out. Almost every plate I picked up on the pass needed cleaning; it looked as if they'd come off a lunch line at an elementary school. The new cooks they'd hired were sloppy. Why was Pa allowing these plates to go out?

At one point, I popped my head into the kitchen, only to see my father standing ramrod straight, looking dazed as the unfamiliar staff worked around him, slopping pasta from the big pot into bowls and ladling out bland-looking tomato sauce without looking.

"Pa," I said from the door, not wanting to cross the threshold into the kitchen. I held up my hand, gesturing for him to come to me.

"What are you doing in here? You need to get back to the dining room," he said, not caring to lower his voice. Several of the new cooks looked over. I could feel my face turn red.

"The plates are messy," I whispered. "I've had to clean them all."

In that moment, I saw my father not as the man I'd looked up to my entire life, but as the flawed human he'd always been. Someone who'd made a series of bad choices who now had to live with the consequences and wasn't sure how. I feared the fight had gone out of him.

It took a moment for what I said to register, but when it did, he clapped his hands twice. Everyone froze and looked at him.

"Attention, everyone. This is my kitchen. I will not let you embarrass me. Cleaner plates, or you are gone."

From the corner, I could see one of the younger new line cooks, who a moment before cowered, trying to make himself invisible, stand a little straighter. At least one of them had some respect.

Unlike the rest of us, Lou didn't get a moment of downtime, and we left right after the last customer as our father had instructed us to. "No lingering around at night. Let the others clean up," he'd told us both. We obliged.

On the walk home, I ran the last two days through my mind. How did I miss what everyone else seemed to know about my father? Had I been too caught up in what I wanted for myself that I couldn't see what was right in front of me? Anxiety and disappointment weighed me down.

"Have you talked to him yet?" Camille asked, pulling me from my thoughts.

"Who?" I responded, still half in my thoughts.

"Ant. Have you talked to Ant yet? You said you were going to at the beach, but you never told me how it went."

I made a low grumbling noise. "No, we didn't get to that. He told me about the gambling issue, though. It shocked me, but

I'm glad I had a heads-up before today. I'm planning to talk to him after church tomorrow."

"It might be harder now, you know. I wouldn't blame him if he didn't want his fiancée working at a place mixed up with the Outfit."

"I know, but I'll have to convince him now. Pa needs me."

Camille grabbed my hand and held it the rest of the way home.

"Coming!" I shouted, racing down the stairs the next morning, my hair still set in its rollers. The doorbell rang again as I reached for the knob, flinging it open.

"Why all the noise?" I asked, expecting to see one of the neighborhood kids asking for Ivana.

"Sorry, I didn't know if the doorbell worked. I've been out here for a few minutes." Lou stood there, sweat dripping down his forehead. It was only ten in the morning, but the summer heat had already saturated the day.

"Oh. It's you." One of my hands flew up to the rollers in my hair, mortified.

"Try to contain your enthusiasm," he said, struggling to grab a handkerchief out of his pocket as he balanced a cardboard box in one hand. Remembering where I was, I took a step down to help him with the box.

"Come inside. My father isn't here, though. You just missed him." We both shuffled inside the tight entryway, rotating around each other like two cats squaring off.

"That's all right. Can I leave these here with you then?"

"Sure."

I peeked into the box to see a large stack of paper that looked fresh from the printer. "Are these new menus?" I asked, pulling the top sheet off the stack.

"Could be. I'm not too sure." He shrugged and set the box down on the bottom step. "They told me to drop them off, so here I am."

"This is all wrong. Where's the ricotta lasagna? And no cannoli? Who do these people think they are?" I spat out, my voice echoing off the entryway walls. "We serve *pizza* now?"

"I guess so. A pizza oven arrived today."

"Well, then. Thank you for stopping by. I will make sure my father sees these when he's back from the market. Edits should be expected," I said, reopening the door so Lou could leave.

Lou lowered his shoulders and leaned toward me as he said in a low, almost mocking voice, "I'm pretty sure he's already approved it. Why else would they have sent it to the printers?"

Stepping back, the wall grazed the backs of my arms, highlighting the lack of space between us. I didn't know if I should shout or laugh. Instead, I dropped my eyes to my skirt, where the keys hanging off his belt loop had brushed against me a moment ago. A University of Chicago tag dangled from the gold chain. So, a smart bartender, then.

As if just noticing the uncomfortable position he'd maneuvered us into, Lou cleared his throat and moved back a few paces.

"My apologies. I'm sure there's still time to make changes, but it will cost an awful lot. I'd advise against it." He opened the door and stepped back out into the sweltering heat.

I shoved the box onto my father's desk in the den and went back upstairs to finish getting ready for church. We would be attending with Anthony's family, as we had done many times in the past. I needed to look put together, every part of the future wife I would be, so Ant would listen. It couldn't wait any longer. We needed to talk about our future, *my* future.

As we entered the Church of Santa Maria Incoronata, where my parents had married and we'd gone every Sunday for the last two decades, a dozen eyes tracked us. One of the only Sicilian churches on this side of town, it was full of the other families who had come from the island. We shared a common sense of familiarity with each other, knowing the customs and history of our people. But as with most Sicilian communities, the gossip mill worked overtime. I shouldn't have been surprised when many of the families who'd normally greet us with hugs and kisses on the cheek turned away, or busied themselves as we passed their pews, even though my family, the Bianchis, had been a respected fixture in this congregation for twenty years.

I held my head high, as did my mother. This was part of the price we'd pay for getting caught up with the Outfit. Hypocritical, to be sure, since most of the men dotting the pews also played the numbers, but, as I learned, it was a different thing altogether to be associated with someone who'd been unlucky.

When Ant squeezed my hand as we filled into our regular pew, grateful to have him by my side. His family had been attending L'Incoronata for longer than we had, and their ties ran deep in this part of Chicago. It meant something to have them sit with us.

As I looked over at my parents, their faces set in a stony silence, my heart cracked. My mother's jaw clenched, her lips forming a tight line as she stared straight ahead. After we sat, I noticed Ant's mother lean over and whisper something in Ma's ear. They'd been close friends since childhood, and if anyone could break through my mother's steely exterior, it'd be her. I couldn't make out what she said, but Ma's face relaxed a few degrees short of a smile.

For the better part of the next hour, we dutifully rose, kneeled, sat, and kneeled again as the old priest delivered his sermon and we said our prayers. The church was old and ornate; as a child, I would get lost in wonder at the stained-glass windows that lined the outer walls. Their scenes terrified my young mind, but the colors danced over the walls in vivid display, as the late morning sun reflected inward like a real-life kaleidoscope. More than once, my mother had jostled me back from my daydreaming with a sharp stab of an elbow. That morning, though, I didn't have the luxury of a wandering mind, as it stayed fixed on my family's circumstances and how I would appeal to Ant later.

Outside, my hand over my forehead to block the glare from the blinding white sun, I asked Ant to go on a walk.

"Sure thing, sweetheart," he'd replied without hesitation.

Most of the time, "going on a walk" was code for time together alone, but it meant more that morning.

We hugged our families goodbye and walked toward the local business district. Before we got too far, I suggested we take the long way through Roosevelt Park, where benches sat along the walkway, one of which my father donated to the park district years ago.

"It's warm out today, but I could use the sunshine," I argued, although I knew Ant wouldn't protest.

After a few minutes of silent walking, we found a bench under a shady willow tree to rest.

"Ant—"

"Rosa—" we both started at the same time. A shy smile swept across my face, and I cringed inside. Now called for confidence, not girlish charm.

Squaring my shoulders toward Ant, I took in a steadying breath.

"Thank you for telling me the truth about my father's… situation the other day. You were right." His expression crumpled into a look of what I thought was pity, but then he reached up and caressed my cheek in his hand.

"I'm sorry you had to find out that way. I thought you knew, but it was insensitive of me to drop it on you like it was nothing. I didn't mean to ruin your day."

"It's all right. It's good I know the whole truth. Cucina Bella is important to my family. To me. And I have a responsibility to ensure we do not lose it."

"Responsibility? Your father got himself into this mess, Rosa. You don't have to answer for his mistakes."

I looked at my hands curled together in my lap before responding.

"What would you do if your father was in jeopardy of losing his business? His livelihood? Would you sit back and do nothing?"

"Of course not. But that is different."

"How?"

Ant held my gaze, the question hanging heavy in the air between us.

At last, he said, "It's my responsibility to take care of you. I'm sorry your father has put you in this situation. And for what it's worth, I do know how much the restaurant means to you. What exactly are you asking me? If you want me to be all right with you working among criminals, I don't think that's something I can agree to."

"Would you have been okay with it before, if my father hadn't gotten himself into this mess?"

"We would have worked something out. But things have changed now," he said, clasping my hands.

Anger bubbled below the surface, threatening to break through. Steeling myself for what I had to say next, I sat back, removing my hands from his.

"Ant, if you love me, if you want to marry me, you will let me help my father. I won't turn away from him now. I understand your concern, but this is something I must do. For my family. After he is through this trial and Bella is safe, we can revisit the topic. Otherwise, I don't know if us getting married is the right thing."

I hadn't meant to give him an ultimatum, but I suddenly realized it was the only way I'd be able to continue to work, to support my father, and ensure our family's legacy stayed intact. And to continue my cooking. As my mother reminded me, I was a woman. And women made hard decisions.

Stunned at my display of defiance, Ant's lips parted then closed into a tight line as he nodded his head once.

"All right then. Let's go get some ice cream." We stood and the conversation was over. For now. I should have been grateful for what seemed like calm acquiescence, but something about it didn't sit right. How could it have been that easy?

After recounting our conversation with Camille that night lying in our dark room, she reassured me that Ant only wanted the best for us and that, apparently, I didn't give his affection enough credit.

"He's loved you since you were both five. He wouldn't let you go over something as silly as working in your father's restaurant."

Still, I knew the conservative Italian family that had raised him. The conversations he had with his mother, which undoubtedly took a similar refrain as those I had with my own, would have weaseled their way into his beliefs by now. Would it be too much for him to accept my small dreams as his own? Our family's insistence on our engagement clouded my judgment, and likely his as well. I prayed he'd stay true to his word, rather than letting me think I'd gotten my way. I couldn't decide whether I was a fool for hoping, or strong enough to take a stand when needed.

Chapter 6

"We have six months to make the money back," I heard a low voice rumble through the cracked office door when I walked into the restaurant kitchen for my lunch shift. It sounded familiar, but I couldn't quite place who it belonged to until a caught a glimpse of his side profile through the office door. Lou stood next to my father, peering over his shoulder at a large ledger on his desk.

"That's it?" my father asked, his voice small.

"Their agreement is ironclad. Unfortunately, six months in standard in these cases. But I've found some ways to cut expenses. You might not like them. They'll only be temporary, until you're paid up."

Maybe Lou had more to do with the menu changes than he mentioned. Although it was atrocious, not a menu I'd be proud to put my name on, we could live with it for a while if it meant getting back to normal sooner.

I wondered how we could have gotten here so fast. Just last week, I was running the kitchen like a well-oiled machine, content to learn the business. Now it felt like an alternate reality. As if we were merely players in a game and outside of our actual bodies, watching as we went through the motions, a ghost of former selves.

Now, the kitchen felt sterile, not friendly. No laughter filled the empty moments, no Ricky coming in late and spilling pasta water all over the counter as usual, no experimenting early in the morning with Pa on a new recipe. In fact, I hadn't a clue where my notebook had gone. My hands had softened because I was no longer washing them fifty or more times a day. I cooked for three hours. That's it. Then I changed into my black uniform and pasted on a friendly smile, my transformation from chef to server complete. Ready now to wait on the customers whose eyes lingered a little too long on my hips, the ones who threw up a hand without making eye contact to get attention. The ones who now watched over the restaurant with a menacing presence.

Ant had made it a habit to meet us every night he could after our dinner shift ended. Camille thought it gentlemanly, her innocence and desperate need for love to be real glossing over the controlling undertones. Almost every night, he walked us home and kissed me goodnight before I climbed the stairs to the bedroom and passed out from boredom and frustration. He could tell. Everyone could. Which is why two weeks into our new routine, Camille suggested we go out for drinks after our shifts. I bristled at the idea, my bed beckoning for another night of blissful unconsciousness.

"When was the last time you dressed up?" she asked, poking at my apron.

"Ant and Jackson are at a business school dinner," I tried to argue. I should have known better.

"Great. In fact, perfect. It'll be you and me and the rest of Chicago," she said, doing a small twirl. Nothing could excite my sister more than an unexpected adventure. The thrill of what could happen, the unknown delights that lay ahead.

"We'd have to change and sneak out. Ma won't be happy if we get caught. She needs our help at the bake sale tomorrow."

"And what she doesn't know won't hurt her. We'll be there to sell banana bread and scones to the ladies who baked the blueberry muffins and sourdough."

It was hard to say no to Camille when she had her mind set. Her optimism infected me in a way that wormed itself straight into my heart, and soon, I was also applying lipstick as if I might run into Frank Sinatra himself that night.

"Where would you like to go, Cinderella?" she asked as soon as we'd passed the farthest streetlight on our block.

I thought for a moment. "Let's go somewhere Ant and Jackson would never take us. Somewhere we're sure not to run into the DePaul girls," I said, my eyes widening in anticipation.

"You can be a real firecracker when you want to be. I know just the place."

Not before long, we were running up the steps to the nearest L station, our skirts fluttering behind in the thick, inky air. After a few stops, we got off at a dimly lit platform. I scanned the area, spotting only a grimy-looking cat. It might have been gray? Or white, once-upon-a-time?

Sensing my hesitation, Camille looped her arm through my elbow and assured me the dance hall was only a few blocks away. We'd already come this far, I told myself, taking one last swig from the bottle of wine we'd wrapped in a paper bag and sipped while on the train.

As we walked, I could smell the lilac perfume my sister always wore. It wafted off her bouncing red curls in waves. Her hair matched her personality. Alive, dimensional, and loud. The only grandchild to inherit my grandmother's coloring, she reminded me of a jewel, even as a young child. Her green eyes shimmered against her light skin and hair the color of an August sunset over Lake Michigan. Ma always crossed herself when someone pointed out the rareness of her features, as if the Virgin Mary herself could save my sister's soul from the devil's mark.

A few blocks and one turn away, Camille led us down a dark alley that smelled of rotting fish and bodily fluids I didn't want to think about.

"Where are you taking us?" I asked, standing back a few paces.

"Don't worry, we're almost there," Camille said, dragging me along behind. And she was right. On the other side of the large, offensive-smelling dumpster, a bright green light illuminated a thick metal door beneath. Camille leaned in and knocked five times in a pattern, and a man wearing a brown fedora low over his brow swung it open as if it weighed nothing.

"What's it to ya?" he asked, not bothering with eye contact.

"The bluejay chirps at six tonight," Camille whispered. At that, the man lifted his chin and presented us with a wide, gleaming smile that held a sliver of a toothpick.

"Welcome, ladies." He ushered us through a short, dark corridor before pulling back a set of black velvet drapes to reveal a room teeming with life. Low, sensual music vibrated up from the floor and floated around us. Men and women, young and middle-aged, milled about in trendy, almost edgy-looking attire. Some perched on high-backed stools around small round tables, while others hovered in tight packs, belly-laughing at someone's joke. This was no dance hall.

The compact bar dominated the crowded space. Through the haze of cigarette smoke, I could barely see our reflection in the large, speckled mirror behind it. It was smaller than the restaurant's bar but looked well-stocked. All brand-name labels on the rows of bottles of whiskey, gin, and vodka.

"Is this a speakeasy?" I breathed into my sister's ear, not wanting anyone to pick up on the fact that I was completely out of place.

"Sure is. Been around since before prohibition, so I've heard."

"How do you know about it?" I raised an eyebrow.

"The new waitress, Sharleen, brought me. I came with her after work when you were off last weekend." Camille pushed us past several groups, making a path to the bar. "Isn't it just the bee's knees?"

"It's something like that," I muttered under my breath. At least we'd be safe from running into anyone from the DePaul crowd here. They wouldn't be caught dead in a place like this.

We shimmied our way up to the bar, filling the last two empty seats. It wasn't my usual place for a Saturday night out, but I didn't feel we were unwelcome either. Something about the intimacy of the place calmed my nerves, like a balm to my exposed edges.

A bartender stood with his back turned to the bar.

"What'll it be tonight?" he said, turning around. I whipped my head up in recognition. Lou. "Oh, well. Hello there."

"Hi. I didn't know you worked here," I responded, caught in his gaze.

"A few nights a week now, after Cucina Bella closes."

My sister cleared her throat, kneeing my thigh under the bar.

"Oh, excuse me. You haven't been properly introduced to my sister, Camille. Camille, this is Lou. He's one of our new bartenders."

"Yes, I've seen him at the restaurant a time or two," she responded, voice huskier than normal. "Nice to officially meet you, Lou."

Lou shook her hand across the narrow bar top and threw his rag over his shoulder with the other. He was wearing a black button-down shirt tucked into black trousers with black and gold suspenders over his shoulders. He fit right in, like another piece of expertly sourced décor.

"So?" he asked, looking between us.

"I'll have a gimlet," Camille replied without missing a beat.

I preferred a bold red over anything else, but I doubted this was the place to order a Barolo.

"Why don't you surprise me?"

Another man's voice piped in over Lou's shoulder from behind the bar. "We don't do that here, honey. House rule. Either know what you want or move aside."

"It's all right, Frank. I know these ladies. I work for their father," Lou shot back.

"Whatever you say," he mumbled before turning back to the other customers waiting for their drinks.

"Be right back," said Lou.

When he turned around to make our drinks, Camille seized the opportunity to spin me in my seat so she could whisper-yell into my ear as if our turned backs would provide any ounce of privacy.

"What a coincidence!" she hissed.

"Mmhmm, coincidence, I'm sure."

She looked up at me with her green saucers for eyes.

"I swear to all that's holy, I did not know he worked here. He wasn't here the other night. But forget about Lou. Did you see the other bartender? He looked like he walked off the pages of Rolling Stone." She fanned herself with the cocktail menu from the bar.

Well, *that* obsession didn't last long.

"I'm going to give him my number," she said, a determined smile playing on her lips.

"What about Jackson?"

"What *about* him? He's likely making eyes at some sorority sweetheart who thinks the South Side is a foreign country. Loyalty isn't his strong suit."

I winced, aware Ant would also be in the same company. I'd be lying if I said a part of me didn't worry about Ant being around women whose families could afford to send them to a school like DePaul. Ant had never given me an outright reason not to trust him, but if his past dalliances were any indication, the playboy version of himself would be hard to shake off.

"Oh, hun. I meant nothing by it. Ant only has eyes for you. You have nothing to worry about," Camille said, squeezing my shoulder. "Come on now. Let's not think about them. We're here to have ourselves a rowdy, fun night. You're not married yet!"

Once we turned around, Lou placed our drinks on small wooden coasters in front of us. Camille's gimlet looked like perfection in a glass, garnished with a lime slice and a small sprig of the daintiest white flowers. As for my mystery cocktail, I didn't recognize it.

"It's sangaree," Lou answered, reading my mind.

I cocked my head, trying to think where I'd heard the name before.

"It's the old-fashioned version of sangria. Speakeasies often served it during prohibition. Thought it might be up your alley."

Odd, I thought. We'd only had two conversations, yet he could tell I wasn't a liquor girl. An observant bartender.

I lifted the wineglass to my lips and took the smallest of sips without breaking eye contact. It tasted like sangria, only with more spice. A hint of nutmeg lingered on my tongue as I set the glass back down.

"What do you think?" he asked, face relaxed to the point that it seemed purposeful.

"It's nice. Thank you."

"You're very welcome." He shifted his weight forward, propping his chin up with one elbow on the bar. "So, what're the Bianchi sisters doing on *this* side of town?"

"Is it a crime to have fun?" Camille asked, shooting him a sideways glance.

"Not at all. But didn't expect the two of you to walk through those doors. Sharleen works quickly, I suppose."

"We'll I'm glad she showed me this place. Much more fun than the uptight dance halls most boys bring us to." Camille pulled a pack of cigarettes from her small, pill-shaped pocketbook and lit one, blowing a billow of smoke in Lou's direction.

"Did I hear someone say something about fun?" Frank said, wiping off the section of bar in front of him. "My shift ends in about ten minutes. Care for a drink and a spin around the dance floor?" he said, peering at Camille like a gazelle he'd like to chase.

I looked over at the small piece of shiny wood flooring in the corner that must have been the "dance floor." Not a single person occupied it, let alone danced.

"Doesn't seem like the dancing sort of place," I said before Camille could respond.

"Oh, it gets hoppin'. You'll see." The corner of Frank's mouth curled upwards, but his smile fell short of his eyes.

"Frank, tone it down. I promised their old man I'd keep an eye out for them," said Lou.

"We're not at the restaurant, and you're not on the clock," I said. "We are perfectly capable of taking care of ourselves."

Camille raised her glass to mine in a toast. "What my sister said. And to answer your question, Frank, I'd love a drink and a spin."

Soon, I sat alone at the bar and watched as the dance floor filled like a bunch of ants fighting over a small crumb of bread. Camille and Frank were the first out there, but it didn't take long for the party to roar to life. Lou refilled my drink and stood back, watching over the small space as if he expected someone to snatch me from my seat.

"You can relax, you know," I said to him finally. "I'm not going anywhere until Camille is ready to go home."

"Well, you might be here for a while then." He stepped closer, and a whiff of cedar mixed with citrus filled the space. Something low in my belly clenched, making me sit up straighter. If anything made me nervous that night, it was him, not the speakeasy. His gaze fell on my left hand and the diamond I'd remembered to slip back over my ring finger, which made him push back to where he'd been standing a moment ago.

"I didn't realize you were engaged," he said, so low I almost missed it.

"Yeah, for a few weeks now. I rarely wear it in the restaurant. Don't want to lose it." I swirled the ring around with my thumb, wondering if I'd ever get used to it.

He held his palms up, showing off the rough and calloused hands. "You don't have to explain anything to me."

"Good. I won't."

He crossed his arms and leaned his hip against the back wall under the mirror. "Tell me something, though. Why does an engaged woman continue to work in a restaurant kitchen of all places? Aren't you going to be doing enough of that at home soon?"

So much for not having to explain anything. Without thinking, I gave him the truth. "Because I like it. And the restaurant will be mine someday. That should be reason enough."

Lou didn't move. He stared down at me, his eyes growing dark and wide as the room narrowed around us and everything else faded to background noise. *A girl could get lost in those eyes*, I thought to myself. A dark, daring part of me wanted to reach up and touch his face to feel the friction of the slight stubble on his chin against my skin.

What was I thinking? I chalked it up to his good looks. I was engaged, not blind.

Clearing my throat, I attempted to bring my unladylike thoughts under control. I'd never met a man so confusing. So hot and cold. Everything about him read as aloof, but there was a protectiveness in the tenor of his voice that I couldn't ignore. It left me uneasy.

"I like your food. I tried some of the lasagna you made for lunch the other night before my shift," he said, finally breaking eye contact. "But you have big dreams. I'd look into making other plans if I were you."

His audacity caught me off guard. He couldn't possibly know enough about me or my family to make such absurd suggestions. For Christ's sake, he'd only worked at Bella for two weeks. Not nearly long enough to hold any strong opinions about my life, let alone my dreams.

I turned my shoulder to him and Camille met my gaze, bounding back to me, beads of sweat forming on her upper lip.

"Rosa, come dance with me!" she shouted over the music, tugging me off the barstool. Normally, I'd protest. I never had much rhythm, but tonight, I didn't care. Anywhere was better than talking to Lou. The dance floor would do.

We danced until blisters formed on the backs of my heels, long past my normal limit. By the time we made our way back to the bar for a much-needed water break, the crowd had thinned to only a handful of youngsters throwing dice at a table. Since finding out about my father's gambling habit, I saw it everywhere. It hardly seemed fair that we'd be paying such a heavy price for a pastime that seemed ubiquitous with living in Chicago.

"We should get going," I said to Camille, rubbing my ankles. "How much cash do you have left? The L stopped running about an hour ago."

I dug through my small handbag. I had only three dollars and some change. During the day, it'd be enough to get home, but at this hour, who knew what cabbies were charging?

We emptied our coin purses onto the bar, pooling what we had, as Frank strolled out the back door. He'd disappeared a while ago after telling Camille he'd be right back. I'd assumed we'd seen the last of him. He struck me as the type to chase a better offer if one came along—and I doubted a girl with an overbearing older sister sounded like one.

"Where ya ladies off to?" he asked, his words slurring together.

"Home," I said without looking up.

"Ahh, so soon? Why don't ya come back to my place? It's just around the corner—" before he could finish his half-baked thought, Lou's hand clasped Frank's shoulder.

"Hey buddy, why don't you get going? I'll make sure everything is closed up." Lou led Frank back toward the door he had come from, but Frank resisted, stumbling back into the shelves of liquor bottles.

"Heya man, watch yourself. I'ma just tryin' to have a little fun," he said.

"Fun's over," Lou said, almost dragging him out the door.

I cleaned up our cash and slipped it back into my purse. We'd have enough to make it close to home. We could walk the rest of the way. I needed to get us out of here.

"Let's go," I whispered over my shoulder.

We slipped out the front door before Lou made it back, but once outside in the dark alleyway, my breath quickened. I didn't feel safe here in this unfamiliar part of town. We made our way back to the main road where we could flag down a taxi. My head spun on a swivel, looking for any potential riffraff we'd need to avoid. The alley still smelled awful, and we both held our breath as we walked, not saying a word.

The night air stood still, and we could only hear the low rumble of the highway in the distance. Either everyone had long gone to bed, or we'd walked onto a deserted movie set. A bubble of panic rose in my throat when I heard footsteps approaching. I spun around to see Lou walking toward us, head down, hands stuffed deep into his trouser pockets.

"I called a cab. Should be here soon," he said once he reached us on the corner. The lone streetlight washed his skin out, but his eyes roamed over the two of us, ensuring we were still intact.

"You didn't have to do that. We'd have found one," I said, turning away. I didn't like this man and his presumptions. But as much as I wanted to put distance between him and me, I was secretly relieved to know we wouldn't have to wait much longer.

Lou didn't care about my chilly tone or the not-so-subtle hints I peppered throughout our conversations.

"No, I didn't have to. But I did. I'll wait with you, if that's alright?" It wasn't a question so much as a statement of fact.

We stood together in a silence that seemed to stretch on longer than Michigan Avenue itself. Camille leaned into me, and we held each other upright as exhaustion crept its way over our bodies, which were encased in a fine layer of dried, salty sweat. Five minutes later, we heard the growl of tires on pavement come toward us before a yellow taxicab with the traditional black-and-white checkered top slowed to a stop in front of us.

I reached to open the back door at the same time as Lou. Our fingers brushed together, sending a jolt of electricity up my arm. I jerked my chin up to face him as I pulled my hand back and placed it on the top of the cab, the cooling sensation of the metal erasing the shock. I caught the expression of surprise on his smooth face, but he quickly righted himself, clamping his jaw shut, sharp edges returning.

We slid onto the cracking leather bench seats and murmured "hello" to the driver.

"Goodnight, ladies. See you at the restaurant," Lou growled before gently closing the door and tapping the roof.

Chapter 7

"You look tired, dear," Ant's mother chirped over the table.

"Morning, Mrs. Russo. Only a poor night's sleep, that's all," I responded, handing her the banana bread she bought. I never understood the point of church bake sales. Every one of these women spent the last week baking pastries to donate. Then each of them intentionally bought back at least as much as they baked. Why not skip all the baking and just donate the money instead?

Mrs. Russo lowered her head across the table toward me. "You know, a woman needs to look her best for her husband. It's your duty. Best not forget that."

"She's not married yet," Camille said in a singsong voice.

"That's right. She's not. Have a wonderful day, ladies. Tell your mother I stopped by."

I turned around to face Camille. "What was that about? Also, how on Earth are you so..." I flapped my hand in front of her. "Awake?"

"A little hair of the dog," she said, opening her tote bag to reveal a bottle of something dark. "Don't pay her any mind. She's only trying to scare you into submission. It's an Italian mother-in-law tradition."

I rolled my eyes.

For the next two hours, we sat in the mid-morning sun, doling out Saran-wrapped goodies to the women of Santa Maria Incoronata.

By the time we finished, I'd nearly forgotten about the plans I had with Ant later that night. I wanted a nap.

The phone let out a loud ring when we arrived home. It was Ant calling to confirm he'd be picking me up at five. I contemplated canceling, but something about Mrs. Russo's tone earlier concerned me. We could use some quality time alone together, me and Ant. Maybe then I'd be able to stop thinking about Lou's calloused hands. I was engaged, for God's sake. Ant deserved my full attention, even if he wasn't ready to fully support my ambitions yet. I'd wear him down with time, I reassured myself.

After splashing some cool water on my face, I ran a brush through my unruly dark curls. Ant's mother was right; I looked worse for wear. Propping myself up on either side of the white porcelain sink, I stared at my reflection for a long time. Things hadn't gone to plan, but I needed to get myself together. Muster up the energy to pick my tired self up and march onward. It was the only thing to do. One foot in front of the other.

I regretted going out.

Pep talk over, I plastered on my face and swept my hair into a low, loose bun at the nape of my neck. It took longer than usual to get ready, but the effort had put me back together. I wanted tonight to be special. I hoped Ant and I could reconnect, and I'd be reminded of all the ways he was good for me. Of why we made sense. Maybe, just maybe, I'd be able to wear his ring without it tightening like a vise around my finger.

"Can we swing by the market?" I asked as we pulled away from the house in his T-bird.

"I made dinner reservations at Salvator's," he responded, shooting a confused look at me.

"Thanks for doing that. But I think I'd prefer to cook for you tonight, if you don't mind? Just the two of us. Jackson's out of town, right?"

"At his cousin's wedding. He'll be back tomorrow night."

"Perfect. What do you say?" Besides the fact that I couldn't stomach another night out, I also wanted to cook. It would steady me like nothing else could, help me get my mind right. Focus back on Ant, on *us*.

"All right. Sure. I wouldn't mind some alone time, either." A small smile played at the corners of his lips.

I'm sure he wouldn't. I waited for the usual thrill of anticipation, but there was nothing. Only the warm afternoon breeze sliding past my cheek as we drove.

Ant's apartment was close to the DePaul University campus but far enough away to say, "I'm an upperclassman with means." He'd roomed with Jackson since freshman year, but moved into a two-bedroom walk-up at the start of the summer. I envied the freedom and independence of college-aged men and women. Sometimes, when sleep evaded me, I played a game of 'what if' with my life. What if I'd gone to college instead of staying home to work with my father? What if I'd met someone other than Ant there? What if I never dated Ant? Never got engaged? What if I studied culinary arts or business management? Did it even matter? Most girls only went to school to find a suitable partner for marriage, anyway.

No one in my family had gone to college. The closest we came was my father's trade schooling. Camille decided early on that college would not be an option as she had a habit of skipping classes and hiding her report cards from our parents each semester. Eventually, they stopped asking. When my Ma was a child, the family merely worked to stay afloat and needed all the hands they could get to operate the produce stand. College or culinary school never felt like much of an option for me either. Cost was a big factor, and I already had the best mentor and teacher one could get: my father. As for my youngest sister… who knew? I hoped she'd have more options. I'd have liked to see one of us escape the domesticity that trapped most young women on our side of town.

We pulled into the small parking lot of a corner market near Ant's apartment to get the ingredients for the chicken cacciatore I planned to make.

"You have pots and pans, don't you?" I asked as we walked together to the shop doors, aware that a bachelor pad may not have a fully outfitted or functional kitchen.

"You know my mother wouldn't let those cabinet shelves sit bare. We have a full set, but you'll probably need to dust them off. I'm not sure either of us has ever touched them," Ant said, turning off the engine.

"Well, it's about time we put them to use, I'd say."

As soon as we stepped into the small but well-stocked market, a jolt of energy had me almost on my tiptoes peering over the rows of neatly packed shelves.

"What can I help you find?" he asked, watching me.

"A nice crusty loaf of bread?"

He nodded, grateful not to be standing around helpless. I'd always admired that about Ant. He never let himself go idle. He would take action, regardless of his duties. You rarely had to ask him for something once, let alone twice. No wonder he'd been named the Illinois State Athlete of the Year two years in a row in high school and awarded a full-ride scholarship to play tennis at DePaul, among others that had given him offers. Not that he needed it; his family would have no problem paying the tuition. Anthony Russo had a bright future ahead of him, one that I'd be a part of, if I stayed the course.

In his narrow galley kitchen, I found everything I needed. Rudimentary at best, but it would work. While chopping the onion, celery, peppers, mushrooms, and herbs, Ant put on a Pat Boone record, and the popular Moody River ballad expanded and floated over the furniture, filling every available space. Before I knew it, every window in the apartment hung open to let in the evening air and give the sauteing vegetables, and us, space to breathe.

For the first time in weeks, my mind tuned everything else out. The urge to cook for the heck of it had been building for too long. Now, time fell away as I chopped, cooked, and tasted. It was only then that I felt true control. Sometimes, I caught myself feeling sorry for people who hadn't yet found their thing, like Camille. The thing that made them whole.

"I love watching you move," Ant said into the space between my shoulder and neck.

I hadn't noticed him enter the kitchen until his arms wrapped around my waist from behind, and for a moment something sharp caught in my throat. My body went rigid and then relaxed back into the solid wall of his chest as if a stage cue had lit up over the stove that read, "You're fine! Show him you're fine!" The truth was that I wanted to be left alone. To cook, uninterrupted, until I felt good and ready to return to reality. I'd emerge a different, stronger woman forged by the flames of this four-burner Kenmore electric stovetop.

Ant sat at the doorway to the kitchen on a small metal chair he'd pulled up to watch me as I finished dinner. We said little; we were never big conversationalists, even as young children. But I could feel his eyes on my body.

"I can't wait to see you in our kitchen one day. The things you'll make. Our kids will be the best fed on the block," Ant said as he helped me set the tiny table for two.

A feeling low in my gut pulsed. It could have been anticipation of the future, our future, or dread. The line between them blurred. Trying to remain focused on the present, I chose anticipation. I had what every girl wanted: a loving man with a steady job who'd take care of me. My mother was right. I needed to get a grip. To make this work.

"Remember that time you tried to cook a soufflé, and Ben Buccatti came running through the house?" he asked, taking the first bite of his cacciatore.

"You about killed him there on the spot," I huffed out a laugh, recalling the long-ago memory.

"Well, you'd been working on it all day. Beating the heck out of those poor egg whites, who did nothing to deserve it. I couldn't let that hoodlum ruin your creation just because he wanted to be loud and obnoxious."

Ant had spent all day with me in my mother's kitchen as I read and reread the recipe for a classic chocolate soufflé, determined to make it. Back then, Ma encouraged my experiments. She likely assumed it would make me a better, more competent housewife one day, not build the foundation upon which our relationship would crumble. I'm sure a psychologist would have a field day with the fact that I don't bake anymore. But back on that early spring day, my ten-year-old self had decided to master the soufflé. I spent hours trying and failing batch after batch. The egg whites would not rise, no matter how long I whipped them.

As I had slid one of my last attempts in the oven, Ben came sprinting through the kitchen, and out the back door, in a game of neighborhood tag. Back then, we neighborhood kids were constantly coming and going through the houses on the block. No one minded because all the families with children were close. But that day, I'd forgotten to lock the front door. And even at ten, I knew loud noises or vibrations could spell disaster for a delicate soufflé.

In the end, no souffles stood up to my satisfaction. But Ben walked away with a black eye on account of Ant sucker-punching him after the third time he ran through the kitchen, ruining my last batch. To be fair, Ant did warn him as I pretended to ignore the whole thing. I wasn't weak, but I avoided confrontation at all costs, something I wouldn't learn to change until much later in life.

When I remembered the incident, I'd always thought of it as proof that Ant cared. He protected me in ways I couldn't. But as I sat at the Formica folding table in front of me, preparing to eat the meal I'd made for us, I realized it was the first of many times Ant acted on my behalf based on an assumption. An assumption I wouldn't or couldn't stick up for myself. And it had became truth, because I didn't learn to do it for myself.

With the kitchen put back together, Ant and I retired to the covered balcony off their living room. While only large enough for two chairs and a small cocktail table in between, I relished the fresh air pumping through my lungs. Ant had opened a nice bottle of wine he must have been saving for a special occasion, because it was old—old enough for the cork to have disintegrated, causing him to have to strain the deep red, almost purple, liquid into a pitcher.

"Don't you have a decanter? You'd think the son of a wine distributor would own such contraptions," I teased him, taking a luxurious sip. The wine was round in flavor yet bold. Its layers had blended over the years, balancing a typically acidic Chianti. Still, I could taste the whispers of its younger years on the edges of my tongue.

"Oh, I'm sure Mother packed one in a box for me, lost now to the depths of my closet," Ant replied, looking up at the night sky. "When we get a house of our own, I'll fish it out for you."

How nice that sounded, a house of our own. I could picture it: a stately brick single-family home built in the early dawn of the century in some hip and up-and-coming neighborhood like Lincoln Park. We'd renovate it, outfitting it with the most modern touches: a brand-new kitchen with an electric stove I would come to loathe, because nothing beats an actual flame, and three bathrooms covered in floor-to-ceiling imported Italian tile. There'd be a backyard, large enough for barbecues and a swing or two. It would be every woman's dream.

"Promise me we can have a natural gas stove in the kitchen," I asked, lacing my fingers through his across the small table between us.

He huffed a small laugh through his nose and squeezed my hand. "Whatever you want, Rosa. It's yours."

I don't remember living anywhere other than the corner townhouse my parents bought a few years after they opened the restaurant when I was only three. But the thought of having my own home, my own things beyond the clothes in the closets I shared with Camille, made me feel giddy that summer evening, sitting atop a balcony, alone with Ant, my future husband. It was all so adult. Suddenly, I could see our lives play out in spectacular color. There would be friendship, travel, children,

I supposed, and Chicago. What the vision didn't include was Cucina Bella.

"I wish you could stay the night," he whispered into the dark.

I barely caught it, but when I realized what he said, I whipped my head around to look at his profile, illuminated by the streetlamps down below. He'd never been so forward. Of course, we'd shared many kisses throughout the year we'd been together, some even passionate to the point of dizziness. But nothing more than that. He knew I wasn't that sort of girl. Or at least he'd assumed and tried nothing else.

"That would be nice, wouldn't it?"

He met my gaze, his brown eyes even darker now with longing. Before we said another word, he stood and led me by the hand back into his dark apartment. The stale air inside still smelled of dinner, but neither of us cared. We searched each other's faces, both standing at the edge of an invisible cliff, waiting to jump.

Ant took a tentative step forward, and I could feel his breath on my cheek; it smelled like expensive wine.

"Anthony," I sighed. Out of lust, out of fear? I didn't quite know.

"Rosa." He cradled the back of my head with his smooth hand, pulling me into him. I could feel the warmth of his chest, stomach, and hips spread through my body. For a moment, he held me there, looking into my eyes before he dipped his chin, bringing his lips to mine. They were still wet and tasted like wine and fruit. A buzzing sensation rose to my head, threatening to float me down the hall. To his bed. Every nerve ending lit up with desire. Such a strange new experience for me, yet magnetic. As if I were being pulled toward something without effort.

The kiss grew more needy as his other hand slid from my neck, over my hip before resting on the small of back. The pressure steadied me, grounding me in place. But I wanted more. I pressed my body into his, arching my back into his palm.

"We don't have to do anything you're not comfortable with," he breathed into my neck, in the space behind my ear. A shiver shot down my spine.

I didn't respond in words. Instead, I broke away, the sudden rush of cool air prickling my skin. Deliberately, I wrapped my fingers around his wrist and led him down the unlit hallway to the last door on the left. His bedroom. This man would soon be my husband. I'd known him all my life, so I had nothing to fear. I had only to let go.

Chapter 8

"**R**osa," Lou shouted as I walked past the bar for the hundredth time that evening. He'd been trying to get my attention for the past half hour, but I ignored him, too busy delivering appetizers to table seven and the drinks over to the large table with a party of ten. This time, though, the table closest to the bar area had turned to look so I couldn't ignore it.

"What is it? I'm a little busy tonight, if you can't tell."

"Oh yes, the Wednesday night rush," he gestured to the half-empty dining room.

My face stayed stony, not caring to debate him. The sooner this conversation ended, the better. Keeping my distance from him at work had become somewhat of a game over the past few days, one I'd been winning until now. I had no time for his confusing banter or his smoldering glances.

After I'd spent the evening at Ant's place, I knew my place and I would not jeopardize it with more inappropriate thoughts of a man I'd just met. While the night had been fine, it didn't match the transformative descriptions of the "first time" I've heard about. Still, I left content and less anxious about the whole "wedding night" fiasco. Ant seemed pleased too, even if he avoided direct eye contact afterwards. I chalked it up to embarrassment. We had taken baths together at one time, after all.

"Your father wants to see you after your shift in the office," Lou said, not breaking eye contact. His palms pressed against the wooden bar edge, learning over as if in deep conversation. But before saying anything else, he pushed himself upright and looked away.

I scrunched up my face in question. "Why isn't he out here?"

"He's in the back, poring over the books. Trying to find a way around things."

"That's right. I forgot; you know the ins and outs of our financials because of your fancy University of Chicago education. How convenient," I said, surprised at the edge in my voice. I hadn't a clue why I said that.

"How do you know where I go?"

I broke from his stare, Aldo catching the corner of my eye. "I saw a keychain dangling from your belt loop the other day."

"So, you were looking at my belt, were you?" His lips clamped together, as if suppressing a smirk.

"Don't flatter yourself," was all I could muster before turning back to the drink station.

The rest of the night crawled to a close as the last few tables cleared.

"Wait for me. I need to talk to Pa, and then we can walk home together," I said to Camille, who had already hung up her apron and slipped her work shoes off in favor of the black kitten heels she loved.

"Okay, but I'm leaving you if you're not out in ten minutes. I've got places to be, people to see," she said with a playful smile.

"Of course you do. I'll try to be quick."

Knocking twice on the office door, I pushed it open a few inches to peek inside before entering. My father sat with his head in his hands over the leather-bound notebook that served as the restaurant's ledger.

"Hey," I said, keeping my voice low, not wanting to startle him.

Pa shot upright but softened his face when he saw me in the doorway.

"Bona sira, bambina mia." *Good evening, my child.*

"Has something happened? Lou said you wanted to see me."

He ran his large hand over his face and blew out air. "Come, sit, sit, please."

"Pa, you're scaring me. What is it?" I asked, fear lacing my rushed words as I sat in the creaky chair opposite him.

"Money is tight. Tighter than I expected," he said, eyes drooping from exhaustion. "I am taking on a second job to help cover expenses while we wait this out, but I need your help."

"A second job? What are you talking about?"

"I've taken a third shift at the Union Stockyards four days a week."

"Packing meat?" I asked. Not wanting to add to his embarrassment, my eyes averted to the small window behind him.

"Yes, only until we're back on our feet. But I need your help here with things. I'll still be able to be here for the dinner service, but the mornings will be difficult. You know this place better than anyone else, and I wouldn't ask if it were not my last option before giving over complete control to *them*." He spat out the last word.

His tone revealed the situation's gravity. "Of course. What do you need me to do?"

Pa explained that I'd oversee making and receiving the regular deliveries in the mornings when he had to work at the stockyard. I'd also go to the market three times a week to handpick our fresh fish and select specialty items.

"But, Rosa, be conservative at market. Things are not like they were before. We must watch every penny." He punctuated his words by poking the ledger with his pointer finger. We both knew my eyes were too big for my purse at the markets. More than once, I'd begged Pa to buy a whole black truffle or ten pounds of fresh scallops driven overnight from New York to the stalls.

"Okay, Pa. I will be good," I said, shoulders pulled back. "Thank you for trusting me to help." A calming sense of pride washed over me. I'd been patient, biding my time in my reduced role, and it had paid off.

"One last thing, and I need you to hear me. Be careful. Things are still not safe here, even less so now that the changes haven't made a dent in the debt. They are not happy with the progress." We sat there for a moment, both absorbing the weight of his words.

A faint knock on the door broke the silence.

"Come in, Lou," Pa said, waving him over to the desk.

I looked between the two of them, eyebrows pinched together. This had nothing to do with Lou.

"Can we help you?" I asked Lou, whipping my head around to face him.

"Rosa, be kind. Lou has offered to help. He'll accompany you in the early mornings for the deliveries, so you are not here by yourself, and he'll take you to the markets. You can show him some of our tricks for picking the best produce," my father explained, like it made all the sense in the world.

"I'll be fine on my own. I don't need a babysitter."

Lou took a half step in my direction. "I won't bother you, I promise. I'll stay out of your way. And make sure we stay on budget."

I ignored him. "Pa, I don't think this is necessary. I can manage a budget just fine."

"It is not up for debate, Piccola. Lou will be with you."

I wanted to argue more, to make my father listen. He wanted me to run the restaurant someday, so I had to learn. And I did not need a gruff bartender-slash-accountant looking over my shoulder. But the look on my father's face told me to drop it.

"When do we start?" I asked, resigned.

"I don't have my first shift until later this week, but I want you to start tomorrow. That way, you can call me if you run into any issues."

"Will you be able to manage?" I shot at Lou. "Or will your shift at the speakeasy wear you out?"

"Don't worry about me."

My eyes nearly rolled to the back of my head. "Oh, I won't."

"Great. Now go on home. I'm going to stay. Get caught up on things," Pa said, ending the discussion.

Making my way back out to the dining room, I expected to see Camille tapping her foot, waiting for me, but it was empty. I turned around to do a final sweep and almost dove headfirst into Lou's broad chest.

"Geez, you seem to be everywhere," I mumbled, stepping back to look up at him.

He steadied me by the shoulders. "Nah, I think you just like being close to me."

Although his shoulders drooped, his eyes were as green as ever, alive and watching. A shiver ran down my spine.

"I have little choice now," I said, half dazed. I cleared my throat, taking another pass around the room. "Um, do you know if Camille left?"

"Someone named Jackson picked her up. She said to tell you she's sorry."

"Of course. At least now she can't rope me into going out with them," I said, grateful I could go straight home and get a full night's sleep before the morning's early wake-up.

The corners of Lou's mouth twitched with amusement.

The weight of the day crawled up my back and nestled into my shoulders, pushing out a long yawn. "I guess I'll see you in the morning. Have a good evening."

"I'm not going to let you walk home alone this late."

"I've been doing it for years. Nothing's changed."

"It's changed because I'm here. Get your things and let's go."

Resisting would spend energy I didn't have, so I gave in. Without saying another word, I untied my apron and walked straight out the front door, not bothering to hold it open for him. He could walk me home, but we didn't need to talk.

When we turned the corner onto my street, he paused on the curb. The ambient streetlights and the moon overhead cast deep shadows underneath his features, making him look more dramatic than he did in normal lighting.

"I'm not the enemy, Rosa," he said, voice sharp around the edges.

I turned on my heel to face him. "Right. So you say. But how do I know that for certain?"

"What do you want to know?"

"It's too late for this," I said, shaking my head. "I want to believe that you have my father's best interests in mind, but trust is a rare commodity for me these days."

"Guess I'll have to prove it to you." He stubbed the toe of his shoe on the concrete. "Well, good night. I'll meet you here at five tomorrow morning."

"You don't have to do that. I can meet you at the restaurant."

He shrugged. "I'll be here. Sleep well." Lou strode across the street and disappeared into the dark alleyway between two rows of houses opposite mine.

"You too," I blew into the night breeze.

My brass alarm clock rang too early the next morning. When I'd climbed under my covers last night, Camille's bed sat empty, sheets and blanket pulled up to the corners, undisturbed. My stomach flipped. Camille had never not come home after one of her nights out. Sure, she'd come in just before dawn a few times, but she always made it back.

Throwing off my covers, I rushed out of the room, careful not to wake the others, and tiptoed as fast as possible down the stairs. Peering over the banister into the family room, I let out a whoosh of air. Camille lay unconscious on the sofa under the front bay window, still in her dress and heels from last night.

As the panic subsided, I made my way over to where she slept and brushed my fingertips along her shoulder, not wanting to frighten her. Her hair sprawled across the green velvet couch cushion, with only a small portion of it still in the gold barrette she must have "borrowed" from me. Her clothes clung to her at odd angles, and her signature red lipstick smudged around her lips.

When will she grow up? I wondered to myself as I applied more pressure to her shoulder.

After a few moments of rustling, her eyes fluttered open.

"Where am I?" she asked, voice raspy.

"Home. You're home. Now hurry on upstairs before Ma catches you down here in this state."

I helped her sit upright and unstrapped one of her heels as she took off the other. Offering her my shoulder, we took the stairs one at a time, careful not to make any noise. Camille stopped twice to double over from nausea.

Once safe and sound in her bed, I returned with a glass of water and two aspirin.

"Take these and drink this entire glass. I've got to run, but I'll call in a few hours," I said before quickly dressing and rushing downstairs.

My heart sank. Camille's behavior had become more and more reckless. I'd have to talk some sense into her. In no way could she continue this routine; it would kill her eventually. I'd been chalking it up to a phase, but after two years, I wasn't so sure she'd grow out of it. If anything awful happened to her during one of her frequent late-night dalliances, I'd never forgive myself.

Once, when Camille was about six, I'd heard her cry my name from the backyard. I remember the morning sun blazing through the kitchen windows as I washed the breakfast dishes, trying to eradicate the dense air that still hung heavily from the overnight thunderstorm that had kept us awake all night.

I wiped my hands dry on a tea towel and rushed outside. Camille had never been a quiet child, but the panic in her voice sounded unfamiliar to my young ears. Pushing through the screen door that led from the kitchen to our fenced patch of grass, I scanned the yard, almost missing her. She had been crouched down at the base of the old maple tree. The one we climbed as kids.

"What are you doing?" I called out, rushing over. When I got to her, I peered over her shoulder and saw a small, almost translucent bird lying on the ground, surrounded by scattered leaves.

Camille looked up, eyes blurry with tears.

"I think it fell from its nest in the storm. We have to save it."

I kneeled beside her to get a better look. The poor bird appeared battered, but its tiny beak still opened and closed, as if gasping for air.

"I'm not sure how," I said. But then, I remembered Pa was home because he had a doctor's appointment later that morning. I sprinted inside to find him. When we came back, Camille sat cross-legged on the floor with a towel draped over her hands, cupping the small bird. Pa sucked in a breath of air at the sight.

"Oh, amore mio, what did you find?"

Camille looked at him, pleading with her eyes. "Papa, can we save it?"

The smell of wet leaves enveloped us as we looked at the baby bird for several seconds, not speaking.

"Let's bring him inside, try to give him some water," Pa suggested, helping Camille up from the ground by her armpits.

Camille choked back sobs as we walked back across the yard.

"It will be okay. We'll do what we can," Pa reassured her.

But as we crossed the threshold into the kitchen, Ma greeted us, hands on her hips.

"What's going on?" she asked, craning her neck to see what Camille held. She took a frightened step back.

"Oh no, no, no." Her head shook. "That thing is not coming inside my house. Drop it! Now!" Her mouth set in a tight line. "And go take a bath."

Pa clasped her shoulder. "Marissa, it's only a baby bird. It must have fallen during the storm. Let's try to give it some water."

Ma snapped her head to look my father square in the face. "No, Marco. This is my house. That thing is nearly dead. They must learn the ways of life. Go throw it away." She pointed back out the door to the side alley where we kept our trash cans.

Camille burst into hysterics. "We can't throw him away!"

I stood frozen in place. It wasn't the first time I'd witnessed my mother's cruelty, but that memory had stuck with me. Camille had always loved taking care of animals, but this she couldn't fix. Not without Ma's approval. Her delicate face turned pale as Pa guided her back to the tree.

I heard him say in his thick accent, "I will take care of it. It's okay. You did the right thing. But your mother is right; he doesn't belong in the house."

The memory of a distraught Camille crying on her bed the entire morning after still haunted me. It was why I made myself a promise to look after Camille as we grew up, to guard her innocence.

Rushing to get to the restaurant on time after a fitful sleep, I did a double take after spotting Lou leaned against the street sign pole, head stuck in a paperback dime novel. He didn't notice me approach, which gave me time to recover from my mild shock at seeing him this early. I'd forgotten. His wavy hair sat atop his head, gelled back like always, and I could still see the marks from the teeth of his comb. His baby-blue button-down shirt, which looked pressed within an inch of its life, was tucked neatly into his navy trousers and leather belt. He looked ready for a job interview, not a morning delivery shift.

"Well, don't you look snazzy this morning. You didn't need to get dressed up on my account," I whistled as I walked past, slowing my pace but not stopping.

"I have class later," he said, pushing upright from the pole and slipping the book into his back pocket.

"Ah, yes, lest we forget, you are smart."

"Not everyone who goes to college is smart," he said, trying to catch up with me. I picked up my pace.

"You don't say?"

We made it to the restaurant, which sat dark and empty at this early hour. I slid the key into the front door, not bothering to hold it open. Lou caught it with his foot before it closed on his face.

"Come on, now. If we're going to work together, you'll need to at least pretend to be cordial to me," Lou said as we stood near the hostess stand.

I drew a long breath before turning around, my shoulders growing tense. I took a deliberate step toward him, trying not to focus on his eyes, which caught the light in the dim entryway.

"Let us get one thing straight. We are not working together. You work for us. If my father weren't concerned for my safety, you would not be here," I said through gritted teeth, surprising myself.

He stared straight back at me, his eyes lingering on my mouth that I'd just used to put him in his place. I couldn't tell if he wanted to leave or shout back at me. For a brief, terrifying moment, I thought he'd kiss me. Instead, he took the smallest of steps forward, until I could feel his breath on my face.

"You know it's more complicated than that, Rosa. And like I tried to explain last night, I'm only here to help. That's all."

Something in his voice made me almost believe him. Before I could formulate a sentence in my malfunctioning brain, the light above us turned on from Lou flipping the switch on the wall, breaking my trance.

"Right, then. Let's get to work," I said, shuffling past him to the office.

For the next two hours, we organized the order slips and met various purveyors outside near the loading dock, many of whom my father had been working with since his first year. Some had watched me grow up, and their surprised faces when I greeted them warmed my heart. It reminded me that Cucina Bella meant more than good food; it meant community, family, and connection. A meaningful life.

To Lou's credit, he made himself useful, counting boxes to reconcile the orders after the deliveries. The time flew by, and after about two hours, I remembered my promise to call Camille.

"I'll be right back," I said, not waiting for his response before leaving the office.

I dialed our home number on the phone that hung on the wall behind the drinks station for privacy. It rang a while before someone picked up.

"Bianchi residence," Ivana chipped into my ear.

"Hi Vanie, is Camille awake yet?"

"Rosa! Where are you?" she asked, surprised to hear my voice on the other end.

"I'm at the restaurant, baby girl. Can you go get Camille?"

The clank the phone being dropped on the table made me wince. At eight-years-old, Ivana was still a child. But as the youngest, she had everyone, including me, wrapped around her little finger. None of us minded.

"Hello," came a half-asleep croak from the receiver.

"Good morning, beautiful. How are you feeling today?"

"You can tone down the sarcasm. I'm..." there was a long pause. "Alive."

"Good. Now get your pretty little behind in the shower and freshen up. We're going to have a talk tonight."

Camille groaned. "Okay, I'm going. Thanks for this morning."

"You're welcome," I said before hanging up, my brows knit together. Camille still didn't sound well. Normally, she bounced back with a few hours of rest and lots of water, but something seemed off. I had a feeling it had to do with Jackson.

Standing in the dark hall, I didn't notice Lou make his way out of the office until I heard a clanking noise behind the bar. Peering around the corner, I watched as he hummed an unrecognizable tune while scrubbing every visible surface. I stayed hidden for a few minutes, curious to see him move when he thought no one was watching. It reminded me of myself when I cooked in the kitchen alone, content to be doing something I loved.

Happy to lurk in the shadows for a moment, I wondered what Lou loved. I couldn't imagine someone being passionate about accounting, which is what he studied. But something about his calm, almost calculated demeanor matched it. Although, watching him behind the bar now, I could tell he felt at ease there. He moved with confidence and near grace as he poured and mixed drinks. Even when the restaurant was at its busiest, Lou never looked rushed or overwhelmed. He knew how to make everything work as if he came out of the womb slinging cocktails.

To hide my snooping, I turned on the tap at the drinks station and washed a few pitchers. When the humming stopped, I took a tentative step out around the corner.

"All clean?" I asked, nodding my head toward the now-gleaming bar top.

"I work better if everything is in its place," Lou said, wringing out the wet rag in the sink. He stopped to look up at me. "I know it's none of my business, but I saw Camille at the speakeasy last night."

I tilted my head, almost glaring at him. Had he been eavesdropping on my phone call?

"She seemed upset before she left, but she'd had a lot to drink."

"Well, she got home fine. A little worse for wear, but nothing I haven't seen her do before." My instinct was to defend Camille, but I shared his concern. "Did you see who she was with?"

"She came with that guy, Jackson. I've seen him around before. Heard he's trouble. Is Camille seeing him?"

Odd. I'd never imagined Lou and Jackson would run in the same circles. As far as I knew, Jackson kept to the DePaul crowd, never one to sully his name with a South Side reputation.

"They're one of those on-again-off-again couples. But I worry he's giving her the runaround," I admitted. "How do you know him?"

"Oh, I don't. Not really. As a bartender, you hear things. She shouldn't get caught up with a man like him. From what I can tell, he enjoys taking risks and doesn't seem to care who gets hurt." Lou's eyes darkened as he spoke, making the back of my neck prickle. He held my stare for another second, then looked away. "I'm sure she knows what she's doing."

"I'm sure she does," I breathed out, as the whooshing in my ears grew louder. It seemed like everyone had secrets. Did Camille know this side of Jackson? It made me wonder what else I was in the dark about. Maybe Lou had exaggerated. He said himself that he didn't know Jackson, only heard rumors. Sometimes, that's all things were: rumors. But as I tried to calm myself, deep down in my gut, I knew the truth. I wanted, I *needed*, Camille to stay far away from whatever he had gotten caught up in. I could see it now: Jackson would only break her heart, or worse.

Chapter 9

"Christ, Rosa, you're not my mother," Camille spat as we walked home together from the restaurant after working one of the busiest nights the restaurant had had in weeks. "I know Jackson; he's a good guy."

"Do you know him, though? Why would Lou say that about him?" I asked, throwing a look her way. "I worry about you. That's all."

We stopped at an intersection to let cars pass before crossing the road to our block. All the way home, Camille had insisted she was fine. That nothing happened last night to be concerned about.

"We're only having fun. And why would you believe Lou over your sister? You were just telling me you had your doubts about his loyalty. For all we know, he's working with *them* and pulling one over on Pa."

I sighed. She didn't understand. Jackson worried me, yes, but her behavior worried me more, and I should have led with that. I grabbed her hand and squeezed.

"Okay, but promise me you'll be careful? No one wants to see you hurt. And please, take it easy on the drinking. If Ma catches you sneaking in sloshed, you'll have more to worry about than a boy."

The city lights backlit Camille's red hair, making it look as if it were glowing. Though she still looked spent from the previous evening's shenanigans, Camille's beauty took your breath away. She didn't need the makeup, pretty dresses, or the high heels she wore. Even in her work smock, hair frizzy from the humid air and not a lick of rouge, she looked ethereal. Almost otherworldly. Wars had been fought over that kind of beauty. The kind that makes men feel the need to control it, cage it in for their own pleasure.

But Camille was an adult now. She had to make her own choices, and she did not need me, of all people, trying to control her.

"I'll take it slower, I promise," she said, squeezing my hand. "I love you."

It had been seven full days since I had cooked anything other than what we served from our pared-down, generic lunch menu, an eternity in my mind. Every morning my fingers twitched at the sight of my chef's knives lined up at my station, clean and begging to be used.

Lou met me at the same spot before our morning deliveries. We walked together in silence, but I noticed he looked far more casual than the day before.

"No class today?" I asked, trying to break up the awkward silence.

"No classes on Wednesdays."

I waited for him to go on, but he didn't. Seemed like we were back to minimal interaction, but I wasn't letting him get off that easily. If Pa was forcing me to spend my mornings with him, I needed more than a few shrugs and tight-lipped responses.

"So... when do you graduate?"

"At the end of the semester. Technically, I already have enough credits to graduate, but I need to—" he paused, "—finish my accounting concentration."

"Concentration? What does that mean?" I knew next to nothing about how degrees worked. Whenever I asked Ant about his classes, he brushed me off by changing the topic. I suspected he thought I couldn't relate, and therefore I couldn't hold a conversation about such things. But just because I didn't go to college, it didn't mean I had zero interest in his experience. It didn't take long for me to stop asking.

"It's like a focus area. Mine is in forensic accounting. It means I can investigate financial records to uncover fraud or help in legal proceedings. It takes a few more credit hours than a typical accounting degree."

So, he was smart. But boring. Still boring.

"Is that more interesting than regular accounting?"

"It can be. But it means a lot more work, too."

"Then, why?"

"I'm good with numbers. Always have been. Plus, it pays well. One day, I want to be able to take care of my father. Like he did for me." His back straightened as he talked, but he kept his gaze down at his feet.

"What about your mother?" I asked before I could stop myself.

His shoulders slumped, and I knew I'd stepped somewhere I shouldn't have.

"I'm sorry—you don't need to answer that if you don't want to," I stammered.

"It's all right. She died of ovarian cancer when I was eight."

"Oh. That's... that's terrible. I'm so sorry." I reached for his forearm as we walked up to the restaurant.

"It's okay. It was a long time ago now. I don't have many memories of her, but my dad did the best he could. He's still in Waukegan, working at the steel factory. That's why he sent me to the city. To get an education, build a better life, and all that."

The sincerity in his tone caught me off guard, almost like whiplash. A few seconds ago, he didn't dare utter a word that wasn't necessary, but now, he let this very personal and devastating piece of information slip.

"Your father must be proud of you. I've heard it's difficult to get into the University of Chicago. A few of my classmates applied, but no one got accepted." Namely, Ant.

"Like I said, I'm good with numbers." He shrugged.

I still knew little about Lou, but the thin layers that had started to peel back showed a different story than the one I'd imagined when I met him a few weeks ago.

Still, I told myself, he could be playing everyone. His story, however tragic, seemed unlikely given the circumstances. Starting work for my father the same week Sal and his gang took over felt like too much of a coincidence. Yet the heaviness in his usually bright eyes caught me off guard. Pain had etched its way across his features, crinkling his forehead to make him look older, more experienced in life and its torments. I wanted to soothe his anguish somehow.

"Why didn't you go to college?" he asked, jolting me back from thinking too deeply about him and his sadness.

"Because I cook. That's what I do. It's all I've ever wanted to do."

"Yeah, but you could have gone to culinary school."

"I guess, but I believe you learn more from doing. Everything I need to know, my father can teach me. I'm lucky." Taking the key from my pocketbook, I opened the creaky front door.

If I were to continue working alongside Lou for the foreseeable future, I'd need to keep myself in check. Caring about him didn't matter, even if we were only being friendly. The image of Ant having intimate conversations with other women didn't delight me. But then again, the thought didn't crush me either. And not for the first time, I wondered why.

As we stepped inside, I swiped my gutter-thoughts away, and a swelling of pride replaced them. I knew my place here, and not once did I ever feel like I missed out by not going to college. I'd received good grades, but all the studying and sitting still drove me crazy. Each hour that ticked by in a classroom could have been better spent in a kitchen, learning. No, Pa's restaurant had taught me everything I needed to know and more. I couldn't afford to forget that.

Heading straight for the kitchen on instinct, I didn't notice Lou follow me in. The cool steel of the prep tables felt refreshing under the graze of my fingers as I ran my hand along the length of my station and picked up the large chef's knife my father had gifted me a little over a year ago. It had seen little use lately, as I reserved it for special occasions only. I didn't trust myself to sharpen it, and having it sent out was expensive, so I tried to preserve the edge as much as possible.

"You're looking at that knife like it's your first-born child," Lou quipped from the doorway, making me almost jump out of my skin.

"You're lucky I didn't drop it on my foot!"

The kitchen looked the same as it always had, yet it begged to be used. And not just by the new staff that stormed in here every evening like a racing crew set on making the fastest time. Kitchens like this deserved respect and attention. You got out what you put in. Lately, I'd given it none, and I suddenly longed to spend intentional, quality time here, not cooking a menu that lacked soul or creativity.

My thoughts rippled over my face like ticker tape. I'd never hidden my emotions well. Ma often told me to quiet my "loud face." That day was no different.

"You know, we're only scheduled for two deliveries this morning. I can handle them. Why don't you whip us up something to eat?"

I jerked my head up to meet his eyes. From my experience, when a man told you to stay in the kitchen and cook something, they weren't doing it out of the kindness of their heart. But coming from him, in that moment, it sounded like a choir of angels singing because I couldn't imagine doing anything else.

"Are you sure? You don't need help with inventory?" I asked, knowing full well he'd be fine on his own for one morning.

"Yeah, yeah. You go ahead and cook your heart out. I've got it," he said, disappearing back through the door to the office. "Better be good, though," He shouted over his shoulder.

When I turned to face the pantry door, my wide, almost half-crazed smile stared back at me in the glass reflection panel.

It didn't take long to gather everything I needed for a new recipe—one that I'd found in a cookbook that someone from the church dropped by last week. Ever since I'd cooked lunch for the women's auxiliary club years ago, a few of them took it upon themselves to gift me with various Italian cookbooks. Some from their own mothers or relatives that they'd already committed to memory.

Mrs. Cuncinelli surprised me last week when I opened the door and saw her standing on the stoop with a package in her arms: a cookbook she had found at a rummage sale. Ever since Pa's gambling debts had become public knowledge, rumors flew around the congregation, causing many former close families to keep their distance. Understandable, given the situation, but still hurtful.

Ma, though, kept her head held high and still attended every function as if nothing had changed. She reassured us, as much as herself, "Things will blow over. When Pa gets Bella back, they will eat my crow." As good as her English sounded, she never quite got the hang of common phrases.

While devouring the yellowing pages of the second-hand cookbook, some covered in faded handwriting I had a hard time making out, I found a recipe for timballo di anelletti. It sometimes made appearances at graduation parties and weddings, but I'd never tasted it. As a young child, it always looked unappetizing, but now I could see how much love and finesse went into it. It combined small, dried pasta rings, ragu similar to Bolognese, ham, cheese, and breadcrumbs that were all baked together in a deep cake pan and turned out onto a large platter when finished.

After organizing the ingredients and equipment, I set to work prepping the ragu, which would take the longest of all the steps. About half an hour in, the entire kitchen smelled of stewing tomatoes, beef, and other vegetables; an aroma I associated with family.

Years ago, back when every new recipe awed me as a young chef, Pa showed me how to make our secret family tomato sauce on that very stove. Over the decades, the women in the family had passed it down by word of mouth through generations until my grandmother taught my father how to make it in Sicily before he moved to America.

Like every Italian family known throughout time, we prized our recipe. Nothing could beat it. It was the best. Unlike most families, though, my father had built an entire restaurant and menu on it. I wondered if the recipe would die with me.

An hour later, Lou popped his head through the swinging doors and asked when the food would be ready. Unfortunately for him, it'd be a while. The thing had to bake and cool, which took a few hours.

"Good things come to those who wait," I teased, relaxed for the first time in a while.

More relaxed than the other night with Ant. The thought made me stop in my tracks.

As I replayed the realization in my mind, bile rose in the back of my throat. I couldn't give this up. It would be like giving up an essential piece of my soul. But I might not have a choice. I'd have to find a way to get used to it. Find fulfillment somewhere else or convince Ant otherwise. Women of every generation had figured it out. I would have to, too.

After Lou accepted the last delivery and finalized the inventory for the day, he joined me in the kitchen as I pulled out the heavy cake pan and flipped it over onto a large baking sheet to cool.

"What *is* it?" he asked, nose scrunched up.

"It's a Sicilian delicacy. I've never tried it, but I found an old recipe for it a few weeks ago in a cookbook that one of the church ladies dropped off for me. It looked like a challenge."

We looked down at what looked like a weird cake made of pasta. I had to admit, it didn't look great. Not like something I'd ever call a "delicacy." But I'd eaten stranger things before, like cow's tongue, and lived to tell the tale. I even liked cow's tongue when cooked well.

"I don't know about that. Might head over to Sammy's to grab a sub," Lou said, crinkling his nose.

"Oh, come on, don't tell me you're scared to try something new, Mr. South Side Bartender with a mysterious past. What could possibly happen after trying some baked pasta?"

"This could be an elaborate ruse to poison me. Wouldn't be the first poisoning I'd seen."

I looked at him, eyes wide. That didn't sound like a joke.

"I'm kidding." He shook his head. "You really don't trust me, do you?"

"I don't know you."

Lou took a step toward me. "You know more than most people. You know about my mom."

My heartbeat hammered in my ears so loudly, I wondered if he could hear it. In the silence, he leaned in, and my breath stopped. I knew I should have backed away, but I couldn't. For a brief second, I closed my eyes, and when I reopened them, Lou had bent over the table and dug into the timballo. He lifted a spoonful to my mouth after taking the first bite. We both moaned with pleasure before swallowing and breaking out in belly-aching laughs. Although it tasted divine, a bitter flavor lingered on my tongue. Guilt.

Why was I reacting to Lou like a silly schoolgirl? Engaged. I was *engaged*.

"You have a true talent, Miss Bianchi. Don't let anyone ever tell you differently," he said, taking another bite. "Do ladies often drop off cookbooks for you?"

"Every once in a while. Less now that our family name is mixed up with...," I gestured around, as if that said enough.

"Ah, I see. People can be cruel and hypocritical. Half of Chicago is in debt to them."

At least someone understood.

Chapter 10

I t didn't take long for our stomachs to fill with the dense pasta, so I wrapped up the leftovers and slipped them into a brown paper box I could carry home for dinner. Lou stayed behind at Bella, but I had the day off and was eager for some time at home. It had been ages since I had had the chance to play with my youngest sister, and since she was home on summer break, it would be the perfect opportunity. And with any luck, Ma would be off at some church meeting or another so I could sneak Ivana out for some ice cream.

As I crossed the threshold into the dark foyer, a blur of red and black made its way down the stairs.

"Where are you off to in such a hurry?" I asked Camille as she hopped on one foot, trying to slip into her sneakers.

"I need to run some errands before work. If I don't hurry, I'll be late. Again."

Her skin looked pale, but her cheeks puffed out. If I hadn't known better, I would have guessed she was sick.

"Are you all right?" I placed a steadying hand on her shoulder.

"Yes, fine. Wish I could chat, but I've got to run," she said, stepping toward the door. "Love you." Then, she was gone.

Before I could get any farther into the house, I heard the unmistakable clatter of my mother in the kitchen. So much for a carefree afternoon with Ivana. As I tiptoed in, not wanting to startle her, she looked up from the sink, hands dripping wet with soapy water.

"What's that?" She jutted her chin out in the box's direction.

"I made timballo di anelletti at the restaurant," I said, sliding it onto the kitchen table. "Thought we could have it for dinner."

"Weren't you supposed to be overseeing the deliveries?"

"Well, yes. But Lou was there, so it was fine," I said, folding a dish towel from a fresh stack.

"Ahh, yes, Lou. The fella your father seems to have taken a liking to. I hope you're keeping your distance and being respectable," my mother said, pausing her washing to give me the once-over.

Without meaning to, I looked away. I could feel the heat rising in my cheeks, threatening to betray me.

My mother gripped the edge of the sink. "Rosa. I don't like you spending time alone with this boy. It's not proper for an engaged woman. I'm going to talk to your father tonight."

"Ma, it's okay. I promise. He's nice, that's all. There aren't many nice people around the restaurant these days. Don't say anything to Pa, please. I can handle it. And myself."

I'd die of mortification if Lou found out my mother didn't trust me around him. Plus, I was twenty, for God's sake. I didn't need to be babysat like a child. Deep down, though, in the corners of my mind where the thoughts I dared not breathe life to struggled for escape, I didn't blame her for being worried.

My mother shook her head. "Well, at least tell me you and Anthony have set a date. His mother will not stop asking about it."

I thought back to the other night at his apartment. Not much talking had been done, but we did briefly discuss the wedding. Of course it would be at the church, but the reception details were yet to be finalized. I'd always imagined it would take place at Bella, but now, as reality encroached upon us, I couldn't picture it. Instead, in my mind's eye, I saw us both in our wedding attire, a generic dress and suit, standing alone in a field looking around for a path we could not find. Strange, considering I had spent countless afternoons as a young girl playing "wedding" with Camille, and always, we ended up pretending to be at the restaurant surrounded by our friends and family, eating the food we loved.

"No date yet. But we know we'll do the service at L'Incoronata."

"Of course, where else would it happen? But you need to figure out the rest. And soon. You don't want him getting cold feet."

I almost laughed before catching myself. I'd never considered the possibility that Ant could change his mind, leaving me the stranded bride at the altar. My stomach turned at the thought, which oddly brought me a sense of comfort. Maybe my inability to picture our wedding was nothing more than pre-wedding jitters. And maybe my mother was right. Time to get this show on the road, especially now that things were picking up steam at the restaurant. The planning would help me put other distractions to rest.

"You're right. We need to set a date. I'll talk to him soon," I promised. "Can I take Vanie out for ice cream?"

My mother sighed but waved me off as she continued to scrub the breakfast dishes.

As soon as we got home, the phone rang. Ant called with surprise tickets to a concert downtown. We'd had loose plans to grab dinner and a movie, but this sounded a thousand times better to both of us. He promised to pick me up at five o'clock sharp.

While getting ready for our date, I thought about how I'd bring up the wedding plans with Ant that night, if only to get our mothers off our backs. I wondered if his mother had been peppering him with the same questions, but knew it wasn't likely. Men didn't bother themselves with silly things like weddings. That was women's work, or so it always had been. Though I knew we needed to move forward, I didn't have the slightest interest in the actual planning of the day. I'd leave the flowers, music, readings, and other arrangements up to Ma and Mrs. Russo, if they'd let me get away with it.

My thoughts careened away from the wedding as I wrapped sections of my hair around the foam rollers I'd been using for years. My brown, curly hair didn't like being tamed into submission and would likely revert to its natural state of disarray by the first song of the evening, but I tried anyway. For Ant.

"Right," I said to my reflection after an hour of primping. "That'll have to do." Compared to Camille's beauty, I'd rate a hair above average, but I didn't mind. Looks faded, I knew that. While Camille turned heads, her exterior demanding attention in every room she walked into, mine simmered just below the surface. Every woman had her own way of turning it on when she wanted.

"Rosaaaa," yelled Ivana from the foot of the stairs. "Ant is here!" I took a quick glance at my watch, a small sterling silver trinket I'd purchased with about a year's worth of green stamps I'd saved years ago, and tsked to myself. Five on the dot.

Ant didn't drive this time; instead, we'd planned to take the train to Grant Park. Parking was always limited downtown during a concert, and he hadn't wanted to waste time looking for a spot. All the same to me, and at least it would give my hair a fair chance of staying put without the convertible to batter it around.

"Well, don't you look lovely," Ant remarked as I walked down the steps to meet him. My closet consisted of plain frocks for work, but I'd found a Kelly green A-line dress with a long white bow at the neckline on Camille's side of the closest. Luckily for me, we wore the same size.

Ant and I walked to the train station hand-in-hand, breathing in the late summer air. Although car horns blared in the distance, and we could hear the train running overhead, the stillness of the neighborhood on such an evening was rare.

"I've missed you," Ant confessed, leaning in until our shoulders bumped. "I'm sorry we haven't spent much time together. This summer statistics class is harder than I imagined. I might even need to hire a tutor to help me pass."

I chuckled. Ant hadn't been at the top of our class, but he held his own. The thought that he'd need to hire someone to help him amused me. Ant had always had an air about him that signaled greatness with little effort. He'd been one of those people born with it. Athlete, well-off family, popular, and handsome.

"What? You think that's funny?" he teased.

"No, no. I'm sure you'll do great. You are Anthony Russo, after all."

Not once did he ask about Cucina Bella, I noticed.

The hum of the crowd intensified as we crossed the street to enter Grant Park. The opener for The Kim Sisters had already gotten the attendees warmed up, and I could see rows upon rows of young people standing around their seats, talking in groups or dancing in the small spaces.

Ant took the tickets from his pocket to locate our seat numbers; we were in the dead middle. As we zigged and zagged our way around the aisles, a slender arm jutted out of a group of people from one row over and landed on Ant's forearm, stopping us in our tracks.

"Anthony!" a high-pitched, yet elegant voice squealed. No trace of a Chicago accent whatsoever lacing the syllables. It had to be a DePaul girl.

After a moment, the disembodied voice had a face that peered at us from between the shoulders of two large men who had their backs turned. She squeezed between them and gracefully slid through the rows of chairs between us. A slender, well-bred woman stood before us, beaming with a smile that could almost blind.

"I didn't know you'd be here tonight. What a surprise," she said, pulling Ant in for a hug, still holding his arm.

"Hey Maggie. I scored a few tickets from the student hall this morning," Ant replied, looking down at her with wide, caught-in-the-headlights eyes.

"You should have told me! I had an extra ticket. Then you could be sitting with us."

"Thanks, but I needed two," Ant said, and Maggie's eyes slowly scanned over to the right where I stood. Her hand fell as she registered my presence.

"Oh my, where are my manners? Of course. You must be Ant's girl. I'm Margaret O'Connor, but you can call me

Maggie," she said, offering an elegant hand with long, slim manicured fingers.

"Hi, Maggie. I'm Rosa. It's nice to meet you." I managed a half smile before turning back to Ant, who flitted his eyes between us unsure of where to focus.

"We have a few extra seats, I believe. Ronnie and Rosann had to cancel last minute. Why don't you come sit with us?"

"Oh, that's kind of you, but we were just heading to our seats. Maybe we'll find you after?" Ant said, looking everywhere but at Maggie.

"Thanks, for the offer," I managed to say before Ant grabbed my hand and led us down the rest of the aisle, scanning the numbers tacked on to the seats with such intensity, you would've thought he was looking for the winning lotto numbers.

It took a few minutes, but we located our seats between two groups of loud teenage girls jumping around and jostling everyone within a ten-foot radius.

"Maybe we should have taken Maggie up on her offer," I joked, but Ant didn't laugh.

"These seats are fine. Let's try to flag down the beverage cart when it comes by."

We sat, waiting for The Kim Sisters to take the stage, but another group of female musicians hopped on as the opening act finished.

Ant sat ramrod straight in his seat but didn't say a word.

"How do you know Maggie?" I shouted over the noise.

"We took a philosophy class together last semester. Her father is the dean of the business school."

We talked little after that. The crowd seemed to grow more and more rambunctious as the opening bands continued to appear until the main act everyone came to see took the stage. I had to admit, it was an impressive show. I'd never been to such a lively performance, but I enjoyed the energy, even if Ant's mood didn't seem to improve until about halfway through. At one point, I grabbed his hand and made him dance, which seemed to loosen him up a bit.

When it ended, we sat back down, allowing everyone to walk past us in a hurry to leave. We weren't. It amazed me to see how quickly the arena emptied, leaving only the various concert detritus scattered around the ground as a sign that anything had happened there at all.

"Thank you for bringing me tonight. I needed a night of fun," I said, tilting my head back to look up at the night sky. All the dancing and singing had cleansed my earlier discomfort.

"I'm sorry for acting strange earlier. The truth is, I almost failed my philosophy class, and Maggie had been in one of my group projects. She helped me through it, but now I feel silly around her," he admitted.

She didn't seem to care, I thought. This was the second time tonight Ant had opened up to me, and I didn't want to scare him off. This was a new thing for him, including me in his other life, his college life.

"Oh, it's all right. I understand. But why did you take a philosophy class in the first place? Doesn't sound like something you'd need for a business degree."

"I thought it would be a good way to meet interesting people outside of the business school. Some of them are boring to the point of tears. But instead, I only embarrassed myself."

"I'm sure that's not true. Maggie seemed happy to see you earlier."

Ant laughed at that. "Enough about school. Let's talk about you." He turned in his seat to face me. "I've been thinking about the meal you made us the other night. What would you say to giving some classes to the girls at DePaul? Many are taking classes until they snag a fella to marry, so I thought it might be helpful. Two birds, one stone kind of thing."

My heart sank, but he didn't notice, taking my silence as a sign to elaborate.

"I know cooking is important to you, so I thought this might be a suitable compromise until we start our family. You know, to give you something to do during the week once we're married, and maybe even some pocket money, not that you'll need it. But I know how important your independence is to you."

His wide eyes and earnest smile said all it needed to. He genuinely thought it would solve the issue. My issue. My passion and dreams boiled down to teaching hopeful housewives to better serve their families.

I'd heard rumblings of the second-wave feminist movement, but I never gave it much thought or consideration until now. Was this what they were fighting against? These assumptions that a woman could only aspire to be a better housewife? How dare she have interests and passions of her own outside of the family? In that moment, I understood the angry faces of the women in the photographs I'd seen of rallies and protests in the paper.

I wanted to scream.

More than that, I wanted to take Ant by the shoulders and shake him. He didn't get it. Still. Even though he'd grown up alongside me and my family, watching as I cooked for hours on end, even helping me when I needed it. Still, he relegated me to devoted wife and future mother. Nothing more.

I straightened my back and looked him in the eye, gathering every ounce of courage and bravado I could muster.

"Ant, I'm a chef. Not a home economics teacher," I said, gritting my teeth. "How could you think that would be something I'd want to do?" and then quieter, "Do you even know me?"

The questions were out of my mouth before I could even consider the implications.

"Of course I know you, Rosa. I'm only trying to make you happy," Ant's voice rose as he spoke.

"Cooking in a restaurant makes me happy. Cooking at Cucina Bella. I realize most people think it's a silly hobby, but it's not. I'm good at it. Damn good, and I want to keep doing it. Why should I have to give up on my dreams while you get to live yours?"

I stood up, looking down at Ant's shocked face. Anger bubbled in my throat, my eyes stinging with tears that I refused to let fall.

Ant broke our stare-off, running his hand through his hair.

"I don't know. It's hard to imagine. If you're working, then when will we have time to start a family? You know I'll need to travel once I take over the business. I want nothing more than to make you happy, but this seems impossible."

For so long, I'd been hoping Ant would support me. That he'd realize the ridiculousness, the unfairness of this conviction society had imprinted upon men and many women. He'd witnessed my passion and talent, so why couldn't he understand it would kill an essential part of me to let it go? I wanted to get off this merry-go-round.

"Impossible? It seems impossible that we could be this far apart." I started walking down the now-empty aisle, avoiding leftover soda cans and empty popcorn bags, discarded like my hopes and dreams, my heart hammering my ribcage.

Chapter 11

"They look like deranged ravioli," I said, staring down at the carton of food Lou pulled out of the refrigerator. "Where did you get them?"

That morning, I had watched Lou balance a box covered in a brown grocery bag through the dining room and into the kitchen before stowing it safely in the walk-in. On our walk, I'd asked him about the bag, but he'd shaken his head, the side of his mouth twitching.

Now, looking at its contents, I wished I hadn't been so interested.

"They're Polish. Pierogies. My mother liked to cook them. I can't be trusted in a kitchen, though. These are from a shop near my place."

"And you want me to try them?" I asked, raising my eyebrows. Although I considered myself an adventurous cook, my exploring stopped at the limits of Italian cuisine.

"I thought I'd repay you for the timballo and introduce you to the food of my people," he said, picking up one of the crescent-shaped dough balls before dipping it in what looked like sour cream.

"I thought you were Italian. Isn't your last name Cuccia?"

"My dad is Italian, and my mother was Polish. We were always closer to her side of the family growing up."

I nodded as if it made perfect sense, which in a way it did. Lou's quiet yet stoic demeanor had set him apart from the other young Italian men around town. Now, maybe I knew why.

"All right. But before I try one, tell me what's in them."

"Nope. That'll ruin the surprise. I trusted you yesterday. Now it's your turn, Chef." He cocked his head to the side as a piece of his brown wavy hair flopped down over his forehead.

Suddenly, I was aware of how close he stood, arm inches away from mine. Heat crawled up my neck, so I stabbed the smallest pierogi on the plate with my fork and bit off the corner to give my body something else to focus on.

I chewed with intention, rolling the food around in my mouth trying to place the taste. Deciding it reminded me of gnocchi, I knew it must have potato in it, but there was something else I couldn't quite place.

"What's in the potato filling?" I asked, mouth still full of the next bite.

"Scallion and seasonings." Lou answered, watching my lips move as I chewed. "Do you like it?"

Lou wanted me to like it. I could see it in the hunch of his shoulders, the silent anticipation.

"I do. They're delicious. Simple yet substantial. They remind me of stuffed pasta and gnocchi, in the best way."

He broke out in a wide grin and slapped the table with a tea towel. In that second, I could picture him as a young boy, sitting at his mother's kitchen table ready to eat her food with that exact expression of anticipation. It cracked a part of my heart to know she'd never see it again, but I was touched that he'd shared it with me.

In all the years I'd been cooking, I'd kept to Italian foods. Chicago had no shortage of culture, but rarely did it mix. The

Italians stayed in their neighborhood, the Polish in theirs, the Mexicans in theirs, and so on. Once in a blue moon, we got a curious couple from a wealthier part of town. But Chicago was as small as it was big. My palate suffered from it. Some chefs spent their entire lives trying to master Italian food alone and I still had so much to learn that I hadn't even looked at other cuisines.

"I'm glad you like it, because tomorrow I'm bringing flaki." I knitted my brows together. "It's tripe soup," he clarified, the right-side of his mouth twitching.

My stomach turned at the mention of tripe, and my disgust must have reached my face because Lou laughed so loud it made me jump.

"I'm kidding. No tripe. But there are other things to try. Let's stop at a place I know for breakfast tomorrow after the market, yeah?"

I wanted to say yes. I wanted to experience more food, different food. But with Lou? It should've been with Ant. I should've been doing that with my fiancé, not the bartender slash bookkeeper my father hired to look after me. As I began to make up an excuse, I remembered last night. The look on Ant's face when he called my dreams impossible.

"Let's do it, but absolutely no tripe."

"Deal," Lou said, jutting his hand out for a shake.

The South Water Market could be intimidating to even the most seasoned buyer. Luckily for us, I had a plan, one that Pa developed over two decades of visits and taught to me during our weekly runs once I was old enough.

First, we hit John McClaire's stand for his zucchini. We waited all year for that first batch of the season, ready to pick out the best, most flavorful of the yellow and green vegetables for our summer ragu. We'd learned through experience that if we didn't get there early, only the smallest, scrawniest produce would be left. Still, anything we bought at the market would be light-years better than what the local grocers sold.

Next, we hustled to the tomato stand near a back corner; the one most people overlooked in favor of the enormous display from a popular commercial farm.

"Look at these beauties, Robert!" I shouted, eyes wide as we pushed our almost empty cart, save for the box of zucchinis, up to the stand.

A man with a full head of white hair rose from his seat behind rows of heirloom tomatoes. His skin had been permanently tanned from decades spent tending his large home garden, but there was still some youth behind his wrinkled eyes.

Lou leaned down to inspect the text on one of Robert's crates.

"Riverbend? Is that where you're from?" he asked Robert.

"Born and raised. Been farming there all my life," he said, releasing me from a hug. "Are you familiar with it? 'Bout an hour west of here by train."

"I used to visit when I was a kid. My aunt lives there," he said.

"What's her name? Riverbend is a small town. Bet I knew her."

"Lucinda Cuccia. She lived in town," Lou responded, cradling a large yellow and red tomato in his palm.

Robert puckered his lips together, as if suppressing a smile, and shook his head up and down.

"Oh, I know Lucinda and knew her husband, Lawrence, before he passed away. Who could miss that stately red brick home smack dab in town central?"

"What a small world," I interjected.

"I love that house," Lou said in a quiet voice. He stared at the red and yellow tomato cradled in his palm.

We ended up with four large bushels of Robert's heirlooms and Romas, which we'd sampled with delight.

"I don't think I've ever had a tomato this flavorful," Lou said, juices running down his chin after taking a bite into one like an apple.

"If you can't get fresh San Marzano from Italy, these are a close second," I said, and Robert saluted in agreement.

For the next hour, we walked around the market, stopping at all the places Pa and I frequented. Everyone asked about his whereabouts, but I simply told them he'd been busy. Rumors being what they were, most already knew about Cucina Bella. No use in rehashing it here.

I taught Lou a few secret tricks to picking out the best produce, but not everything I knew. It had taken me years to learn them from my father, so it had to be earned.

A few times, I'd caught Lou watching me. It sent prickles up and down my skin, every nerve ending awake and on alert. I'd never been self-conscious at the market, which was full of loud and rugged farmer types who didn't take any shit. Normally, I didn't pay the men much mind and they let me do my shopping in peace. Being here with Lou, though, made me aware of my every movement. I was showing him a part of my life no one else ever saw, except my father, a part that defined me. Here, I was the expert. Lou the student.

Ant would never see this side of me. As the thought crept into my mind, my lower stomach churned. My mind kept going to places it had no business visiting. Ma had a point. I'd made a promise.

We dropped our purchases at the delivery truck and started the walk back to the restaurant. The sun had turned the city streets into a sauna. Steam hovered in waves off the pavement, creating mirages of colors ahead on the dark asphalt.

"How did we do on the budget?" I asked Lou. Pa had been right; I needed someone to keep me accountable.

Lou laughed. "Surprisingly not too bad, but I'll watch the totals more closely next time. I got distracted." He shoved his hands into his pockets as he walked. "By all the vegetables."

I let a tight, "Right," slip out. "What was that about your aunt? Are you close?"

Lou sighed as he whipped away sweat beads forming on his neck with the small handkerchief he always carried. "Used to be. I spent a lot of time with her after my mother passed away. She never had kids of her own and is older than my mom by fifteen years. I think she felt a sense of duty to look after us."

"I'm glad you had someone," was all I could manage to say. I had no idea what it felt like to lose a parent or anyone close to me. I considered myself lucky, although if I thought too hard about it, I'd have to admit it terrified me.

A few blocks from the restaurant, Lou took a sharp left down a narrow alley between two storefronts. My mind went back to the speakeasy. This guy had a thing for alleyways.

Stopping in front of a red metal door with peeling paint, Lou knocked twice without saying a word. He stepped back, and it swung open, a slim arm holding it open at a forty-five-degree angle.

"Hey Elizabeth, you still got some of those chocolate croissants left?" Lou asked, craning his neck around the door to see inside.

"Lou! Only for you, my dear," a hoarse yet confident voice called back from behind the cracked door.

The skinny arm belonged to a woman of indeterminate age. At least over forty. Her tight curly hair sprang out from under her white chef's hat, a mix of salt and pepper, but her bright blue eyes pierced through the dimness of the alleyway. Although short, she looked as if she could jump ten feet into the air with all the energy bursting from her.

When she saw me, her chin jutted up to Lou. "Not like you to bring a date. She must be special." Her voice was thickly accented, but I couldn't place it. French, maybe?

"Elizabeth, meet Rosa. She's a chef at Cucina Bella in Little Italy. I'm working the books and bar there," he explained.

"Any female chef in this city is a friend of mine. Why don't you two come inside?"

All three of us crammed ourselves into the small backroom that doubled as storage. Boxes upon boxes leaned stacked against the walls, but the room smelled yeasty and felt comfortably warm. A small ray of light illuminated a walkway as we followed Elizabeth through to the cozy, albeit dated, kitchen. If I thought it was hot outside, this must have been the seventh ring of hell. Elizabeth didn't seem to notice.

"So, we have some chocolate pastries left, but take your pick from the case. I'll be right back." She disappeared around the corner and left us to choose.

Fluffy golden pastries lined the shelves in a windowed display case running along the checkout counter near the back of the shop. In the front, a single refrigerated display held cakes, pies, and other desserts I'd never seen. They all looked delicious.

"What would you like?" Lou asked, watching me scan the selection.

"What kind of pastries are these? They look too beautiful to eat," I said, voice full of admiration.

"Elizabeth grew up in a small town near Provence, France. She's been here since she was nineteen. Her family ran a pastry shop in her hometown for decades, so she opened this place after she'd immigrated, wanting to bring French technique to America," Lou explained. "Best pastry chef I know."

I narrowed my eyes at him. "Do you know many pastry chefs?"

"Nope. Just the one." He leaned in and plucked a perfectly golden rectangular pastry off a shelf and bit into it. "I've known her since I was a boy, but more recently helped her with some accounting paperwork."

I could see the chocolate filling ooze out of its shell, and my mouth watered. I needed to try one. It was a matter of life and death.

"Shouldn't we pay for them?" I murmured, staring at the delicacies.

He shook his head. "I worked for free, but she still tries to pay me back with carbs."

Lou grabbed another pastry, placing it on a napkin, and we walked around to the other side of the store to sit at a small table. It was already in my mouth before I sat down. The buttery crust of the croissant melted as I bit into it, giving way to a rich but still very sweet center filling of chocolate. Another flavor danced on my taste buds, but I didn't have a name for it.

"Is this chocolate?" I asked through a bite. When I looked up at him, his eyes were locked on my lips, and I stilled, aware of the soft moan I'd let escape. My cheeks must have turned several shades of red because his lip curved upwards in a sly grin.

"It's hazelnut chocolate. My favorite." He kept his eyes on my mouth. "Sounds like it might be yours, too."

I coughed after inhaling the crusty flakes. Elizabeth returned to set down two mugs of what looked like cappuccino, and I took a sip to regain my composure. The taste was different from what I expected—silkier and less bitter.

"It's café au lait. Coffee and milk. It's how we drink our caffeine in France most of the time," Elizabeth said. "Enjoy."

"Kind of like cappuccino," I said to myself.

"Except no espresso," Lou added.

The sugar in the food and drink made my head buzz. I couldn't believe I'd never had a hazelnut croissant before or realized coffee and milk could taste so wonderful. It struck me how similar yet different these simple dishes were from Italian food. They shared a bloodline but remained cousins in their differences, much like the French and Italians.

I finished my pastry in four bites and downed my café au lait before Lou even touched his.

"It's meant to be savored, you know."

Lou leaned over the table and brushed something from the side of my mouth. The feel of his skin on my face sent a jolt through my core. I stood up.

"This was lovely. Now, we better get a move on," I said, heading for the exit.

Chapter 12

"Are you going to show us, or do I need to come in there?" I shouted through the closed dressing room door.

"I look like a wedding cake," whined Ivana.

Camille jiggled the doorknob. "I'm sure it's not that bad. Please, come out."

Ivana cracked open the door to make sure the hallway was clear. When she stepped out, I had to suppress a giggle. She did look like a layered cake. So many ruffles.

Camille spun her around by the hand, skirt flying out like a pinwheel. "Well, no one would miss you on the pulpit."

Camille and I had taken Ivana dress shopping for her First Holy Communion ceremony since Ma was busy making ten dozen cannoli for the Ladies' Auxiliary fundraiser that afternoon.

"Come on, let's go to Marshall Field's. They'll have a better, more... modern selection of dresses," Camille suggested, holding up another frilly dress the salesperson had recommended.

Ivana dove back into the dressing room to change. Every Bianchi sister had gone to R.L. Bernstein's shop for our communion dresses, but it had been years since we had stepped foot in the store. It looked its age, as did their selections of attire.

Two bus transfers later, we pushed our way through the revolving front doors of the massive department store, thankful for the glorious invention of air conditioning. The young ladies' section had moved to the top floor, so we hopped on the new escalators and rode them up, to Vanie's delight.

"The stairs, they move!" she exclaimed, eyes wide as we stepped on. "We're living in a Captain Z-Ro episode!"

It didn't take long for Camille to pluck out an armful of dresses for Ivana to try. Once in the enormous dressing room, we found a waiting area, complete with couches and a tea service.

"How much do these dresses cost?" I whispered in Camille's ear after a service gal set down two cups of brewed tea and cookies in front of us.

"They're not cheap. But I've been saving up and can cover the difference from what Ma gave us to spend."

That was the thing about Camille. Her personality came across as flighty and vain sometimes but scrape away those layers and you'd find a generous heart that ached for the love of those around her. She'd put herself out one hundred times if it meant you got what you needed just once.

I squeezed her hand. "I'll pitch in, too."

Ivana had it tougher than any of the Bianchi sisters. As the youngest child, she was the apple of my mother's eye. Soon she'd be nine, but still more than a decade younger than me and Camille. Ma didn't go easy on her because of her age, though. If anything, Vanie got it double time to satisfy Ma's need to "get it right." Both Camille and I fell short of what she pictured as the ideal Italian daughter, so she put extra pressure on Ivana.

"Hey, how was that concert? I heard Ant took you to see The Kim Sisters."

I took a long sip of my tea, taking my time to set it back down on its small saucer.

"It was good…"

"I hear a 'but' coming," Camille goaded.

"Ant and I got into an argument and haven't talked since." A rush of air left my lungs, loosening my chest.

"Oh, hun," she said, turning to face me. "Tell me all about it."

And I did, starting with Ant's "friend," Maggie.

"Should I be worried about her? I mean, besides the fact that he clearly doesn't want me working at the restaurant after we get married, do I also have to worry about him stepping out?" I lowered my voice on the last part, as if someone might overhear us in the little girls' section.

Camille sat back on the velvet-upholstered sofa and peered into her teacup.

"If you'd asked me two weeks ago, I'd have said no way. But now, I honestly don't know."

That wasn't the answer I'd been hoping for.

She went on. "Look, I know Ant loves you. He has been pining after you since before you even hit the seventh grade. But they're university boys. Pretty, smart young women surround them every day."

"We're pretty and smart," I said, sitting up straight.

"You know what I mean, Rosa."

I'd never seen Camille so unsure of herself. Her usual confidence, which radiated through a room and magnified in bright light, had lost some of its luster.

"All I'm saying is you'll get used to it. Most women do. It's normal for men to sneak around so long as they come back home."

"No, Camille. It is not." I wanted to shake some sense into her, tell her she didn't have to settle. But more than anything, I wanted to punish Jackson for whatever he did to hurt my beautiful, luminous sister.

Just then, Vanie swung the door open and twirled her dress.

"I want this one," she beamed.

On the bus ride back home, Ivana fell asleep on my lap. Camille and I continued our conversation, and I told her about the night at Ant's apartment. After the initial shock wore off, she told me to be careful and demanded I get fitted for a diaphragm.

"Why does my little sister know about diaphragms?" I asked, eyebrows to the heavens. But of course, she would know. It shouldn't have shocked me.

Camille opened her pocketbook and handed me a discreet business card. It contained only a name and phone number printed in black ink.

"He helps unmarried women," she explained, looking out the window as the city zoomed by in a blur. "But you'll have to pay out of pocket."

I took the card, knowing I wouldn't use it. I'd decided my first time would be the last as an unmarried woman. What did concern me, though, was Camille's tone and overall seriousness throughout the day.

"Are you okay?" I asked, looking at her.

"I will be," she said before falling silent.

When we arrived home, a note on a small piece of paper, scrawled in my mother's handwriting, waited for me next to the telephone in the downstairs hall:

Rosa—Mrs. Russo called to invite you to dinner tomorrow at six for Anthony's birthday. Bring bread from the restaurant.

I stood on the Russos' front stoop trying to calm myself by taking in slow breaths, one after another. The collar on my yellow dress with a white daisy print dug into my neck, making it feel more like a noose than a pretty frock. I pulled at it to no avail. At least it looked nice. Who cared if I suffocated in it, right?

The bag of Italian bread in my arms had crumpled during the walk, but the loaves still felt warm. Pa must have baked them fresh.

Before I could even ring the doorbell, the ornate wooden door swung open.

"Hi, Rosa! So glad to see you," Maria, Ant's younger sister, said as she pulled me into a long hug.

"Hey. You, too. It's been a while," I said when we parted. We hadn't seen each other since the day on the beach.

Mr. Russo and Ant popped around the corner from the sitting room to greet me. Looking at Mr. Russo was like looking into Ant's future. The only differences I could spot were the strands of gray hair speckling Mr. Russo's sandy brown hair and the wrinkles crinkling his caramel-colored skin that outlined his big, almond-shaped eyes. Other than that, they were carbon copies.

Ant grabbed me around the waist and placed a quick kiss on my cheek.

"Happy birthday," I said, handing him the loaves of bread and a card I'd picked up at the A&P on the corner.

I studied his face for any lingering resentment from the concert but saw only his genuine smile. We had talked little since then, only one quick phone call the previous night before his tennis practice, so I half expected him to give me the cold shoulder. Instead, he acted as if nothing had happened at all.

"Thanks for coming. Mom is in the kitchen getting the food ready. Can I get you a glass of wine?"

"No, thanks. I'll go check on her to see if she needs help."

Mr. Russo and Ant nodded, heading back to their seats in the sitting room to finish their pre-dinner drinks.

The house smelled wonderful, and I knew Mrs. Russo must have been making Ant's favorite, ossobuco ala Milanese—braised veal shanks with gremolata and risotto. I inhaled the delicious aromas before making my way to their large kitchen in the back of the house.

Although my family had been close with the Russos for decades now, we did not share the same comforts or sizable bank accounts. The Russos had done well for themselves in the years since Mr. Russo started his wine distribution business as a young man fresh out of business school. Unlike my parents, who immigrated as children, Mr. and Mrs. Russo were both born in Chicago to immigrant parents who insisted they get their educations. Albeit only two years for Mrs. Russo, who met and married Ant's father at age twenty.

The Russos' house stood on a large lot one street over from us. Its elegant light-colored greystone exterior contrasted the dark trim around the front bay windows, door frame, and the dark, gas-lit lanterns on the front vestibule. Ant and I had climbed onto the balcony over the front stoop several times as children. As one of the few single-family homes in our neighborhood, it demanded respect and oozed status.

Of course, the kitchen would suit such a grand home. Upon entering, my eyes were drawn to the back wall of curved bay windows, which illuminated a dinette set. In front of the table, a large workstation flanked the double oven and stove range, which sat under an impressive stained wooden hood with intricate latticework adorning its edges.

I had fallen in love with the kitchen as a child and had often imagined myself cooking in it. Not that Mrs. Russo would ever give up her beautiful home to anyone, even Ant, but I dreamed one day I'd be able to build myself something similar, if not better.

Mrs. Russo stood under the hood, stirring a massive pot of risotto on the stove.

"I'm almost finished here. Go check on the men. Top off their drinks." Just like that, she dismissed me from her kitchen without a glance in my direction.

Turning on my heels, I headed straight back the way I came. Maybe one of these nights, she'd let me cook.

Before I could reach the sitting room, Maria intercepted me, pulling my hand up the stairs.

"Let me show you what Daddy got me for my sweet sixteen."

We raced up the curving staircase to the second floor and down the hall to her bedroom. Her room was larger than all three of our bedrooms combined, but it still looked girlish with pink lace curtains on the two windows that flanked her Victorian-era four-poster bed.

Near the foot of her bed stood a table with a new record player on top.

"It's a Zenith!" she squealed. "Daddy got it direct from the factory. It's not even in stores yet."

Maria reached under the table to finger through her collection of records before plucking one out and placing it on the turntable. Ricky Nelson's *Travelin' Man* crackled through the speaker and filled the room. She threw her head back and sang along.

"Isn't it wonderful?"

I had to say, it was impressive. I'd never owned anything as extravagant. The only record player we had sat in the bar area of the restaurant for parties and special occasions, although I wondered if it even still worked. Its large wooden frame served as a staging station for the wait staff now. But Maria's record player was no larger than a briefcase. It even had a locking lid and handle.

"It is," I said, running my hand over its smooth top.

Maria pulled the box of records to the middle of the floor. Sitting next to me, she began to alphabetize the collection. When we got to the Ds, she paused to look at me.

"Why didn't you go to college?" she asked.

Not expecting this turn of conversation, I set the Elvis Presley "Don't Be Cruel" record I had in my hands on top of the pile before responding.

"I've always wanted to be a chef. You don't need a fancy degree for that."

"Yeah, but it'll be different once you're married," she said, looking at the caramel-colored carpet. I shrugged, not knowing how to answer that.

"I don't think I want to get married. I want a career."

I reached over to touch her hand. "You're young and smart, Maria. You can do whatever you want. Who says you can't have both?"

She cocked her chin to the side.

"Do you really believe that? More than anything, I want to attend veterinary school, but I doubt my parents will pay for it. They expect me to find a husband and pop out babies," she said.

"Have you told them?" I asked, knowing she didn't have anyone else to talk to. I was the closest she had to a sister.

"No. My mother has already picked out the secretarial school I'll attend after graduation."

Before I could respond, Ant knocked at the door.

"Dinner is ready," he said, smiling at the two of us crouched over on the floor, records in heaping piles.

Maria jolted up and headed for the stairs, while I stayed put. She couldn't have known how her own anxiety struck a chord, and I wondered how many other young women battled the same pull, the same pressure. Much like being split in two.

I stood, smoothing my dress and rolling my shoulders back to clear my mind. It wasn't the time to dwell on such things. Eventually I'd have to muster the courage to fight for my own dreams.

"Thanks for coming tonight. And for entertaining my sister." He laughed, but the space between his eyebrows wrinkled in concentration.

"Look, Ant, I'm sorry for being rude the other night," I started before he cut me off.

"No need to be sorry. I should be the one apologizing," he said. "There's a lot of pressure on me, but that's no excuse to treat you poorly. You deserve better."

I took his hand, holding it between mine. It meant something that he acknowledged our conversation, but I still didn't think he understood the gravity of the situation and its impact on my life. To move forward, we'd have to see eye to eye on this. I didn't see any other option.

"Thank you for apologizing, but it doesn't solve anything. We need to be on the same page. Preferably *before* we're married," I said.

"I know. Let's not talk about it tonight. Let's celebrate. Can we do that? For my birthday?" he asked, eyes pleading for me to drop it.

"Of course."

We made our way down the stairs to the formal dining room, where the Russo's housekeeper had set an elaborate table using the family's finest porcelain dinnerware. It looked fit for royalty.

"This looks beautiful," I said, marveling at the array of summer flowers overflowing their vases along the center of the long table.

"It's not every day your son becomes a man," Mrs. Russo said, stepping into the room. She looked immaculate. The exact opposite of me after hours in a kitchen.

She pecked Ant on the cheek and said, "Happy Birthday, Anthony."

"Thanks, Mom. Rosa is right; this is all wonderful."

Mr. Russo said a quick prayer over the food and took his seat at the head of the table in a large wooden chair that reached up to his shoulders. We followed suit.

"Let's eat."

After the first few bites, I relaxed enough to enjoy the food while listening to Ant recount his summer business course curriculum to his father. When together, that's all the two talked about: business or school. Ant's father was a nice man, but when it came to his children, he had a very hands-off approach unless it intersected with his interests. Now that Ant was taking over the business, they spent every spare moment together, with Mr. Russo attempting to impart his wisdom from over three decades in the wine industry to his successor.

Mrs. Russo, on the other hand, knew every detail of her children's lives, whether they liked it or not. That's why her chilly attitude toward me lately had wormed its way under my skin. If this was how she responded to me continuing to work at the restaurant, how would she act when Ant and I disagreed on larger issues throughout our marriage? Would it always be me against them? The thought weighed heavily on my chest as I munched on olives and bread.

During a lull in the riveting conversation about Ant's statistics class, Mrs. Russo cleared her throat.

"Maria has an announcement," she said, staring across the table at her daughter, lips set in a straight line. "Go on, tell them."

Her eyes darted over to me for a second before she pulled her chin down to say, "I received an early acceptance to Rosary College."

Mr. Russo beamed. "That's wonderful, darling. Though I didn't realize you were applying. Isn't it early yet?"

Maria opened her mouth to answer, but Mrs. Russo beat her to it. "I might have put a birdie in the ear of the admissions director's wife. She's on the church women's club board." Mrs. Russo sat up proud, like she'd announced she'd solved world hunger.

The self-satisfied look on her face made my mouth sour. *Poor Maria*, I thought. Rosary College was a Catholic all-girls school, specializing in a few concentrations: home economics, education, and secretarial sciences. Nothing that would prepare her for vet school or even give her the basis to apply.

"I don't know if I'll accept yet. I'm keeping my options open," Maria said softly.

"Keeping your options open for what? You won't get into a better school than that, my dear. Don't waste your time," Mrs. Russo chuckled.

I offered Maria a small smile across the table. It wasn't much, but I hoped it said, "I know, I see you, and it's not fair."

To Mr. Russo's credit, he looked disappointed at his wife's flippant comment. He turned to Maria and told her, "You still have plenty of time to decide. At least now you have an option."

No one said much else until dessert, when the question of setting our wedding date lingered in the air.

"We haven't figured everything out yet, but we will," I promised.

"Don't want to wait too long. You don't want Ant changing his mind," she chided through a rueful grin.

"Mother, we have it under control. No one is changing their mind."

She hummed in response, taking a bite of her lemon cake. Ant's jaw clenched so hard, the veins in his neck popped out.

After dinner, I offered to help clear the plates and, to my surprise, she didn't decline. The housekeeper had been dismissed hours ago.

Chapter 13

"Thank you, Rosa, for helping." Mrs. Russo dried while I plunged my hands into the gray soapy sink water and scrubbed. "I'm glad to have some time with you alone."

My shoulder muscles tensed. I couldn't deal with a lecture, and especially not from her. More than anything, I longed to be home curled up on the couch with the new cookbook that had come for me by mail the day before. The small gift had surprised me with only a short note of explanation attached:

For your collection.

-Lou

At first, it perplexed me. Why would Lou send me a cookbook? Then I remembered our conversation in Bella's kitchen over the timballo and it made sense. The book wasn't new; it looked well-loved, and it was French—the first non-Italian collection of recipes I'd owned or even read. I couldn't wait to dig in.

Mrs. Russo's hand landed on my shoulder as I finished up the last of the washing, bringing me back to the moment.

"You will be my daughter soon, so I want to be honest about my reservations," she said.

I turned to face her, hands braced behind me on the sink's edge. My fingers dug into the porcelain.

"My son deserves a devoted wife and partner. And that's exactly what married couples are—partners. But you will play different roles. Do you understand me?" Her eyes narrowed. "It's time to take your role seriously. Lord knows plenty of other women would line up for the chance."

My mouth fell open. Mrs. Russo not only insulted my intelligence by talking to me as if I were a child, but she also threatened my relationship with her son. I bit my tongue to keep from snapping back.

She let out a short huff through her nose, making her nostrils flare. "I'll make it as clear as I can: you need to give up your silly notions of becoming a chef."

Before she could go on, I spat out, "I am a chef."

"No, you're a girl who cannot let go of childish dreams. I blame your father for indulging you for far too long. Your mother agrees. But now, it's over. Anthony needs a devoted woman by his side. Not a career girl with no time for her family."

The insult stung. I'd worked hard for so long that it hit me in the gut to hear someone discredit my efforts in one fell swoop. All in the name of wifely duties, time-honored stereotypes I could not escape. Echo after echo of the same refrain: women should aspire to be in the home only. The pressure condensed behind my eyes, forming a tight, piercing headache that blurred my vision. I took a quick breath before responding.

"Mrs. Russo, with respect, this is between me and Ant. What we decide to do with our lives is our business, not yours."

She pushed herself upright from where she'd been leaning on the counter. "It certainly is my business. We will be sharing a last name, which I intend to protect. I am on your side. Your family has been close to ours for years. But make no mistake,

Rosa. Anthony has options. The phone still rings here for him. You'd do well not to forget that."

My brain seized in that moment, but my heartbeat blazed in my ears. I turned my focus to the sink, attempting to steady my breath when Ant walked in.

"Ready to go?" he quipped, smile falling at the sight of the two of us and our serious faces. "Everything all right?"

I snapped out of it, brushing past Mrs. Russo as I walked to the door. "Yes, but let me say goodbye to your sister."

Neither of us said much on the short walk back to my house, although Ant reached for my hand as soon as we hit the sidewalk. I wondered if he could sense my distress through my clammy palm.

How did we get here? I thought. Ant knew more about me and my childhood than anyone besides Camille. He'd stood up for me in middle school when a group of girls taunted me for wearing "Coke bottle" glasses. I'd helped him study in high school for his advanced biology final so he could ace it. We'd stayed up all night for three evenings in a row. I'd made flashcards and quizzed him until we both fell asleep on the kitchen table, drool running all over our textbooks. We had walked home from school together every day that he didn't have practice since elementary school. He even went with me to pick out my prom dress with Camille. We attended with a group of our friends, but not together.

Ant had always been the popular kid, the one with the most friends, and he'd pulled me along with them any chance he got. It wasn't that I didn't have friends, I had a few. Mostly, I kept my head down, spending my free time at the restaurant. Ant knew I needed entertainment and was always willing to provide it.

I wanted that version of us back, the unlikely duo that always covered for each other. Yet now, I was incapable of mentioning the awkward exchange I'd had with his mother. We were two ships drifting farther apart with each passing day. The gulf between becoming so wide, I had no idea how to close it. It might have even been too late to try.

When we arrived at my front door, I almost invited Ant in for a nightcap but stopped myself when I spotted Pa through the window in the sitting room. More than a week had gone by since I'd seen him and he'd started his extra job. We needed to catch up.

Ant kissed me on the cheek, thanking me for celebrating his birthday. "Soon, we'll be hosting our own dinner parties," he said, pushing a piece of hair behind my ear. "Everyone will want an invitation."

I winced at the implication but hid it under a smile. At some point soon, I would have to be honest with Ant and tell him the raw truth about my feelings. That meant confessing everything, not just my desire to continue cooking at the restaurant, but my concerns about the growing distance between us as well. He deserved that. I did too.

When I turned the overhead light on in the sitting room, my father looked up at me like I'd surprised him. Exhaustion etched his face, making him appear ten years older than the last time I saw him. His slumped shoulders leaned forward in a way that looked as if he were balancing heavy weights on them.

I crossed the room to sit next to him on the small settee.

"How are you holding up, old man?"

"Who are you calling 'old man'? I worked fifteen hours straight, and I'm still upright."

"Barely," I murmured. "Are you all right?"

"I'm tired," he answered. "But I'll be okay. We'll be okay if we stick to the plan."

His voice sounded confident, but the look on his face said otherwise. He was worried. I could see it behind his drooping eyes and lopsided smile that didn't reach the top half of his face.

"What can I do?"

"Oh, piccolina, you're already doing so much." He patted my knee, looking forward into the dark kitchen. "Without you, we would have lost her already. It's unfair to put so much on you. You have a wedding to plan."

"I'm not worried about the wedding," I said, realizing I meant it. "I'm worried about you. About the restaurant and our family."

"That's a lot of weight for a young person to carry," he said. "Let me do the worrying. You just look forward to marrying Ant."

Silence stretched between us. I could hear the clock on the wall ticking as the house sat quiet for once, smoothing my rough edges. Camille was working, and Ma and Ivana were attending a youth play at church.

Confident we were alone, I plowed ahead. Pa might have been the only one to give me an honest reading of my situation with Ant.

"What if I don't want to marry Ant?" I asked.

My father craned his head toward me, studying my expression.

"Don't you love him?" He tilted his head to the side, chin pointing up, eyes squinting.

"I care about him. I think I always will. But love? Who knows for sure?" The couch's scratchy fabric rubbed against the backs of my calves. "Plus, I don't think he knows either. Love seems… big."

Pa only hummed, nodding his head for me to go on.

"And he wants me to give up the restaurant."

"Ah, there it is," he said.

I quickly added, "But that's not the only thing giving me pause. I'm worried we'll grow to resent one another. What if we realize we've made a mistake, and then we're stuck? I don't want to regret my life."

"Those are normal concerns. Everyone who has ever gotten married has dealt with them. I know I did when I met your mother. But my love for her outweighed everything else."

My parents' love transcended time. I think from the moment they met, they knew their destiny. Although the two couldn't be more different, they somehow fit. When I was young, I used to catch them dancing together in the living room after they'd put me and Camille to bed. I'd watch them from the top step, through the banister spindles. They never played music, instead they simply held each other close, cheeks pressed together as they swayed to imaginary music. Even now, I saw their stolen glances across the room, communicating without words. Their love had changed over two decades of marriage, but it was strong. No longer a smoldering fire of passion but a rock-solid foundation that only death could break. It was always a hard notion to reconcile with the distant mother I knew.

I thought about what Pa said. I didn't want to hurt Ant, but I couldn't be trapped in a future I didn't control, either. Then, my father asked me the real question.

"Can you learn to love him? And are you willing to give up your passion for the chance at love?"

"With Ant?"

"Well, yes. Who else?"

That night, I sat in bed with the cookbook Lou had dropped off propped up on my knees. The reading lamp on my small nightstand lit up the pages like a spotlight as I flipped through the heavy book. This one didn't contain pictures or illustrations like all the new Betty Crocker cookbooks I had seen in store windows on Michigan Avenue, but it had clear instructions, even if I didn't recognize a good portion of the ingredients.

Every so often, I ran across a page with handwriting. Those notes were in French, so I couldn't understand it, but some phrases were underlined or circled along with various stain marks from what looked like cooking oil or splattered butter, which the French seemed to use a lot.

When I found a recipe for coq au vin, I stopped and read it several times. The chicken dish, braised in wine, reminded me of chicken cacciatore, something I'd been making for years at Cucina Bella. It was a local favorite, of sorts. Scanning the ingredients list, I realized I had everything I needed to make it the next day, which was exactly what I needed: to cook. When I cooked, things became clearer, the clouds in my head cleared and I could hear my inner voice better.

As I closed the book, a note fell out of the back, landing in my lap. I unfolded the yellowing paper with faded handwriting and read:

My Dear Patrice,

This book taught me everything I needed to know about French cooking and is the reason I moved to America all those years ago. The fire that burns inside me was lit between these pages.

During some of my darkest moments, this old cookbook provided me comfort and refuge. You are embarking on a journey to forge your own path, and I'm so very proud of you. But I won't lie, it will be lonely. Cook from this book when you need comfort or courage. It is yours now.

With all my love and admiration,
Elizabeth

I read and reread the note several times trying to decipher who Patrice and Elizabeth were to each other. A few scenarios ran through my head before it clicked. Elizabeth. The woman Lou had introduced me to a few days ago at the bakery. This must have been hers. But I couldn't figure out how I had ended up with it. Where would Lou have found it? I welcomed the puzzle to distract me from the thoughts lurking at the corners of my consciousness.

Mrs. Russo's reservations and hostile warnings chipped away at the thin illusion I'd been holding onto for months now. I knew if Ant spent any real time thinking about our match and our impending marriage, he'd agree. We were playacting the roles our parents assigned to us years ago. A self-fulfilling prophecy of our own making. I felt it more. After all, Ant had been promised the world and he would get it, with or without me by his side.

Chapter 14

The next week flew by with the steadiness of routine etching itself in place. Lou and I met by the lamppost in the morning and walked to the restaurant as the sun rose. Most days, I'd find an hour or two to cook us something new. Sometimes trying a French recipe from the book he'd given me, other times working on my own dishes. For lunch, Lou brought food for us to try from different places around the city. Tacos from a Mexican place he frequented, butter chicken from an Indian restaurant a few blocks from his apartment, and even an egg and noodle dish he picked up in Chinatown.

The different flavors and textures of the dishes opened my eyes to a new way of experiencing food. These exotic foods provided a glimpse into another world altogether, one that I wanted to devour.

The first morning after Ant's birthday party, I thanked Lou for the book on our short walk to Bella. I found it easier to talk to him while we walked; our eyes could face forward and I didn't run the risk of being ensnared in his intense gaze.

"It's nothing," Lou said with a shake of his head.

"No, it's something. You remembered what I'd told you about the church ladies and their cookbooks…" I trailed off, straining to find the right words. "I really enjoyed reading about French cuisine." I decided not to tell him about the letter I had found. I didn't have the words to explain it, nor did I want him to feel obligated to explain it to me.

Thursday afternoon, I took the bus to the library to look for other cookbooks outside of Italian food. Unsurprisingly, there weren't many actual cookbooks to check out, but the Chicago Public Library did have a decent food history section I pored over.

The receptionist rolled her eyes at the stack I brought to the desk and informed me of their five-book limit with only a cursory glance in my direction. The task of narrowing the books down to five felt like giving up the keys to an unlocked repository of knowledge. Each book seemed to hold precious information that I needed to know. I rationalized I could come back the following week to rescue the others from their lonely homes on dusty shelves.

I had the night off, and instead of meeting Ant and his crew for drinks, I opted for an evening with my new books. Camille would be appalled, but she had to work the closing shift at Bella, so at least I'd be spared the pleading.

Armed with a notebook and pen, I planned to devour as much as I could, taking copious notes along the way for future reference. As I read the pages on my bed under the dim light, I began to think about the hundreds, even thousands of other restaurants in Chicago alone that I had yet to visit. It suddenly felt like a sin to live in such a large and diverse city yet restrict oneself to the five-block radius of the neighborhood one grew up in, which was by far the norm.

While at the library, *The Alice B. Toklas Cook Book* seemed to call my name from the stacks, so that's what I started reading first. Part recipes, part memoir, it followed Alice's bohemian life in Paris during the early to mid-twentieth century. How different her experience was from my own. She told of the famous artists and literary icons she dined with and cooked for, along with personal anecdotes sprinkled throughout the recipes. Her tone and often dry wit made me shriek with laughter. The recipes themselves ranged from complicated to rustic, and I copied down a few to try later. At one point, the bowl of spaghetti I'd whipped up for myself sat cold, forgotten. I wanted to taste the food between the pages of that book.

Each recipe, each story, fascinated me more than the previous, and I read faster than I ever had. Oh, how I longed for illustrations in the book so I could see the food she described in detail. I imagined the pictures that could have been taken at the parties she hosted. It was almost too much to bear.

One line struck me hard. Alice wrote, "It was not that I was learning to cook, but that I was learning to become a cook," and it was like looking in a mirror. All my life, I'd been learning to cook, like Alice. We had both become chefs along the way.

While my life would never resemble Alice's Parisian rhapsody of color and intrigue, I desperately wanted my own version of it. My destiny had not yet been sealed, I told myself. There was still time to chase those high-flung, somewhat delusional dreams I'd only now allowed myself to look at in the full light.

For the first time in weeks, sleep arrived unchallenged.

Around three in the morning, muffled voices rose from the stairwell. Concerned someone had fallen, I rose without bothering to pull on my robe and swung the door open, not checking if Camille had made it home or not.

Squinting in the darkness, I could see large shapes swaying on the stairs. My heart raced at the awful thoughts swirling through my half-awake brain. Panic rose in my throat until I heard a voice cry out.

"Watch it, buster." Camille's words slurred into each other.

"Camille," I whispered her name as forcefully as I could without reaching full volume. "What's going on?"

"Rosa, it's Lou. I'm with Camille," came a low voice from the darkness.

I rubbed my arm, pinching it to make sure I was awake and not still dreaming, then I heard one of them take another stumble on the steps.

I sprang to life.

"Shhh. Be quiet. Get in the bedroom." I took Camille's other arm, the one Lou wasn't already propping up over his shoulder, and guided them back to the bedroom, praying my parents didn't hear.

We plopped Camille down on her bed, and she flopped onto her back with the dramatic and uncoordinated flair of a drunk woman. I flicked the lamp on. Camille's French twist dropped to one side, the bright red lipstick she always wore smeared down her chin, and black mascara streaks flowed over her cheeks. The strong odor of liquor and bile permeated the room.

"I'm fiiiine," she whined. "I don't know what the big deal is. Can't a girl have a liiiittle fun?"

Scanning the room from Camille to Lou, I realized my state of undress. The thin, short nightgown I wore left nothing to the imagination, and embarrassment rose in my stomach. I quickly grabbed my robe.

"What happened?" I asked, tying the belt tight around my waist.

"Her friends left her at the club."

"What do you mean, left her? Who?"

Lou ran his hand down his face, turning away toward the window. The moonlight created shadows across his sharp nose and deep-set eyes.

"Lou, tell me."

"Jackson. I didn't recognize the other guy."

Anger roared up my spine. The audacity of that man! How could he abandon her in that part of the city? No doubt he was the one who'd gotten her this drunk, too. I wanted to grab him by the neck and squeeze until the life drained from his face.

Before I could find the words to respond, the bedroom door swung open. My mother appeared in the doorway.

"What in the world?" she asked, rubbing her eyes.

Taking in the scene, her posture went ramrod straight.

"Marco, get in here. Now."

Dread replaced my anger.

No one slept that night except Camille. After all the commotion, Ivana insisted on sleeping with me, too scared to be alone. I lay in bed with her, staring at the water stain on the ceiling while a battle of thoughts raged in my head.

I knew Camille would have hell to pay in the morning, and part of me sympathized with her. There was no telling what retribution Ma would demand for her actions. She hadn't said much after I explained that Lou had brought Camille home after his shift to ensure her safety. Other than a stern, "The night's over. We will deal with this tomorrow," she didn't say much once Pa had come in to witness his daughter fall-down inebriated. Lou had silently followed Pa down the stairs to the front door.

No one wanted to be left alone at a bar at two in the morning, but this proved Camille's pattern of recklessness had to stop. Her infatuation with Jackson had become dangerous. He'd shown himself to be nothing more than a fast talker with a slow conscience.

Failure gnawed at me. As her older sister, I should have protected her from boys like him. Of all the talks I'd given her lately, none stuck. Playing the nice sister hadn't been working, and now the situation called for tough love.

As I listened to her deep breathing, blissfully unaware of what waited for her come daybreak, I vowed to talk to Ant. He and Jackson were close, maybe he could talk some sense into his friend or at the very least convince him to leave her alone. The heartbreak would wound Camille, but it wouldn't kill her.

If she refused to protect herself, then we'd do it for her.

At breakfast, my parents avoided conversation, their exhaustion clear from the darkness that hung around their eyes. Coffee was poured, toast was buttered, cereal was crunched. No one broke the spell, not even Ivana, as we sat around the oval-shaped table, missing only Camille. My nerves jittered under my skin from the espresso.

Finally, Ma spoke.

"Rosa, go wake your sister." The edge in her voice was unmistakable. "Tell her to meet me and your father in the den in ten minutes."

Although grown, Camille and I both feared our mother something fierce. Her hard-eyed looks alone could crumble anyone into a puddle on the floor. No doubt this talk would be unpleasant, but I took solace in the fact that she needed it.

Camille lay on her side, in the same position as when I'd left thirty minutes ago. I gripped her shoulder and shook it. "Hey, it's time to wake up." Nothing. I sat on the edge of the bed and turned her over. A soft moan escaped her throat.

"What time is it?" she mumbled.

"Ten past eight. Does your head hurt?"

"Yes. Water. Please."

A minute later, I returned with a full glass of water, helping her to sit up and drink small sips. She looked like death warmed over and smelled even worse.

"Why is the room spinning?" she asked, looking uneasy.

I rubbed her back as she caught her breath.

"I wish I could stay with you until you felt better, but Ma and Pa want to see you in the den. Now." I softened my voice as I spoke. Seeing her like that threatened to dissolve my plans to give her tough love until she started making better decisions.

Camille started to rise but stumbled back onto the bed. "How mad do you think she is?"

"I don't know. She said barely a word at breakfast. I don't think she got any sleep."

Camille groaned. "Great." This time, she made it to the door.

"Who were you with last night?" I asked as she fumbled with the doorknob.

"Jackson and Ant."

"Just a minute!" Ant shouted behind the metal apartment door.

I kept pounding, even louder. Not twenty minutes before, I had called him and hung up as soon as I heard his voice on the other end. I needed to know he was home. Then, I'd gathered my purse and hopped on the L train to take the short ride over, seething with rage. How could he have left Camille alone? What kind of man would do that? Certainly not the man I'd agreed to marry.

I stood in front of his door as my pulse pounded in my ears until I heard steps on the Linoleum floor behind the door. It creaked open, but I could only see half of Ant's face.

"Rosa, what are you doing here?" he asked, his eyes darting back over his shoulder.

"I came to see you. Care to let me in? Or do you plan to make me stand out here?"

"Now's not the best time. Can you come back in an hour?"

"No. We need to talk," I said, my patience growing very thin. He saw from the look on my face that this wasn't a social call. "Why on earth would you leave Camille at the bar alone last night?"

"Rosa, please come back or call me in a bit. I'm in the middle of something." It was as if he didn't even hear me.

I cocked my head to the side and stared at him. For a moment, my anger gave way to confusion. Then I heard rustling on the other side of the door. If it were only Jackson and Ant in the apartment, there'd be no reason not to let me in. Only the large armchair in the living room was visible from over his shoulder, but I knew someone else was in there.

"What's going on, Ant?" I asked, my voice raising a few octaves. "Open the door."

The anger returned with a vengeance—I wanted, no, needed, to get beyond his front door and see for myself. Maybe he'd been studying, or working on a wedding surprise, I briefly told myself before pushing past him. I had to know for sure, even at the risk of looking like a jealous, unhinged fiancée. Ant tried to stop me but surrendered after I stuck my foot out to keep the door from shutting.

I heard him rasp, "Rosa, please," as I made my way into the small entry.

Light from the fixture above blinded me as I looked around the small living room. It took a second before my eyes adjusted and caught a woman hunched over on the sofa. At first, I couldn't make out what she was doing. Her brown hair hung in tumbling waves over her shoulder, obscuring her face. Then, I saw the pantyhose dangling from her hand as she tried to slip it over her bare foot. Her head shot up, and she looked me dead in the eye when she heard me gasp. My face flushed with heat as hers drained of color. I knew instantly who she was.

Maggie from the concert. I guess they weren't just studying together after all.

Things like this happened in the movies or dime-store novels, not in real life. Not my life. In the movies, the scorned woman either stormed off in tears or crumpled to the floor in a sad heap, and while I felt capable of doing either, my feet stayed rooted to the floor. Drama was for other people. But now everything stood still. My entire future narrowed down to this single second in time.

I turned to Ant, whose face looked so twisted in pain I didn't recognize some of his features.

"Why?" My voice was barely a whisper. It felt as if the wind had been knocked out of me.

"I'm sorry," he breathed, looking past me.

The woman, the one from the concert, gave up on the pantyhose and grabbed her handbag before rushing past me. Her hand landed on Ant's arm for a brief second, and then she was gone.

"You said she was only a friend. Someone you studied with. Why would you lie to me?" I genuinely wanted to know.

If Ant didn't want to marry me, then he should have simply said so. The distant gap between us had grown wide since the engagement, but to do this instead, to carry on with another woman, damaged not only our fragile courtship but also our friendship. I didn't care about the pending marriage. Ant had been one of my closest friends for two decades. Camille had been right. A sharp pain in my chest made my breathing ragged, but I would not cry. Not now, at least.

"I didn't mean for it to happen, Rosa. I really didn't. I don't want to hurt you."

"So, you'd lie to me instead?"

We stood only a few feet apart, but there might as well have been an ocean between us.

Ant took a deep breath, his shoulders rising with it.

"Come on. You know you haven't been completely honest with me either. I've heard how close you've become with that boy, Lou." I started to deny anything between us before Ant put a hand up to stop me.

"It doesn't matter, though. You never wanted to marry me. I think I always knew that. You never loved me like I loved you."

I let out a short laugh. "Neither of us knows what love is, Ant. Don't kid yourself."

"That's not true. You love cooking and the restaurant. They mean more to you than trying to love me ever could."

At that, I could not argue. We'd both lied to each other, but I still wasn't letting him off the hook. He'd left Camille alone in a strange bar in a rough part of the city, *drunk*.

"Why did you leave Camille last night? She had to be taken home and could barely stand up straight. How could you put her in danger like that?" I squared my shoulders to face him. While it might've been over for us, we were still tied together by our families.

"What are you talking about? She was with Jackson when I left."

That made sense. I let the breath I'd been holding since last night go until I realized he'd probably left with Maggie.

"I swear I'd never leave her. You know me better than that."

"I thought I did." The words left my mouth before I could stop them.

Ant looked like he'd taken a blow to the stomach. "You do. Better than anyone."

"None of that matters now."

Chapter 15

"Rosa, I'd like a word after dinner," my mother said as we set the table.

I nodded without a word. Of course, she'd known about me and Ant. I prayed I would have at least a day to process everything before the interrogation. It was only a few hours ago that her disappointment rested with Camille. Now it was my turn.

I'd opted to walk the forty-five minutes back to the restaurant after leaving Ant's that morning, even if it meant I'd be late for the lunch shift. For once, I didn't care about being the responsible one. The staff could wait for me like I'd done for them a hundred times before.

The pressure built inside me, feeling as if I'd swallowed my own heart. As I walked in the mild morning air, my body loosened, releasing the weight I'd been carrying since the night of the engagement.

Yes, I was still angry with Ant for lying to me and for betraying my trust. But deep down, part of me knew I wouldn't have left him on my own either. If I hadn't caught him with Maggie, I would have married him and fallen into the life I'd seen so many other women live. And who knows? Maybe I'd have made peace with it, but not likely.

Of course, there'd be fallout now. But it meant I still held the pen. I could write my future without the fear of being held back by duty.

Ant and I decided that morning that we'd call off our engagement. He offered to take the brunt of the blame. Part of me wanted to resist, because I knew I played a large role in our downfall, too. But he'd insisted. Guilt can make martyrs of us all. He never explained exactly who Maggie was to him, and I didn't ask.

"You mean a lot to me, and that will never change. But you're right; we both deserve to know genuine love and the opportunity to find ourselves," Ant had explained that morning in his living room.

I squeezed his hand as he continued, "I only want the best for you. You need someone who shares your unconventional dreams. Ours are too different to coexist, and I realize that now."

"Our families are built on convention," I half-laughed.

"And it's what I want."

"I know." A sad smile reached my lips.

"I'm rooting for you. Always will."

And I knew he would. I also knew we were over.

At dinner that night, my mother didn't say much of anything. Ivana fussed over a new doll and the rest of us, Camille included, ate our rigatoni in silence. Pa, bless his heart, tried to make conversation, but it fell flat with one-word responses.

"Camille, you're on cleanup duty tonight. Ivana, help your sister clear the table, and then you can go outside and play before bed. Rosa, go to the den," Ma said, standing from her chair. "You too, Marco."

I tried to catch Camille's eye to share one of our conspiratorial eye rolls, but she kept her face turned down at the table while Ivana cleared her plate. Pa didn't move until after Ma had left the kitchen. He squeezed Camille's shoulder for a second as he passed. My fingers gripped the edge of the dining table, hoping to steal some of the oak wood's strength.

I made my way through the dark living room into the den, where my parents sat in two leather armchairs. The wall clock ticked in the silence, and Ma motioned for me to take a seat in the desk chair facing them.

My resolve to tell them the truth grew as I sat under their stares. This was my life, and I needed to claim it. For far too long, I'd let her expectations dictate my decisions. That was over now. The spell broke the moment I knocked on Ant's door that morning.

"Ant's mother called this afternoon," Ma said. She let the words linger in the air. My father looked uncomfortable, shifting in his chair.

"I suppose she told you, then," I finally said.

"Told you what?" Pa asked, turning his shoulders to face my mother.

"Go on, Rosa. Tell your father the news you've neglected to share with us all day."

I glared at her for a long second before continuing.

"We've called off the engagement."

Ma shook her head, as if it were the worst news she'd heard in years. My father didn't say anything. I wasn't sure if I'd imagined it, but I thought I saw a slight upturn at the corner of his mouth.

"I want to know why," Ma demanded.

"Mrs. Russo didn't tell you?"

"No, she said it was a private matter between the two of you. But I don't agree. We were going to be family. I deserve to know why you've thrown that future away."

"My future, you mean."

"Don't talk back to me. I want answers. Surely this can be fixed?"

"It can't," I said. "Ant and I are not getting married. I went along with the engagement to make everyone happy, but I should have said no from the start. I'm done trying to please other people at my own expense."

My mother sighed, and Pa picked at his cuticle. Just once, I wished he would stand up for me, but I knew better. With family matters, he'd always defer to my mother.

"Part of growing up is realizing your role in life. Dreams are for children. You're a woman now, and if you're set on playing "Miss Independent," I won't stop you. You'll have to learn the hard way like your sister. Both of you have three months," she paused. "I'm so disappointed."

"Three months for what?" I asked, cocking my head to the side.

"Until you're out. I won't have two grown women living here like heathens. You'll need to stand on your own feet, without our help."

At this, my father snapped his head up. "Don't you think that's a bit harsh, Marissa?"

"They need to learn, and I'm done coddling them. You left your family at ten to move to a foreign country not speaking a word of English, Marco! We've given them too much as it is. Three months is more than generous."

No words came to me. I sat like a fish, mouth gaping.

"Now go help Camille." My mother dismissed me with a flick of her wrist.

I did as I was told, walking to the kitchen on autopilot. Camille had already finished and was heading up the stairs back to our room, so I followed her.

She collapsed onto her bed.

"Still hungover?"

"You could say that. I feel like a bus hit me." She rolled over to face me. "What happened?"

I sat and filled her in on the day's events.

"Wow, I can't say I'm surprised about you and Ant, but I am shocked they're kicking us both out."

"It's Ma's decision, not Pa's." I correct.

She narrowed her eyes.

"What?"

"Pa could speak up and stop it if he wanted to. You've always made excuses for him, but you know I'm right."

Of course she was, but I didn't feel like getting into that. We had other things to discuss.

"Ant said Jackson was with you when he left last night. Is that true?"

"He was, but not for long. I accused him of cheating on me with the hostess, who'd been staring daggers into my back the entire night, and he stormed off."

"I can't believe he left you there alone. What a prick."

Camille shrugged. "I deserved it, I guess. I knew better than to pick a fight, even if we were both plastered."

That broke something inside me. Camille still didn't know her own worth. All her life, she lived in the shadows of others, trying on their personalities like dresses, hoping one would fit.

As if hearing my thoughts, she said, "It's so hard trying to be everything everyone expects me to be. It's like you and I were built in the same factory, but they forgot to install a few of my parts. I can't seem to find them either. Meanwhile, you're becoming more you, every day. It's beautiful and heartbreaking at the same time. The more you become, the less I am."

"Oh, Camille. You're beautifully imperfect. And you're not alone. I'm not going anywhere. We'll get through this."

At this, Camille crumpled into a tight ball and cried hard into her hands. I moved to her bed to rub her back, making shushing noises to soothe her. Between her sobs, I heard her mutter, "I'm pregnant."

For the second time in twenty-four hours, words failed me.

The next week limped by without fanfare. Camille and I resembled zombies as we methodically went through the motions of the day until we collapsed in our beds at night. We exchanged little conversation, too. And although I appeared half-awake, inside, questions bounced around in my skull like a ping-pong ball:

Where would we go in three months? Did I make enough money to afford rent in the city? Would Camille keep the baby? Was Jackson the father? Did he know? Did Ant know?

The only person to notice anything amiss was Lou. He'd skipped a few mornings at the restaurant because of his fall classes starting back up, but as soon as he'd returned, he clocked my sullen mood. We worked alongside each other in silence until he caught me staring into a large pot of tomato sauce I'd put on for the lunch rush.

"Earth to Rosa. Everything okay?" He waved his hand in front of me.

I blinked hard a few times before turning slowly to face him. "Oh, yes. I'm fine. Didn't get enough sleep, that's all."

"Uh-huh. You've been like this all week. What's going on?"

Before I could answer him, my father clattered through the kitchen door and headed straight back to the office.

What's he doing here? Lou must have been wondering the same thing because he tapped the metal table next to us with his knuckles and blew out a long breath before following my father.

If I'd learned anything from that week, it was that I didn't have as much control as I'd thought. Part of me felt relieved, but a smaller part of me wilted under the harsh reality of my situation. I knew I'd have to pull myself together and figure out the next steps not only for me, but for Camille as well. For now, though, I'd allow myself some time to wallow. The determination I felt the night Ma confronted me had all but disappeared.

Under normal circumstances, I'd turn to Camille for advice. Or Ant. These weren't normal circumstances. I'd have to do this alone. Never had I felt such loneliness—it descended on me like a gray cloud that swallowed my days and especially my nights. My world had consisted of my family and Cucina Bella. How sad that at age twenty, I still lived the same relative life I'd led at fifteen, twelve, even ten. The realization deflated me.

Muffled voices rose from behind the closed office door, and for once I was grateful to be left out of it. Let Lou handle whatever my father had going on; I didn't have the mental capacity to deal with it.

A few minutes later my father stepped out, face pinched in concern. For me, his family, or the restaurant, who knew? But when he caught me watching him, he screwed on a polite smile and made his way over.

"How long have you been babysitting this sauce?" he teased.

"Oh, I don't know. It probably needs another hour or so." My eyes roamed to the clock on the wall.

Pa sighed. "You should go home and get some rest, bambina mia. You look tired."

The thought of home deepened my creeping depression. It didn't feel safe anymore. When I laid down at night, an invisible ticking clock teased me, counting down the days until Camille and I would have to move out, which was why I'd taken every shift I could the past week. If I worked my body hard enough, only then would my mind quiet enough to sleep.

"Everyone keeps saying that, but I'm okay. I am." I looked at him with what I hoped came across as sincerity. "How do the numbers look?"

If we saved the restaurant, maybe I still had a future in the kitchen. It was my only hope.

Pa's face fell, but he tried to recover before I could notice. "Slower than we'd hoped, but we're still heading in the right direction. Lou's looking over the books to see where we can trim."   "I thought we were catching up?" This news alarmed me so much I stopped stirring the pot.

He ran his hands through his tight curly hair and rubbed the back of his neck. He smelled of raw meat from his morning shift at the factory.

"Sal has doubled our weekly payments."

"But why? According to Lou, we haven't missed a payment."

"I don't make the rules, amore mio."

Chapter 16

Lou never went home. I couldn't tell when he had time for classes anymore. We both spent every possible waking minute at Bellas. Him in the office or helping with the deliveries, and me in the kitchen working on new recipes when no one else was around. Camille came and went with her shifts and no more. Often, I caught her lying in bed, covers pulled over her head.

During my daily lunch and dinner shifts, I did my best to stay out of the way of the new crew and let them handle the rushes, but I ached to get back to the stove. My determination shifted after the conversation with my father. We couldn't lose any more time moping around. I'd felt sorry for myself long enough; it was time to do something about it.

Of course, my solution involved more cooking. It was the only thing I knew how to do. My grand plan was to convince Pa and Lou to add a few high-end Italian dishes to the weekend dinner menu. I hoped that if we could get more people in or even gain some attention from the local papers, the debt could be paid back faster and things would go back to normal. Pa and I could get back to our plan for the restaurant.

The constant cooking and working left little time to apartment hunt. Camille and I had talked about it a few times, but hadn't agreed to anything. Only once did I ask her about the father. The question was met with a pointed glare, and I dropped it. We both knew who it was.

One evening, about two weeks after the night Lou brought Camille home from the bar, a group of young women who I'd gone to high school with stopped by Bella for dinner. I asked our new hostess to seat them outside my section, as I was one of only two servers that night. The other called out sick, and I didn't want to lose time with small talk.

The hostess looked at the dining room and turned back to me, shrugging. There was only one open table, and of course, it was in my section. I turned on my heel and sped back to the kitchen to pick up one of my orders. On my way, Lou caught my eye behind the bar and threw me a sympathetic look, even though he was getting killed that evening, too.

It took me longer than usual to reach the table of four women. By then, I knew I probably looked a little scattered, but all I could do was keep moving.

"Good evening, ladies. Sorry for the wait, we're busy tonight. What can I get you to drink?"

Rhonda, the busty blonde ringleader of the group, spoke up first. "Hi Rosa. I don't mean to complain, but it's been ten whole minutes since we were sat. Why doesn't your father hire more servers? Where's Camille? Is she too busy to help?"

This drew a few nervous chuckles around the table. Rhonda had always been the confrontational type, but I'd never paid her much mind until Ant and I started dating. She'd always had a thing for him, even though she could have had any boy this side of Lake Michigan.

"She has the night off. We're short a server because of the flu that's going around. What would you like to drink?" I didn't have time for her games while I had other tables waiting on their orders.

I wrote down their drink orders, all white wine, and headed back to Lou to put them in.

"Hey, take a minute. Here's some water," Lou said, sliding a glass of tall ice water behind the register on the bar.

When I turned, I saw my reflection in the mirror behind the liquor bottles on the wall and grimaced at the splotchy red face looking back at me. My bangs were plastered to my forehead from the sweat I'd worked up running around my tables.

"Dear Lord, I hope Gemma is better by tomorrow," I said before I gulped the water down. "Thanks for this," I said, lifting the empty glass before heading back to the table with a tray full of wine glasses.

As I sat the last drink down in front of Rhonda, her fingers latched onto my wrist.

"I'd heard the rumors but thought nothing of them, Rosa! Oh, my dear, I'm so sorry," she said, feigning sympathy while showing off my empty ring finger.

Murmured apologies and gasps echoed in the small booth.

I snatched my hand back and wiped it on my trousers. "It's quite all right. We're better off as friends."

"My thoughts exactly. To be honest, I was shocked when he proposed. I knew it'd only be a matter of time before it fell apart, though. After all, what's a working girl got to offer a man like Anthony? No offense...," she trailed off, not trying to hide the smirk on her face. "I'm sure you're a wonderful cook."

Everyone nodded along, except for Lydia, who sat at the back of the booth, fiddling with her wineglass stem.

I wished the floor would swallow me whole. I'd always been underestimated by girls like Rhonda. They'd written me off as a nobody, just another Italian from an immigrant family who would never escape the neighborhood she'd grown up in.

And truthfully, I never let it bother me much because I had a passion and purpose, something almost all of them lacked. Rhonda, like most of the girls my age, went on to secretarial school, biding her time until she walked down the aisle. But at that moment, standing in front of one of the many women who saw Ant as the prize, I snapped.

"Rhonda, if you must know, I broke it off with Ant. Not because I'm not good enough for him, but because I want more than marriage. Something I know might be hard for your pretty head to wrap itself around. Now, what can I get you to eat?"

In all the years we'd gone to school together, I'd not said over three full sentences to her. Her mouth gaped open as she stumbled to open her menu.

"I'll give you some more time, but please be ready when I come back. You're not the only table I have tonight," I said, turning away.

When I got back to the bar, my hands shook as I lifted the tray of beers for one of my regular tables.

"Whoa, let's set those down, why don't we?" Lou said, stopping me before I could walk away and spill all five mugs. His hand landed on my shoulder as he took the tray. "Take a breath. Your tables can wait."

I shook my shoulders out to loosen the tight knot behind my neck. Even though every seat at the bar was filled, Lou's attention stayed on me.

"Need to talk about it?" he asked.

"No—well, not right now." I wiped my hands on my apron, straightened my back, and lifted the tray once more.

This was my restaurant. No one could rattle me here.

Dinner service concluded later than usual but went by in a flash after the initial rush. Rhonda and the other ladies devoured their meals, giving only polite responses to my visits to their table after our heated exchange.

After they paid, but before heading out, Lydia cornered me near the restrooms.

She looked over her shoulder before whispering, "Ignore Rhonda. You know how she can be. And I'm so sorry to hear about you and Anthony. If you ever need a friend, I'm only a phone call away."

Shocked, I managed a tight "thank you" before she squeezed my hand.

"I'd better catch up with the girls. Hope things slow down for you tonight!"

I desperately did not want things to slow down. Not only because it kept my mind busy, but because we needed the revenue more than ever. But her kind words had soothed my loneliness a bit. Even if I never took her up on her offer, at least she'd tried, and that had to count for something, right?

I watched as Lydia bounced through the dining room, zig-zagging through the busy tables and out the front door where her friends waited for her. I wondered what it would be like to have a group of people outside my family who knew me well. Would my dreams and outlook on life be the same, or would I want what they wanted?

Looking around Bella, I imagined a different life, one that didn't include this restaurant, but one that I shaped, not the predestined path to motherhood and marriage I'd nearly escaped. It exhilarated me. It terrified me.

That night, after everyone had left and the only thing left to do was lock up, I collapsed in the back booth. My feet ached from being on them all night. When I cooked in the kitchen during a busy night, my entire body felt used, but it invigorated my mind. This was a different kind of exhaustion. One that seeped down to my bones and left my thoughts in a murky puddle somewhere under the table.

"I made you some tea," I heard a low voice say. I looked up to see Lou slide into the seat in front of me.

"Thanks," I said, wrapping my hands around the warm mug. "Aren't you tired? The bar was slammed tonight."

"Nah, I'm used to it by now. Old hat. A few years of bartending will do that to you."

"Do you have to go to the speakeasy tonight?" I couldn't imagine having to work another shift.

"Nope. I'm off tonight. Want me to walk you home? Everyone's gone now."

He didn't seem at all tired. He looked like he could stay up all night and be fine to be back here at six in the morning again.

"Sure, but in a minute. I need to sit."

Lou leaned back to rest on the high back of the booth, folding his hands on the table in front of him. A strand of hair fell across his forehead like an apostrophe. I sipped my tea.

"Want to tell me what happened tonight with those women? Do you know them?" he finally asked, brushing his hair back into place.

Warmth crawled up my chest to my face. I'd hoped he'd missed all of that and had chalked up my attitude to a busy and understaffed night. A sigh escaped through my nose.

"I went to school with them."

"Friends of yours, then?"

"Not exactly. No."

He waited for me to go on, but I didn't know where to start. After a minute, he changed tactics.

"Rosa, where's your ring? Did something happen between you and Anthony?"

About a month ago, I'd started to wear my engagement ring at the restaurant out of guilt. I should have realized people would notice when it disappeared.

"I'm surprised my father didn't tell you. We broke off our engagement," I said, like I was reading him the weather forecast.

"Your father and I don't talk about you. Just the restaurant."

For some reason, that stung.

As if he could tell, Lou added, "But I know he cares about you. We all do. Are you all right?"

"I'm fine, actually. I'm not sure I ever wanted to marry him in the first place."

Lou nodded as if he already knew this.

"Then what's been bothering you? You haven't been yourself lately."

Lou and I didn't confide in each other this way. We limited our conversations to work, food, and his school. Rarely did I ever discuss my personal life, but I needed to talk about this, and he was asking. Plus, the way his eyes crinkled around the corners melted any resolve I had left.

"I'm not sure what comes next."

"What do you mean?" He leaned forward.

"My mother is kicking me and Camille out. And I don't know what's going to happen to Bella," I motioned around. "Everything I thought my future would hold is uncertain now."

"Well, the future is always uncertain. But I'm sorry if this has anything to do with the night I brought Camille home."

"It does, but it's okay. I never thanked you for what you did." I lifted my chin to look him in the eye. "I don't know what would have happened if you hadn't stepped in. I'm grateful you were there."

"Any decent man would have," he said. "But you're welcome."

"Any decent man..." I echoed, looking away.

"I'm guessing things didn't end amicably between you and Anthony?"

I didn't know how to respond because the answer was somewhere in the middle. I still hadn't quite figured out how I felt about Ant's betrayal. Was I upset because he cheated on me, or because he lied and tainted our decades-long friendship?

"Let's just say our relationship became a bit too crowded for my taste."

"He cheated on you?" Lou's voice dropped to a low rumble.

I nodded but then waved my hand as if I were swatting it away. "It doesn't matter, though. We would have ended it one way or another. That's not what I've been worried about." "Camille?"

"Yes, Camille. She's been so reckless lately, and I'm concerned she's one decision away from something truly terrible." I felt the floodgates open as hot tears began streaming down my cheeks.

I choked back a sob, "And she's pregnant."

Why was I telling him this? I thought. *Camille would kill me.*

Lou reached across the table to wrap his hands around mine.

"Oh, Rosa. I'm so sorry. You have so much on your shoulders." Then he looked at me. Really looked at me like no one ever had.

"But a baby? A baby is always a good thing."

Then I realized that I'd been waiting to tell *him*. My loneliness was self-inflicted because he was the only person I'd wanted to share my secrets with. Somehow, I knew he wouldn't judge. That he'd say the right thing. And he did. I couldn't look away from his searching eyes, his perfectly imperfect face.

He squeezed my hands, which snapped me back to reality. I tried to stand but knocked my knee on the table and doubled over to check the instant bump forming. When I stood back upright, Lou positioned himself in front of me. He was so close I could feel the warmth radiating from his body. He smelled of aftershave and whiskey.

Lou took a half step forward, closing the small gap between us before gliding his hand up the back of my neck. My breath hitched in my throat as his gentle touch electrified my skin. My eyes locked onto his lips. I needed to know what he tasted like.

We stood centimeters apart for what seemed like forever before he rested his forehead on mine. My heartbeat only grew more rapid.

"Rosa," he whispered. "I want this to be okay."

"It is," I breathed into his ear.

And in an instant his mouth came crashing down on mine. My hands wrapped around the firm muscles of his back and his fingers wove into my hair. It wasn't gentle, but it felt exhilarating. Pure exhilarating desire.

Carnal passion ripped through me as our hips met. His body was warm but hard. Strong, yet welcoming. I ran my fingertips down the length of his back as he pushed me up against the wall. Everything below my waist throbbed. I wanted this.

For a few wonderful moments we tasted, held, and explored. Lou's muscles moved under his shirt as he pushed his body against mine, closing any remaining distance between us. I heard a low, sensual growl come from him as my fingers slipped below his belt. He untied my apron and let it slide down to the floor before his cool hand met the hot skin on my back, under my shirt.

Then, as abruptly as it started, it ended. Lou pushed back from the wall and scrambled to pick up my apron. I didn't move an inch, stunned at the sudden rush of cold air on my face.

"I'm so sorry," he stammered, looking anywhere but at me.

I grabbed his arm. He needed to know this was okay. I was okay. Because now I knew what had been missing all along.

Chapter 17

When I got home that night, Camille was still awake, waiting for me in our room. She wore a bright peach dress and makeup. For the first time in weeks, she looked like herself, not the pale, lifeless version that had been haunting the house of late.

"You look like you're ready to go dancing," I quipped, my mind still focused on how Lou tasted like tobacco and mint.

When she didn't respond, I whirled around to face her. "Tell me you're not going out." The look on her face made my stomach drop.

"Jackson called this afternoon. He's picking me up in ten minutes."

"You're kidding, right? The guy who left you stumbling drunk at a nightclub on the south side?" I lowered my voice. "The one who knocked you up? We can't be talking about the same person."

"What choice do I have? I need to make things right between us before I tell him about the baby. I don't want to be an unwed, single mother. What would Ma say?"

"I'm going to help you figure it out. You won't need him. What kind of father would he be, anyway? Look at everything he's done to you," I said as I motioned up and down to an imaginary list of grievances.

I wanted to ask if she'd thought through all her options, *really* thought about them, but it was useless. Although we zoned out most of church every Sunday, we'd been born bearing the weight of Catholic guilt. She was keeping the baby.

Earlier that night, after Lou had kissed me, he walked me back to the house. After a few awkward moments of silence, he told me to warn Camille about Jackson. At first, it startled me to hear his voice through the dark, inky night, even though we walked side by side. I blinked to concentrate on what he said, because my mind had been far away from Jackson. My mind had been on Lou's lips, his body, his strong back.

He confessed Jackson had connections to the mob and that he often gambled sizable sums of money from his rich daddy, who'd paid off more than one high-ranking officer in the Outfit. He'd also been a regular at the club Lou bartended and was often thrown out for starting fights or over-drinking.

"He thinks because he comes from money that he can do whatever he pleases. But the past always has a way of catching up, and I wouldn't want your sister be caught up in something dangerous."

The truth about Jackson rang loud in my ears. Damage had already been done, but I feared we hadn't seen the worst of it yet. I didn't know a whole lot about babies or being a mother, but I knew they didn't make life easier. From the sound of it, Jackson was used to *easy*. He'd never had to deal with a real consequence his whole life.

Camille sighed and sat on the edge of her twin bed. "I have to make this work. Ma would never forgive me, you know that. And Pa won't defend me, either. It's this or lose my family."

"I wish it were different. But no matter what happens, you'll never lose me. I'll always be your sister, through thick and thin."

If it came down to it, I'd give up everything for her and that baby. It would hurt, but I'd do it. More than anything, I wanted to save her from Jackson, but I knew had to be careful, or she'd run right into his arms.

"How was work tonight? You looked happy when you came in. I haven't seen a smile on your face in days," Camille asked, changing the subject. It was a tactic she'd mastered young.

I could feel my cheeks turn red, and I looked away. That loud face of mine betrayed me again.

"Tell me! I need to hear something good."

I hesitated, not sure if talking about it would break the spell and force me to look my reality in the face again. Before I could overthink, I spilled it all, and once I started, I couldn't stop. It felt so good to tell someone everything that I'd been suppressing for months.

"Camille, I'd never felt that before. With Ant, it was polite and nice, but nothing like this," I confessed. "It almost hurt when Lou pulled away. He caught me completely off-guard."

"I knew there was something between you two. The chemistry has been off the charts since the first day he stepped in the restaurant."

I thought back to all the lingering glances, the way my breath caught in my throat when his skin brushed against mine, or how he encouraged my cooking in subtle reassuring ways.

I'd be lying if I said I never thought about him or what it would be like to feel his body against mine, but I didn't allow myself to get swept along. Whenever my mind wandered there, I shut it off. Tucked it deep down, insisting it was my body's way of rebelling against my engagement to Ant. A completely normal reaction for someone who was about to commit their entire life to loving—and touching—only one other person.

But tonight opened my mind to the terrifying realization that I had almost robbed myself of the pleasure and pain I'd only read about in books or seen on the silver screen. Desire was a powerful drug, and one taste had me yearning for the next time I could touch Lou again.

Was this how Camille felt about Jackson? If so, it made more sense to me now.

"Now it's my turn to tell you to be careful," said Camille. "Lou's a nice guy and all, but he still works for Pa. And I'm not convinced he's not involved in other stuff."

My head jerked up. "What do you mean, 'other stuff'? What do you know?"

"Nothing. Only, I find it strange that Pa hired him the same day Sal took over Bella, that's all."

"He's done nothing but try to help us. He practically lives at the restaurant, looking for ways to increase our revenue."

Camille nodded. "Yes, you're right. I'm wary of all men right now. Don't listen to me. Have your moment. I'm happy for you. I'm happy you're happy."

Who could blame her for not trusting men? And honestly, I was glad to hear her question his motives if it meant she'd start doing it for herself, too. But Lou wasn't Jackson. Wherever the thing between us went, Lou was a decent man. It might have taken me a while to realize that, but was glad I'd been wrong about him at first.

"You don't have to tell Jackson, you know. Just because he's the father doesn't mean you need to be with him. We can do this together. It'll be hard, but I know we can do it."

I saw the doubt in her pursed lips.

"Either way, whatever you decide, I'll support you. Always."

After Camille snuck out for her date with Jackson, I curled up in my bed with the cookbook from Lou. Holding it this time felt different somehow, and the letter I'd found inside weeks ago piqued my curiosity once again. Lou never told me the name of his late mother, but I wondered if the recipient, Patrice, might be her. Either way, the two women had a closeness that reminded me of my relationship with Camille. Growing up, I never had strong friendships with other girls. Because of Camille and Ant, though, I didn't lack companionship.

Maybe that was part of why I couldn't open myself up to Ant, or anyone else. I'd learned to become a deeply independent person through my childhood, preferring the company of a few to that of many. Some might have said I was cold or off-putting. And they might not be wrong. Although Camille could not see it, I often felt as much an outsider as she, my hopes and dreams labeled obscure and even inappropriate for a woman.

Sometimes, I wondered if parts of our personalities got switched. Maybe Camille was the one who was supposed to fall in love with cooking and become obsessed with being a chef. She had the fire and determination that it called for, while my need for approval and distate for confrontation would suit a married woman well.

My mind ached from all the thinking I'd been doing. It never seemed to turn off.

So, for the first time since I'd met Lou, I let myself get lost in thoughts of him. I tried to relive the feeling of his hands in my hair and the way his mouth searched mine, as if kissing me felt like breathing for the very first time.

Confessing my innermost thoughts to him had unlocked a need to be seen—and I wanted *him* to see *me*.

I had the next day off, but I couldn't stay away. Even if my mind kept flashing back to the night before, I had a plan to put in motion. First, I'd need to convince Lou to help me, to talk to my father about my idea for a few updated menu items. Then, I'd have to impress Pa enough with the dishes that he'd invite Sal for dinner one evening so he could taste them in person, too.

If Sal could only see, *taste*, what we could make at Bella, maybe he'd cut us some slack or take our business more seriously. Beyond pulling my father out of this self-imposed debt, I yearned for validation. Plus, it couldn't hurt to have the Outfit on our side when operating a business in Chicago. We'd have to learn to go along to get along. For better, and hopefully not for worse.

Ivana called my name up the stairs. "Someone's on the phone for you!"

Camille had gotten home at a decent hour last night. For once, she didn't smell of alcohol, and that gave me a boost of confidence that she was taking things a little more seriously now.

As I dressed, she still lay in bed, asleep. Her peaceful face squeezed my heart. I hoped her night with Jackson went well, that he was kind to her.

In a rush, I buttoned my shirt up as I walked down the hall to the phone. I picked it up, cradling it between my ear and shoulder, doing up the last few buttons.

"I've got it, Vanie. Thanks," I said into the receiver. I waited to hear to click from the kitchen phone.

"Hey, Rosa."

"Hi," I said, more breathless than I intended.

"It's Lou."

"I know."

"Oh, okay. I wasn't sure. You all right?"

"I'm fine," I said, a small smile breaking free. I could feel my insides warm at the sound of his voice. "Are you okay?" I asked, hoping he didn't regret our kiss.

"I'm super. Calling to see if I can take you out for lunch since we both have the day off?"

My stomach jumped into my throat. Of course I wanted to go to lunch with him, but I didn't want to seem overeager.

I took a deep breath to get a hold of myself. Just two weeks ago, I was engaged to be married to someone else. The last thing I needed was for more rumors to fly about my love life, and for Ant to be vindicated in his premature suspicions about my relationship with Lou. Taking things slow, for several reasons, was the safe and logical thing to do. And for all I knew, the kiss was a fluke. Camille's warning also rang in my head. She'd caught on to the same trepidations I'd first had about Lou, too. That seemed a lifetime ago now, though. Now I knew more about the brooding, dark, and handsome man he was.

"Sure, lunch would be lovely. Can you meet me at Bella's, though? I'm heading there now to get some cooking done for a few new dishes I want to try," I responded.

"Of course you are. One of your only days off this week and you choose to spend half of it at work. Very admirable."

"It's called an obsession," I corrected.

"You're wrong. It's passion with a healthy dose of talent."

I laughed. "Does noon work?"

"I'll pick you up then."

After we hung up, I wondered if Lou had a car, or if we'd take the train. I'd only ever seen him arrive by train, but he said he'd pick me up as if he'd be driving.

When I arrived at the restaurant, the staff had already opened, and they were prepping the dining room for lunch service. The kitchen crew had become used to me sneaking in a few hours here and there to practice. One of the line cooks, Frankie, maybe seventeen at most, followed me around like a puppy. He wanted to know what I was cooking, how long things took to bake, why I used one spice over another, and so on. At first, the attention worried me. I didn't want to press my luck using the kitchen this way after Pa's instructions to practice at home. But I'd tried that. It didn't work. Ma hated her kitchen being overrun. My only option had been to sneak in early to Bella's to try things out.

After I tied my apron and gathered what I'd need to make seafood risotto, I looked around for the kid. No one said a word to me; most avoided eye contact altogether. If they didn't acknowledge me, they could claim ignorance if anyone asked what I was doing. They were all aware of their boss's stance on women working in the kitchen.

Not seeing him anywhere, I got to work. By nine, I already had multiple versions of risotto I wanted to try before Lou met me. Stirring the rice for twenty straight minutes gave me time to think. I missed showing the young cook how I did things; teaching came naturally to me, as it did to my father. His questions, sometimes obvious, often sparked curiosity in me and propelled me down rabbit holes I'd never considered in my cooking.

At some point he had asked if I'd ever used saffron as a spice in anything. I remember giving him an incredulous look. If you knew anything about saffron, it was that it was expensive and scarce. No, I had never cooked with it, I told him.

But that had made me *want* to cook with it. I couldn't stop thinking about it for days afterward. I'd never tasted saffron, which made me determined to find some. The books I'd been poring over in my off time had mentioned the use of it in several recipes, which I skipped because of the impossibility of finding it. Not to mention the price.

One morning, while going over that week's orders with Lou, I had scanned the pamphlet from one of our purveyors. It listed all their items and their prices. I scanned down to the bottom, "s" section for saffron. Lo-and-behold, they sold it.

"Do you have anything else you'd like to add to the order?" Lou asked, clocking my interest in the item sheet.

"No. Well…" I looked over my shoulder, uncomfortable asking for what I wanted. "…yes, but we can't afford it."

"I'll be the one to decide that," he said, cocking his chin down to look at me through hooded eyes. "What is it?"

"Saffron. It's a spice, but it's too much."

Lou looked over my shoulder at the list, where I pointed to the line item.

"I've heard of it. Elizabeth's bakery uses it every once in a while. Let me talk to her. I can't imagine she'd pay a price like that," he said.

The next morning, a small paper bag tied with string sat at my workstation in the kitchen. I took a quick peek inside. Saffron.

Lou popped his head out of the back office. "Put it to good use," he shouted before disappearing.

I knew what I'd do with it. For the next two hours, I'd abandoned my responsibilities to receive the daily deliveries, leaving it in the capable hands of Lou while I worked on our sumptuous lunch: ravioli filled with ricotta, lemon, and a pinch of saffron in a simple tomato sauce.

I remembered the threads had to be soaked in water before using them. A cookbook I'd read long ago had taught me as much. While making the fresh pasta dough, I let the saffron sit in a shallow bowl of water, hoping that a little would go a long way.

It paid off. The ravioli had been incredible.

Lou agreed. He hadn't said a word while eating lunch that day. It was all the confirmation I needed.

The rest of the small pouch went home with me that evening. No way I would have left it in the kitchen for the other cooks to use. They wouldn't know it from floss, anyway. Saffron was as good as gold, and I'd treat it as so. It didn't matter to me how Lou got it, only that he had. For me.

Lost in the memory over a pot of cooking rice, I startled when one of the line cooks dropped a full pan of dough.

"Gino, what the hell?" yelled the lead cook, who avoided me at all costs.

"Sorry, I rarely do the bread. Where's Frankie?"

"I dunno know who you're talkin' about."

"Sure, you do. You know the young guy who made the bread every morning? All doe-eyed and unsure of himself?"

"Nope, and neither do you. And I don't want to hear that name ever again. You understand?"

Gino stumbled to pick the heavy dough balls off the floor, eyes growing wide. No one said a word, keeping their heads down, focused on whatever they'd been doing. I took a quick look around, and then I understood.

I turned the burner off to save my risotto and pushed my way past the others to the office. I let the door close with a thud behind me.

"Where's Frankie?" I asked Lou, who sat at Pa's desk looking at the large leather-bound ledger.

I saw a muscle twitch near his jaw.

"They let him go. That's all I know."

"As a cost-cutting measure?" I asked, hoping that'd be the end.

"The order didn't come from me. From what I heard, it came from above, if you know what I mean." He lowered his voice as he spoke.

"Do you know if he's okay?"

Lou shrugged.

I sat down in the creaky seat across the desk from him. "I hope he didn't get into trouble for talking to me. He wanted to know how to be a better cook, is all."

"Ah, that might explain it then."

"Explain what?"

"I'm not going to lie to you, the new staff were told to keep their distance from the Bianchi sisters. Sounds like Frankie didn't listen."

"Neither did you," I snapped back.

Lou leaned forward onto his forearms, a devilish smile curling his lips. "You're right, I didn't. Do you want me to start now?"

It felt dangerous and electrifying at the same time. Something low in my body hummed to life, and I couldn't stand to look at him without melting into a puddle.

"Couldn't they make you?"

The spell broke, and he shifted back into the chair.

"I suppose. But we'll be careful. Plus, I think your father likes me, so that's gotta help."

"I don't think Pa is the one calling the shots around here," I said, standing to leave.

"No, you're right." He opened his mouth again before closing it into a tight line.

"Will you do me a favor and ask around about Frankie? I want to make sure he's all right. I wouldn't be able to live with myself if something terrible happened to him on my account."

Lou nodded, and I went back to my rice.

Just as things began to feel normal again, the kitchen, once my sanctuary, felt foreign again. I couldn't stop thinking about what more than friendship with Lou might cost. As far as I knew, he didn't work for Sal, he worked for Pa. In theory, it wouldn't be a problem. In theory.

All the more reason to convince Lou and Pa of my plan. I wanted my life back.

Gino and the rest of the crew scurried around the warm kitchen, struggling to get the food prepped for lunch service, but I paid them no mind. If they could ignore me, I sure as hell could do the same. No two-bit deep-fry slinger would intimidate me out of my kitchen.

For the next two hours I stirred, pan-fried, and plated two separate seafood risotto dishes, tasting each and tweaking the flavor of the creamy grains that held the right amount of bite until Lou popped his head out and gave me an almost imperceptible nod to meet him in the back outside.

I left the plates on the communal work bench. If these guys refused to talk to me, maybe they'd take a chance on my food.

The alleyway behind Bella's had always been a damp, dark mess of a place that communities of large rodents called home. I hated it back here. When we were little, Pa would make Camille and me take the trash out to the large, commercial-sized dumpster during the dinner rush when everyone else was too busy to be bothered. We'd count to three at the back door and run together with one hand pinching our noses as we hurled the bags over the side of the metal dumpster.

Lou stood near the same dumpster, not daring to lean against its grimy side. The small ray of sunlight that the end of the alley let in backlit him, but I could make out his teeth glowing in the darkness, which reminded me of the Cheshire Cat, making me giggle.

"What's so funny?" he asked, stepping out of the shadows.

"Nothing, you just looked like the Cheshire Cat there for a moment."

He laughed. "I promise I'm not trying to trick you. My intentions are noble." He paused and looked up. "Well, maybe not entirely."

My skin broke out in goosebumps even though the heavy, sticky air clung to me.

"Can we get out of this place?" I asked.

Lou strode up to me and laced his fingers through mine. "Follow me."

Chapter 18

"Can we take a quick detour to the library?" I asked, sitting next to Lou in his palatial Lincoln Continental. The car did not match the man.

Lou glanced over the wide bench-style seat we both sat on, cocking his head.

I held up the tote bag I'd been carrying. "I need to return a few books before they're overdue."

He nodded and turned the car down a back alley. "I know a shortcut."

The car puzzled me. Its front bench seat felt as large as my twin bed, and the steering wheel was enormous, with chrome spokes that gleamed in the sunlight. Every detail looked intentional, right down to the tight stitching on the upholstery.

I'd been in nice cars before, and Ant's was nothing to turn your nose up at. But this one felt brand-new. It even smelled different. A mix of leather and polish hung in the air.

As I ran my fingers over the armrest, I noticed buttons on a small panel. Automatic windows. I pushed one for the novelty of it, unable to conceal my delight as the window hummed and lowered.

"This is such a nice car," I said, looking out the open window.

"It's not mine. My uncle lets me borrow it while I'm in school," he explained. He'd never mentioned an uncle before.

"That's very kind of him. Does your uncle live close?" I hoped he did, since his father lived about an hour away and it didn't seem like they saw much of each other.

"He lives here in Chicago, but he's a busy man. I don't see much of him."

Before I could probe further, we pulled up in front of a small branch of the Chicago Public Library that sat nestled into a shopping mall.

"I'll be right back," I said, sliding out of the car, feeling conspicuous in this part of the city where most people drove old Chevy pickups.

Lou slid the gear into park and turned on the blinker. I could feel his eyes scanning my backside as I made my way up the sidewalk, and goosebumps rose on my skin at the thought. I slipped the books one by one into the small opening cut into the glass front door. They were open, so the lady at the front desk gave me a polite wave through the window and went back to helping the line of customers queued to check out books. This neighborhood branch seemed much more pleasant than the grandiose library I'd visited downtown last time.

Back inside the Lincoln, Lou waited, bopping his hand on the wheel to a song that played through the vehicle's smooth stereo system.

"So, what kind of books do you read?" he asked after I'd slid back into the car. He reached for the silver knob on the dashboard to lower the volume.

"Mostly cookbooks. Sometimes other things, but that's all I've had time for in a while."

"I should have guessed."

I thought of the cookbook he'd dropped off at my house weeks ago and its forgotten letter.

"In a way, you inspired me to check out the cooking section at the library."

"Oh, yeah? How's that?" A faint smile turned up the corners of his lips.

"After reading the book you left, I wanted more, so I thought I'd check out the library. And lo and behold, they have a whole cooking section!"

He laughed an easy, but amused chuckle.

"Glad I could be of service. How did you like the cookbook, anyway? My aunt gave it to my mother when she got married, but my dad and I don't cook, so it was collecting dust on my kitchen counter."

"Was your mother's name Patrice?" I blurted out before realizing it might be hard for him to hear her name out loud.

Lou shook his head. "No, Patrice is my aunt." He turned toward me for a second. "Why?"

"Does your aunt know Elizabeth? The one who owns the bakery?"

"I'm confused how you know that, but yes. They were neighbors and friends years ago here in Chicago, before my aunt moved to Riverbend."

"Such a small world," I whispered to myself. Patrice must be the aunt he mentioned at the market. I wondered if she still lived here or if he visited her often.

"It is indeed," Lou replied with a soft nod.

"So, are you stalking me?" he said in a low, serious voice before knocking his knee against mine.

"What?" I asked, my voice wobbling. "No, of course not! I found a letter that Elizabeth wrote to your aunt tucked into the back of the cookbook. It fell out when I opened the cover, and I couldn't help but read it and make some educated guesses. That's all."

"Oh," he said, looking surprised. "What did the letter say?"

"Not a lot. Elizabeth gave your aunt some encouraging words for an upcoming journey. It was sweet, actually. Reminded me of how I talk to Camille sometimes."

I don't know why I added last part. He didn't need to know how much I thought about the letter since finding it weeks ago. And while it reminded me of my relationship with my sister, it also highlighted the distance between me and my mother. Words like that would have never been exchanged between us.

"That must have been when she moved. I remember growing up, my dad would poke fun at her for living in the sticks when she called. Elizabeth and my aunt used to cook together, even though they were decades apart in age." Lou paused, taking in a deep breath that raised his chest. "My dad's mother died giving birth to him, so my aunt took on a parent role in his life but never learned to cook the Italian way. Elizabeth helped her learn."

Lou looked out his side window and took a slow turn onto a busier street toward downtown.

"You've had cooking in your blood all along, then," I said, looking at his side profile.

"I guess. But after my mom died, I didn't have a taste for anything. Certain foods reminded me of her, which hurt too much. She made the best Polish food this side of the Mississippi. Even my aunt's Italian cooking tasted bland and stale through my grief. It wasn't until I started bartending that I rediscovered my love for good food, although I still can't cook to save my life." He paused. "I bet that's why I like you so much."

My stomach did a flip that took my breath away.

"Why did your aunt move to Riverbend? Seems like a big change from the city."

Lou didn't answer right away, but his knuckles tightened around the steering wheel, turning white.

After a long moment, he said, "There was some drama with my uncle, her brother, so they left the city. She and her husband built a house on a piece of land they owned."

"She still lives there, then?" I let the question linger between us as his grip tightened even more. He knew my entire family and some of our worst secrets, so I felt my prying was only fair.

"Yes, but we're not in touch. We grew apart when I went to high school, after her husband passed away. My dad still talks to her every few months, though, and gives me updates. She has lung cancer."

"Oh, Lou. I'm so sorry." I felt the urge to grab his hand, but when I looked over, he sat stiff and upright in his seat, unblinking as if he'd told me the weather. My gaze cast down into my lap and I pressed my lips together. There was more to this story, and he'd tell me when he was ready.

Fortunately, the awkward silence only lasted a few seconds as we pulled into a small parking lot off Halsted Street.

"We're here," Lou stated, parking the car in one of the few open spots and turning off the engine in one smooth move. The shadow from a tall, old building cast the entire lot in an eerie darkness. A faded advertisement for an old brand of tobacco loomed large in front of us on the brick facade.

"Did you bring me to a tobacco shop for lunch?" I asked, throwing him a goofy grin over the top of the Lincoln as we both climbed out.

"No, no. You'll see. This way." Lou gestured for me to follow him around the building to a brown door with what looked like apartment numbers listed down the side trim piece.

Once inside, it took a moment for my eyes to adjust to the small, dim entryway. Lou flicked on the light switch before we climbed a flight of steep stairs.

"Is this some kind of secret restaurant? Like the speakeasy?" I asked with a nervous chuckle.

Lou turned, extending his arm to me. I reached forward, folding my hand into his, which felt giant and warm. His touch sent a jolt of white-hot yearning through me. If he were touching me, I'd follow him anywhere.

"Cucina Cuccia, I like to call it," he said, heading up the staircase into the darkness.

My brain stuttered. *Cuccia?* At first, I couldn't place where I'd heard that name before, but a few steps from the top, it hit me. Cuccia was Lou's last name. How could I have forgotten?

"I hope you don't mind that I brought you to my place," he said, stopping in front of a nondescript door at the top of the staircase.

Lou could sense my hesitation as I pulled back from the door. It wasn't that I didn't want to see where he lived. On the contrary, I had thought about it so many times. I'd imagined it to be a simple efficiency room, with a small bed in one corner, a hot plate and a bathroom. Uncomplicated and easy. Or sometimes I'd let my thoughts run wild and envisioned him living in a grand penthouse suite with a butler, a large kitchen that he never cooked in, and a view of Lake Michigan through a window that took up the entire wall of his living room. Mysterious and well-thought-out, like Lou.

A growing sense of unease bloomed in chest. Would the versions of Lou I'd conjured in my head evaporate once I saw this private part of his life?

"That's okay, but what about lunch?" I asked.

Lou's face brightened with a smile that lit up his eyes. "That's why I brought you here. I made my mother's stuffed cabbage rolls last night. I thought it would be better to eat them here, just the two of us."

His sincerity amused me. Lou had always insisted he couldn't cook. Once, he'd admitted to burning three grilled cheese sandwiches in a row before giving up and settling for canned soup instead.

"You made them last night? We didn't leave Bella until after eleven."

Lou looked down at his feet and rubbed the back of his neck.

"Yeah, well, I was inspired," he said before turning the key in the lock and opening his door.

The space was bright, even with the lights off, a marked contrast from the hallway. An ornate fireplace with wood trim and two short pillars flanking each side served as the centerpiece of the living room. A large bay window lit the space at the far end, making the honey oak trim glow. While the apartment was small, it felt warm and inviting. I found myself looking for the bedroom door down the small hallway to the left.

"Make yourself at home," Lou said, pulling my attention back to the living room. "I'm going to pop the pan of cabbage rolls in the oven to warm them up. Would you like anything to drink? Water, lemonade, or...?" He poked his head into the small refrigerator. "Yeah, sorry. That's all I have."

I suppressed a smile at his nervous energy.

"Water would be great. Thanks." I sat down on the armchair closest to the window, watching people walk by below. After a few minutes, I could hear the clanging around of someone unfamiliar with working in a kitchen. As I sat, looking down at the city, my previous excitement morphed into a constricting pressure behind my rib cage.

There were so many reasons it should have felt wrong to be here. For one, it was too soon to be seen with anyone after calling off an engagement. Two, if Ma ever found out I was alone with a man she didn't know, she'd accuse me of disgracing the family. And three, the things I felt around Lou scared me so much I questioned reality. It was all too much, too fast.

My fingertips dug into the worn upholstery of the chair. To steady myself, I focused on the soft feel of the velvet-striped pattern and the smell of pine, as if Lou had just mopped the floor. Which, maybe he had, because the hardwood glimmered in the sunlight.

Only a few minutes later, Lou returned with a tray of glasses filled with lemonade that he set on the antique table in front of us.

"It'll take about twenty minutes to heat," he said, wiping invisible crumbs from his trousers as he sat in the chair beside me.

"Thank you—," I started to say.

"I wanted to—," he said.

We both half-laughed.

"You go ahead," Lou said.

"Thank you for inviting me today."

"I know it's not a fancy lunch downtown, but I wanted to return the favor."

I shifted in my seat to face him. "Return the favor?"

"You've cooked for me dozens of times now; it only seemed right that I should cook for you. Or at least try to cook."

I stared at him, mesmerized by the faint lines that crinkled at the corners of his eyes when he grinned. His teeth looked slightly crooked on the bottom, but the top row gleamed straight and white, and I appreciated his face wasn't perfect, like Ant's. Lou's had personality, grit.

"Your cooking can't be beat. We both know that. But I found my mom's handwritten recipe for her family's cabbage rolls when I moved from Waukegan a few years ago. Back then, I stuffed it in a drawer along with takeout menus. Until last night. Watching you cook at the restaurant gave me the confidence to try it out. I'll admit, it was rough going at first. I think I reread her notes a dozen times before attempting, so it's anyone's guess how they turned out."

"I'm sure they'll be delicious," I assured him. "And if they're not, I clocked a sub sandwich shop next door."

"Taylor's Place, yeah, they know me well. Would probably give us a discount, too, since I keep their place open most weeks," he joked.

After that, we sat in silence. The awkwardness settled into a simple comfort as my body relaxed back into the soft chair while I sipped on the ice-cold lemonade, which had the distinct flavor of being mixed from concentrate.

"How's Camille?" Lou asked, breaking the trance after a while.

I filled him in on her dalliance with Jackson the previous evening, omitting my blatant disapproval though my voice dripped with it. He didn't say much, listening as I spoke and nodding along. At one point he reassured me that things had a way of working out in the end, if one could be patient enough. His calm demeanor contrasted against Ant's need to fix everything, and I appreciated the vote of confidence to navigate my life without interference from a man.

A few moments later, a loud ding came from the kitchen oven, and I followed Lou into the galley-style space to help set the small table pressed against its far wall. Without asking, I opened cabinets and drawers in search of utensils, plates, and napkins, finding them with relative ease, given there were only a handful of cupboards to search.

The mismatched plates and cutlery looked charming atop the white and gold speckled Formica top table with room for two. Lou sat the steaming baking dish on a hot pad in the middle of the table and tossed a quick salad in a large bowl. The smell of the cabbage, mixed with whatever meat filling and tomato sauce he'd poured over top, made my stomach grumble in anticipation.

Sitting down, I tried to recall the last time someone other than Ma or Pa cooked a meal for me. Nothing came to mind. Cooking had always been something I did for other people. My way of showing love and appreciation. But for a man to put so much thought into attempting something I loved while also sharing a part of themselves, I appreciated the effort tenfold. It didn't matter how it tasted.

We tucked into the meal, savoring each bite. The edges tasted slightly bitter from overbrowning, but the inside of the rolls filled my mouth with the savory, comforting flavor of a hearty meal.

"So…?" Lou asked. He hadn't touched his plate.

Mouth still full, I mumbled, "It's great. Thank you." I wasn't chewing like a lady, but I couldn't help it; the day had left me ravenous.

"You can be honest...," he said. "They're not as good as my mother's, but I wanted you to taste Polish food, the way my family made it."

His earnest, puppy-dog face slowed me down, and I swallowed so I could talk to him without my voice breaking.

"It's delicious, honestly." I reached across the table to touch his hand. "I'm very impressed, *Mr. Cuccia*," I said with a wink. "Not a lot of people cook for me."

"That's a shame. Your passion for cooking is inspiring, and you deserve to have someone take care of you for a change. It's a shame no one has yet."

"Until now," I added.

A light blush of pink spread across his cheeks.

"Until now," Lou echoed.

After my stomach settled into a satisfied fullness, I slowed down enough to hold a proper conversation. I needed to use this time to convince Lou to help me execute my plan to save Cucina Bella.

Wiping the corners of my mouth with the light blue napkin I'd found in a drawer earlier, I took a deep breath.

"I have an idea I need your help with," I started.

Lou's eyebrows raised a hair.

"I've been experimenting with different Italian dishes, perfecting them."

"Yes, I know. I've been watching you. They're great."

"Well, I want to add a few new items to the menu." Lou opened his mouth to talk, but I raised my palm to indicate that I knew he didn't make the menu decisions, but that I needed him to hear me out.

"I'm thinking higher-end additions to the weekend dinner menu. Things like ossobuco, seafood risotto, and a few others.

I think they might draw in a wealthier crowd, with the more expensive dishes helping to chip away at the higher monthly payments. We could take pictures of the dishes and write to the *Tribune* or *Sun Times* since they have covered us before. And we could also try to bring back events. We haven't held a wedding reception or retirement party since the spring. They bring in a lot of cash." I was rambling and sounded out of breath, but I couldn't help it. This felt like the last Hail Mary we had left.

Lou leaned back in his metal chair, and the plastic cushion squeaked. "That simple, huh?" he said, a grin pulling at the corners of his mouth.

Chapter 19

The food in front of us went cold as we discussed how to elevate the menu. We also decided Cucina Bella would start hosting events again. No one told us we couldn't in the first place. We'd assumed by the staffing changes and the general lockdown on the restaurant after Pa's indiscretions that events were off limits.

We drew up sample menus on the backs of envelopes, estimated the wholesale costs, and calculated new, higher prices for certain dishes.

Sitting hunched over Lou's small kitchen table, the afternoon flew by with little notice. Soon, shadows from early evening crept up the walls.

Exhausted but satisfied with our detailed plan we'd take to Pa the next day, we celebrated with a bottle of wine Lou had been saving for a special occasion.

"It's late enough in the afternoon," I said, as he popped the cork out and poured two healthy glasses. "Plus, we deserve it for working on our afternoon off."

He joined me back at the table, and we clinked glasses. It felt good to have a partner, someone who shared my desire to save the Bella and get things back to normal.

After gulping down a few liberal sips of the wine, I asked him how he got the job working for my father.

Lou swirled the dark purple liquid in his glass and looked up at the ceiling before answering.

"You're not going to like the answer," he finally said.

I steeled myself for something awful. Maybe my initial suspicions and Camille's hesitations were right; maybe he worked for Sal after all.

"I met Marco at a pool hall one night." He looked me in the eye. "They were broadcasting a horse race. Your father had won a sizable amount the previous week and was betting it all on one horse. He was a bundle of nerves, so we chatted about our lives to pass the time until the race started. That's when he told me about the restaurant and his challenges. I offered to help," he explained.

"Why would you do that? You didn't even know him."

"He seemed like a good man down on his luck. And I wanted to do more than sling drinks. I thought we could help each other."

Before I could respond, Lou took my hand in his. "But I'd be lying if I said it hasn't become more to me. I care about your family, and I want to help protect what you've built. And I care about you. More than I wisely should. I hadn't counted on meeting anyone quite like you and it ..." his eyes met mine, "...complicates things."

I was aware of the complications on my side, but I wondered what he meant. How did this complicate things for Lou?

Reading my mind, he elaborated. "We should be careful until your family has control of Bella again. I don't want us to get caught in the crossfire. From what I've seen, the organization can be ruthless when it benefits them. I wouldn't blame you if you kept your distance. God knows, I've tried to keep mine, but it's your decision."

I squeezed his hand, searching his face. Earlier that day, I would have said my feelings for Lou were a response to my breakup from Ant, that it didn't, couldn't mean anything more than a welcome distraction. But now, I doubted that.

"The restaurant will always be my priority, but you've changed things for me, Lou." I didn't know how to put into words the swirl of highs and lows exploding inside of me. Every cell in my body reached for him, wanting to feel him again.

"That's what I'm worried about," he said, shaking his head. "I should take you home." He rose to his feet, face set in stone.

My stomach fell. Was he worried that my feelings for him were different, stronger than what he felt for me? I was a fool. Of course, this couldn't work. It was only a fun flirtation, nothing more. Lou was a nice guy. End of story.

Snapping to attention, I also stood, looking around for my things.

"Okay. Let me grab my handbag." Frazzled, I pushed past him into the living room where I'd left my purse. The streetlights below had turned on, and the sky blazed with the orange of a late August sunset.

Looping the strap of my bag over my shoulder, I took one last look at the brilliant sky and turned toward the door and ran straight into Lou.

"What are you doing?" he said, words running together, eyes narrowed.

"You're right. This is silly. I shouldn't have come here. I shouldn't have allowed myself to get caught up in..."

"Us." He finished and took another step toward me, closing the gap between us.

I could feel the heat coming off his body as my gaze fell to his mouth. I wanted to taste him again, but I couldn't. This was stupid of me. I was acting like a love-crazed teenager. The same thing I'd admonished Camille for.

"Rosa, I've tried to stay away. I pushed you away on purpose. I'm sorry. But the thing is, I can't stop thinking about you. There's not a day that goes by that I don't yearn to be near you. And it's not fair, or at least it wasn't when you were engaged, but now you're not, so it's your decision, not mine."

I looked away. The push and pull of him left me dizzy.

"Do you want this?"

I shook my head yes. Before I could even look back, he'd wrapped his arm around my waist and pulled me against his body, our mouths finding each other with the hunger of a spark dying to erupt.

His hands wound through my hair, pulling it out my French twist, my waves tumbling down my back. He tasted like the wine: dark, spicy, and complex. My entire body came to life, each touch a flame igniting.

His lips trailed down my neck to the space between my shoulder and back, sending a thrill straight to my core. In slow circles his fingertips traced circles on my sides, where he'd wrapped his arms.

What started fast and breathless, grew into a slow, smoldering embrace that deepened with every touch, every exploration of our mouths.

My hands found the top edge of his pants, and I drug my fingers along the seam and then up his spine, feeling his bare skin warm mine.

A deep moan escaped him as I made my way to his hips, pulling them closer against mine, so I could feel all of him pressed against me. On instinct, I pushed my body into him, wanting to close every possible space between us. He smelled like spice and cooked tomato sauce, in the best way.

Lou lifted me as if I weighed nothing more than a scrap of paper and guided us to the armchair. He sat without taking his eyes off mine as I straddled him, bunching the skirt of my dress around my thighs. All these clothes, layers upon layers between us, and I wanted nothing more than to feel his bare skin against mine. I sat back on his thighs, memorizing his face glowing in the last rays of the sun. His eyes still lingered on mine, like the pull was too strong to look away. His pure desire was plain for me to see. No hiding or pushing me away now.

Sitting back on his hips, I reached for the strap of my dress and pushed it off my shoulder, down my arm. Lou didn't move. He watched as I slid the other down. After, he reached behind me, pulling himself up to my chest, and unzipped the back of my dress down to my waist. When he sat back, the top of my dress fell between us, and his eyes went wide. I hadn't worn a bra that day because of the hot, sticky weather.

Lou cupped one of my breasts and took my taut nipple between his wet lips, trailing his tongue over it. My head tilted back in pleasure.

The scrape of his rough skin teased up my side and around my back, wrapping me in his embrace. In one swift motion he pulled me closer, and I felt him strain against my underwear, only the fabric of his pants and my undergarments between us.

My hips moved back and forth as he guided me. When he looked back up at me, I couldn't miss how his pupils took over his once green eyes.

"Do you want to go to your bed?" I asked without thinking.

A low sound escaped from deep within him, and he looked away.

"More than anything." It came out more like a growl. "But we shouldn't." He turned his head back to me.

"I think you're done deciding what we should and shouldn't do," I said, teasing him, but meaning it all the same.

In a flash he'd gripped my body to his and we were making our way down the hall with my legs still wrapped around his middle.

The sky had turned inky black by the time Lou drove me back home that night, but I felt lighter than I had in years. I couldn't help but wonder if Lou felt the same, and judging by the lazy smile plastered on his face since we'd left his bedroom, I imagined he did.

Although we stopped short of doing anything I might regret later, what we did left me breathless and wanting more. With Lou, it all clicked into place. My body moved in rhythm with his until we forced ourselves to relax, slow down. Even lying together, arms twisted around our hot, sweaty bodies, felt more real than anything else.

When we pulled up to the house, dark except for a few bedroom lights, Lou leaned over and kissed me goodnight.

"Thank you for such an unexpected day. I wish it didn't have to end," he exhaled, pulling back to rest his face against mine.

For a split second, I worried it had all been too fast. Our rush toward each other, this head-on collision that had turned my world upside down. Then I leaned my shoulder into his and remembered I was in control this time.

"I should go."

"You should."

"Okay." Sliding from his warm body toward the handle, Lou grabbed my hand that lingered behind and lifted it to his mouth, placing one last lingering kiss on the inside of my palm.

"See you tomorrow?" he asked, lips brushing against my hand.

"Tomorrow."

When the front door creaked open, I imagined Ma on the other side, ready to pounce. But then I stepped inside, remembering how she wanted us gone, which dissolved my need to please her. Control felt good.

Lou and I fell into an easy routine the rest of that week. He waited for me each morning at the corner, and we walked to Bella's like we'd done a dozen times before. We didn't dare hold hands, in fear of the gossip mill that seemed to be spewing rumors left and right. The latest rumor was that I'd fallen pregnant with another man's baby. If Lou hadn't been there to distract me, I was positive I'd have gone mad with all the unfair accusations, but they did little to penetrate the protective bubble of happiness that had cocooned around me.

I should have known Ma would feel it all, though.

She had started to work short shifts at Bella again to keep overhead low. I avoided her at the restaurant, keeping to the back of the dining room and kitchen, but I knew she'd confront me sooner or later.

One evening while filling up water glasses for a table of eight, she cornered me. I'd just returned from the walk-in fridge, where Lou and I had started to meet in private. We'd become experts at navigating the always-busy restaurant, finding the in-between spaces.

"For someone who broke off their engagement only a few weeks ago, you look like nothing happened. Happy, even," she quipped over my shoulder. If she had been any other type of mother, I wouldn't have been offended. But from her, it could only mean disapproval of my behavior.

"I'm happy I won't be stuck in a loveless marriage, if that's what you mean," I shot back. Her eyes went wide at my backtalk.

"You should be ashamed. Mrs. Russo says Ant is miserable. Do you have no decency?"

I felt trapped. What did she expect me to? Hide myself away in shame?

"Well, it wasn't very decent of him to cheat on me. I'd say we're even. Now, if you'll excuse me, I have tables." I tried to push past Ma, but she shot an arm out to block my escape.

"I don't know what's gotten into you, Rosa, but I'm warning you, do not bring any more shame on this family," she hissed.

The layered emotions inside me tumbled, straining to break free. Before she could see the tears well up, I turned my back to lift the large tray of water glasses and walked toward her. She could either get out of my way or cause a commotion.

She stepped aside at the very last second, allowing me to pass.

Later that night, after a non-stop rush of customers, Camille tracked me down in the women's restroom.

"Rosa, it's me," she said through the thin wood. "Let me in."

I stood from the small chair in the corner and unlocked the door.

"Were you looking for me?" I asked.

"No, but Lou asked if I'd seen you." She tilted her head sideways.

"What did he want?"

"I think you know what he wanted." Camille suppressed a smile, her lips crinkling together in a line.

I told her about the earlier confrontation with Ma, and she rubbed my back.

"Is that why you're hiding?"

"I needed a minute to myself. Everything has been happening so fast. I can't keep my head on straight. Between the situation with the restaurant, Ant, Lou, and the thought of having to move, I might as well be a puddle on the floor," I confessed. Rarely did I let myself feel pity, and it was even rarer for me to tell Camille about my anxieties. She had enough to worry about. But as happy as I felt around Lou, the rest of my life had tangled into a giant web of problems.

And the one thing keeping me sane, the one person holding me together, had to be kept a secret. *For now*, I told myself. *For now.*

"Tell me."

Confused, I knitted my brows together, tilting my chin up.

"Lou, silly. Tell me about Lou."

And I did. I told her about how he swept the stray hair off my face before kissing me. How his rough hands grounded me. How the low tenor of his voice somehow calmed my nerves, even in a crowded room.

"Love looks good on you," Camille said before we left the restroom to join the cleanup crew.

Chapter 20

"Oh! A two-bedroom, two-bath! Circle that one, too," Camille exclaimed over my shoulder.

We sat at the very back booth of the restaurant before lunch service, poring over the "for rent" section of the newspaper, looking for places to check out later that afternoon. We needed a plan fast. Our eviction date was barreling toward us, and Camille had worn loose-fitting dresses she found at the Salvation Army to cover up her growing belly.

I circled the ad, but knew we'd never be able to afford an apartment like that. We'd be lucky enough to get a one-bedroom that wasn't an efficiency at this point. Everything seemed light-years out of our measly budget of ninety dollars a month, even if we pooled our earnings.

The few places we'd gone to see over the weekend had been dreadful. All three of them backed onto the highway, only had one or two windows in the entire unit, and the last one smelled like decomposing flesh.

But all hope wasn't lost yet. Lou had informed me that Pa was on board with the changes we wanted to propose to the menu and was even bringing back a few smaller events to offset costs. It turned out that Sal, in fact, had brought up hosting his niece's sweet sixteen birthday dinner at the restaurant a few days ago. Lou and I decided it would be the perfect time to debut some of the new high-end menu items to get Sal's support, but I needed to perfect them first. Pa insisted on a taste test before the big night.

Camille slid out of the booth to stretch her back.

"Everything all right?" I asked, watching her knead her knuckles into her hip joints.

"We're fine. Just gets hard to sit for long periods of time. Or stand, for that matter." She flashed me a half-hearted smile.

"When do you go to the clinic?" I asked for the hundredth time since finding out about the pregnancy.

Camille winced. "I have an appointment tomorrow, but I'm hoping Jackson will come with me."

My eyebrows rose. As far as I knew, she hadn't worked up the courage to tell Jackson anything yet. I hoped she wouldn't, and that we could go on dealing with this ourselves.

"He's picking me up after work tonight, and I'm going to tell him. He deserves to know, Rosa. Plus, he's called me every night this week to talk. I think he wants our relationship to work. He's trying, at least." Camille wiped her hands down the front of the faded blue and white striped frock that made her seem more like a chambermaid than a waitress.

Although the baby sucked all her energy, Camille never looked more beautiful with her full, glowing face and thick, luscious locks. I could imagine why Jackson was so keen on seeing her. Despite the growing belly she hid well, she looked like a fresh-faced model.

"Maybe if it all works out, we won't have to get an apartment after all."

I looked up at her, confused.

"If Jackson asks me to marry him after he finds out about..." she lowered her voice so no one could overhear, "...you know. Then, we can both move in with him."

My lips parted, but no words came out.

Camille raised her palms in front of her face. "I know, I know. It would only be until you figure out what you want to do next. Temporary."

To steady myself, I drew in a long breath and placed both hands on the table, pushing myself to standing so Camille would pay attention.

"Camille, I don't want to hurt your feelings, but please, *please* don't get your hopes up. That man has let you down more times than I can count. What makes you think he's going to do the honorable thing here? Besides, I can't imagine he is the man you'd want to spend the rest of your life trying to please. I'm begging you not to fall for that. Your life and your happiness are worth too much for that."

"That's rich coming from the woman who was too scared to call off her own engagement to the wrong man. If you hadn't caught Ant cheating on you, you'd still be walking down that aisle, and you know it."

She took a step closer, and I could feel her breath on my face.

"You act like you're so strong and independent, but you were ready to give up your entire world to not disappoint mommy and daddy. It's all an act. So don't you dare tell me how to live my life and decide for my future family."

Her words stung. Not because they were false, but because deep down, they explained everything there was to know about me. My worst fear, my harshest reality laid bare at my feet.

I stepped around her, heading nowhere in particular but needing distance. "I hope you get what you want, Camille. Until then, we still need to look at apartments. Meet me out front in twenty minutes," I called over my shoulder without looking back.

The reality of the situation with Camille and my life had sunk to the pit of my stomach.

Although flashes of anger flared in response to Camille's hurtful words, I also knew she said them out of fear. I was scared, too. Both of us had big decisions to make, changes that would shape the rest of our lives.

For me, it was more than just moving out of my parent's house. It meant taking a stand on what I wanted for my future and defying the expectations that had controlled my life since birth. The more I thought about cooking, pursuing it as a career, the more confused I became. For so long, I'd pictured myself taking over Cucina Bella one day, running it like Pa had and maybe even growing it into something more. But now, the thought of staying here in my tiny neighborhood until I died seemed suffocating. One step at a time. That's all I could handle, which meant looking at more apartments with Camille on our only afternoon off together.

We met the realtor, a friend of Lou's who'd agreed to help us for free, outside an apartment complex across town that took two bus changes and a brief ride on the L train to reach.

"I don't know about this," Camille whined as we stood huddled under an umbrella to keep out of the drizzling rain.

"It's far, but it's within our budget," I countered. "And it looks more modern than anything else we've seen, so that could be good?"   Camille narrowed her eyes at me.

"Let's just keep an open mind. We have two others to see today as well," I told her.

The first place we toured had everything we wanted, but Camille was right. It was too far from the restaurant. It would take an hour to get there and back, which was out of the question, especially for Camille with a baby. The next place only had one shared bathroom on the entire floor of the small apartment building, to be used by ten people. Automatic no.

Then, as we began to lose all hope, the realtor brought us to a small house about fifteen minutes from our neighborhood. From the outside, it looked like all the other row houses around it. Squat brick with no identifiable differences on the outside. But he informed us that the owner had lived there for decades and turned the upstairs into an apartment, complete with a small kitchenette, one bathroom, and two "cozy" bedrooms.

Upon seeing the space, we learned "cozy" was code for small. Tiny, but we both fell in love. I could picture making breakfast on the hot plate, not ideal but workable for the three of us. The small living space had enough room for a loveseat and chair, and we could eat dinner on our laps around the coffee table. Most importantly, we'd each have our own rooms. Camille would get the larger of the two, so she could fit a small crib up against one wall.

"We'll take it," I exclaimed to the realtor before we even made it back down the stairs to the front door.

"Let's talk outside," he said, not bothering to turn around to look at me.

It turned out we weren't the only ones interested in renting the apartment. The landlady was reviewing another application, but she had been picky, turning down three people who'd already applied.

"You'll have to wait and see what happens with it. And I'm not sure she'll like the idea of an unwed mother living under her roof," he said, gesturing to Camille's stomach. We hadn't told him that Camille was expecting, but he'd figured it out by our space planning.

"But you never know. People can surprise you. It's worth inquiring about." The sympathetic look on his face made the hope I'd felt moments earlier evaporate.

Still, we filled out the paperwork to be safe and made our way back to the restaurant for our dinner shifts.

Lou ended up walking me home, as he did most nights we worked together now. Pa had noticed, but had said nothing to either of us, just watched, head tilted, as we found reasons to talk to each other throughout our shifts.

On the way back, I filled him in on the apartment search, lamenting about finding the perfect place only for it to be taken already. Not to mention the unwed mother part of it all.

He squeezed my hand and told me it would all work out. I wished that I could have believed him. For all his earlier grumpiness when we first met, Lou had turned out to be one of the most optimistic people I'd ever met. If only some of that could rub off, I'd have been grateful.

Camille had come home earlier than usual that night. I'd expected her to be out with Jackson past a respectable hour, like usual. But around midnight, I heard the jangle of the bedroom door and for a moment thought it was Ivanna who sometimes had nightmares, only to see Camille's bright head of hair poke through. Maybe pregnancy had given her some perspective and calmed down the inner party girl she often indulged in.

"You're still up," she said flatly.

"Getting ready to turn in for the night. How was everything?" Curiosity crawled up my spine, resting like an unruly monkey.

Camille unbuttoned the back of her dress and kicked off her high-heeled shoes before plopping down on the twin bed across from me.

"Fine, I guess. He didn't say much after I told him. Only asked if I was keeping it and then offered to drive me back, since I 'must be tired'." She used air quotes. "So, I don't know what he's thinking. Maybe just needs time to process the information. I know I did."

"Where did he take you?"

"A small tavern by the lake. We ate a late dinner, and he was nothing but a gentleman."

I could tell Camille wished the conversation had landed better. She had had a version in her mind that ended in a proposal and a sweeping declaration of love from Jackson. But I, for one, was surprised to find that he hadn't acted like a complete heel, which was the very least he could do for her at this point.

Flopping backward on the bed, Camille let her arms go wide as she stared at the ceiling. "Distract me, please. Tell me something about your love life. It has to be better than mine. Anything is better than this." She waved her hand over her abdomen with the dramatic flair of a stage actress.

Instead of talking about Lou, I brought her up to speed on the new menu items, the sweet sixteen party we were planning for Friday, and my hope that it would be enough to pay Sal back in a few more months.

"Then everything will be normal again."

"Normal," she said before falling asleep.

Chapter 21

"Twirl!" I shouted at Ivana as she stepped off the last stair to show us all her communion dress.

Her hair swooped back in a low ponytail, but it had been curled by Camille earlier that morning and reminded me of whipped cream in soft peaks. She smiled wide, but I could tell the nerves were creeping in by the way she kept chewing on the inside of her cheek, the Bianchi tell.

"You look beautiful, Vanie," Pa said. "Grab your shawl and let's get going. We don't want to be late for your big day."

The dress we got Ivana fit her perfectly after the alterations. She looked like a girl straddling the line between adolescence and womanhood, unsure of which way to lean. The blue flowers around the neckline highlighted her youth, but the way it cinched in the middle hinted at something more grown.

"Hold on, Pa." Camille started up the stairs. "I need to grab my pocketbook."

Ma rounded the corner into the front hall, shooting a sharp look at my father. He hung his head before looking at me, then at Camille on the staircase.

"Girls, can I have a quick word in the kitchen?" he asked.

I narrowed my eyes. "Sure."

Out of the earshot of my two youngest sisters, Pa huddled us near the stove.

"I'm sorry, girls, but your mother doesn't think it's wise for you to join us today at the communion ceremony. We'll meet you at Bella afterwards," he explained, not daring to look either of us in the face.

"What?" I asked, still not believing she could prevent us from going.

"Your mother wants the attention to be on Ivana today without distractions. Please don't fight her on this. I want a nice day. For your sister and everyone else."

"How could you, Pa? How are you all right with the fact that she's ashamed of her own daughters for doing nothing but living?" Camille spat at him. "Will you ever stand up for us?"

He looked at his rough hands curled inward from the arthritis he'd never admit to having.

"Let's try to get along. Neither of you has bothered to come to mass for over a month, anyway."

"Of course. Why would you stand up for your daughters?" Camille brushed against my shoulder in a huff.

"I'm sorry, Rosa," he said, looking past me.

In that moment, I realized he'd never change. Looking at this broken man, I wondered if this is what it meant to grow up. Did the illusion end for everyone? Did all parents lose their magic eventually?

I followed Camille outside, and we sat on the concrete steps together, looking at the large maple tree that had grown so large its branches hung over almost half of the small backyard. We listened for the clunk of the front door before either of us spoke.

"What's going to happen when she finds out?" Camille asked into the wind. "I can't keep it hidden for much longer."

"We'll be out of the house by then, so it won't much matter what she thinks," I replied, more confident than I felt. I knew she'd make it hard on us. At the very least, she'd cut us off altogether. I only hoped Pa would continue to let us work at Bella. She couldn't take that from us. From me.

I laced Camille's fingers through mine. "We're in this together."

After our little pity party on the back steps, we dusted off our dresses and marched, heads high, to the church. We wouldn't let her pride separate us from our family. However, to be safe, we entered late, sliding into the rear pew.

While no one noticed us tiptoe in, a few gazes lingered as we filed out like normal. The priest shook our hands as we made it past the vestibule out into the blazing sun.

Once out in the open air, we felt exposed, scanning the walkway for the easiest exit to avoid our family while snaking through everyone else.

As we made it to the small sidewalk flanking the church and wound around back, I glanced once more behind us, feeling a set of eyes between my shoulder blades. Ant stood twenty feet away near his family, who'd joined another in conversation. I slowed and returned his stare, softening my face at the sadness I could see even from this distance. Then, in a flash, it was gone. He nodded once and turned his back on me.

That's how it would be between us now. Our past friendship only a memory. We'd ruined it. That realization should have gutted me, but I felt nothing other than relief. Relief that we didn't have to pretend everything was fine between us. I didn't think I could stand trying to make everything feel normal again. And our silent refusal of one another said all it needed to.

Camille caught my wrist. "Let's go."

Neither of us could stomach lunch at the restaurant with the rest of them. Instead, I hugged Camille and told her I was going to find Lou. She needed rest anyway.

I knew he wasn't working this weekend because he had told me about an important upcoming mid-term exam he'd been studying for, which would determine if he'd graduate early or not.

He answered his door on the second knock.

"Well, aren't you the perfect distraction from reading about cost-volume-profit analysis?" he joked, the left side of his mouth curling upwards.

"I have no idea what you said, but I'm here to deliver lunch," I responded, holding up a paper sack of sub sandwiches from the shop below.

"If Steve looked like you, I'd order his sandwiches every day."

Lou pulled me in for a lingering kiss, and I could smell the coffee he'd been drinking on his breath.

"Sorry to barge in on you while you're studying. Hope it's okay that I came."

He played with the hair at the nape of my neck, leaving a small trail of kisses along the top of my shoulder, which was almost bare from the spaghetti-strapped dress I'd been wearing.

"I can't blame you for not being able to stay away."

I batted his arm with the bag. "Let's eat."

"If we have to," he grumbled into my neck, slumping forward.

In the kitchen, I tidied the small table to make room. As I stacked his papers and books into a neat pile, I noticed a large, unopened manila envelope with a return address from Riverbend, Illinois.

"You have an unopened letter here," I said, pressing my finger into the thick piece of mail.

"Oh, it's from my aunt, but haven't gotten around to opening it yet. She sometimes saves newspaper clippings about baseball games and mails them to me."

"Baseball?" I asked, tilting my head. Lou didn't seem like an All-American sports-type.

"Used to play a long time ago," he said. "Before I broke my ankle in high school. Wasn't any good, anyway." He waved off my pitying look before we could dwell on his lost future as a White Sox player.

"You're still a mystery to me."

"There's not much more to me than what you see," he retorted, biting into the crusty bread of the Italian sub I'd ordered for him.

"For some reason, I doubt that very much, Mr. Cuccia."

Lou tried in earnest to get me to stay longer after we finished lunch, but I knew it was best to get back home. Though I almost caved when he trailed his fingers up my spine whispering, "I want to see you in my bed again." My knees wobbled a bit before I remembered Camille was waiting for me.

I needed to be there when Ma and Pa returned to give Camille a buffer. She had looked exhausted earlier, and dealing with Ma's snide remarks alone could crumble anyone, let alone someone harboring a secret that would be the very downfall of our family name in my mother's eyes.

Despite Camille, I didn't want to leave. I wanted to explore these feelings for him, these feelings that were veering towards dangerous territory. I liked him. A lot. More than just with my body. Over the past weeks, we'd grown close, both physically and otherwise. I found myself wanting to tell him all my secrets, the ones he couldn't read on my face. And I wanted to know his, too.

But I could still feel him holding back, even after our evening at his apartment weeks ago. Every time I got close to touching something real with Lou, I felt him retreat. A thin coating of doubt clouded my judgment.

Pancetta. Veal flanks. Vegetables. Stock. Risotto. Lobster. Parmigiano Reggiano. Wine.

I looked at the ingredients stacked on my workstation that Lou had helped me buy for that afternoon's tasting with my father. He'd talked to all our purveyors and taken a few trips to the open-air market to ensure we could stock everything we needed if we were to add the new menu items as regular offerings each weekend, haggling down an agreed-upon price.

"You have your work cut out for you," Lou teased, standing so close to my back that I could feel his warm breath on my neck. "Need any help?" He ran his fingertips around my hip.

I jabbed him with an elbow. It was already nine in the morning, and the kitchen staff had filed in. We didn't need to make it any more obvious.

"I know I make cooking look easy," I said. "But I need you to leave so I can concentrate."

"Oh, you have a hard time focusing around me, do you?"

I spun on my heels and pointed to the kitchen door. "Out."

His hands shot up in the air, and he backed away, keeping me in his sights.

I had three hours until all the dishes needed to be ready for Pa's tasting. Although I knew he'd give his approval, I still wanted to impress him. He'd been my teacher my entire life, and I owed my passion and talent to him alone. Of course, I still hadn't gotten over his blatant betrayal the morning of Ivana's communion, but I could separate that man from the person he was in the kitchen.

Setting to work, I tuned the radio to the classical music station, which made the other staff groan, but I ignored them. I worked best with minimal distractions, and the fluid melody that classical music offered helped me stay in a rhythm. They'd get over it.

Lou brought me tall glasses of water every few minutes, and I gulped them down. Between my cooking and all the morning prep, the temperature in the kitchen had reached a fever pitch by ten o'clock.

"Rosa thinks she's cookin' an eight-course meal for President Kennedy!" one man shouted as I stirred the stock into the risotto while checking on the veal shanks.

Ignoring him, I sped up my work. There needed to be time to taste-test everything myself and adjust, if needed, before Pa. One of the hallmark lessons he'd taught me himself.

A skilled chef never sends out a dish they haven't tasted themselves.

I did, however, find it funny that every single cook working that morning stopped and watched me as I plated the three dishes. No one said a word then.

Veal ossobuco with Saffron Risotto.

Lobster Ravioli in Cream Sauce.

Buttermilk and Sage Panna Cotta.

Lou joined the small crowd that had circled around my station and beamed up at me as I whipped down each plate with a napkin, cleaning them to perfection.

"You did it," he said under his breath.

"Did what?" the lead cook huffed. "Cooked fancy food that no one will order? Can you even pronounce whatever this is?"

"Can you, Dario?" Gino asked, shooting him a pointed look.

Poor Dario had tried to assert his dominance in the kitchen, but it kept backfiring on him. He shuffled back to the wash station.

"Smells good in here!" Pa said, sticking his head through the pass. "All ready to go, Chef?"

I nodded in his direction, but my hands trembled as I picked up the plates. Lou took one from me, winking before we navigated the busy dining room.

"Ready for a feast?" Lou joked, setting the plate down as we reached Pa. I wiped my clammy hands over the front of my chef's apron and explained each dish to my father, who eyed them like a hungry wolf.

"Okay, okay. Am I supposed to eat with you watching me?"

"Yes—" Lou said.

"No," I demanded at the same time.

"Who's in charge here?" Pa looked between the both of us standing over his table.

"I am," I said, shoulders back, chin raised.

"Good. Come back in ten minutes."

I waited in the office, with Lou staring at me the whole time.

"You know he's going to love it. How could he not?"

Despite his reassurance my heart pounded hard against my chest, threatening to jump out and land on the linoleum floor. Before I could get up and check on my father at the ten-minute mark, he'd barged through the office door, looking half-crazed.

"Rosa. My bambina, where did you learn to cook like that? Not from this old man," he beamed, arms wide for one of his famous bear hugs.

He loved the dishes. No notes.

Chapter 22

The doctor from the clinic said she was already sixteen weeks along, which matched Camille's best guess. She wouldn't start showing in earnest for a few more weeks.

Still, the pressure to find an apartment mounted.

Trying to push that aside and focus on the upcoming sweet sixteen party, I plunged into a day of planning, organizing, and food prep.

The new menu items wouldn't be a silver bullet to fix the issues we had with the restaurant, but I hoped they would help. Anything had to beat doing nothing, as the hole Pa had dug kept getting deeper and deeper with each passing week. Tonight's party would determine if the restaurant would sink or swim.

Lou serenaded me with pep talks all week after Pa's tasting, but a pit in my stomach grew each time I imagined Sal taking a bite of the fancy dinner food. He'd made it clear he didn't think women belonged in commercial kitchens, only in the home. In fact, he thought little of women at all, besides arm candy. *To be seen, not heard.*

So that morning, I woke up extra early to get to the restaurant before anyone else. I wanted my mind clear and my senses sharp.

To my luck, as I opened the front door, the phone rang. I ran to pick it up, hoping it hadn't woken up the rest of the house.

With an edge in my voice, I whispered, "Hello."

"Morning, ma'am. Is Miss Rosa available?"

"This is," I responded, peeking around the stair banister for any signs of life. "How can I help you?"

"This is Reggie. Your realtor. I'm calling to let you know that Cannon Street apartment management approved your rental application. The upstairs space with the two bedrooms?"

I let out a high-pitched shriek and then rushed to cover my mouth. Now I was the one being loud. A shot of adrenaline coursed through my body, and I couldn't wait to tell Camille. Things were falling into place. I thought about waking her up, but she looked exhausted last night. She needed her rest. It could wait until later.

Gathering my purse and knife set, I rushed out the door. The sun had peeked over the tops of the buildings, and bright white rays filtered through the trees as I hurried my way to Bella. It had been weeks since I'd done this walk alone. Lou had been my constant companion, even meeting me on his mornings off before class. And while I missed him, it felt good to soak in the silence before the storm.

The "closed for private event" sign had already hung in the front window. Normally, we still ran lunch service when we held events, but not that day. Later, dozens of members of *the family* would walk through those doors. We needed them impressed and well-fed. Our future depended on it.

Cucina Bella had a special quality to it when no one else was around. She welcomed me with a soft embrace; sometimes it felt like the hug I needed, and other times the nudge to reach for more. To try harder. That day, I needed both.

Running my hands across the metal top of my workbench, I organized my materials: knives, bowls, whisks, pots, salt, seasonings, and all the ingredients. There was still so much to do. Grabbing my notebook from my bag, I jotted down a schedule that I'd worked up in my mind the previous night and posted it front and center next to the ovens for everyone to see.

Our kitchen staff tonight would consist of cooks from our usual crew and a few others I'd worked with in the past. They rarely turned down catering work. Pa had advised me to stay out of sight as much as possible when people started arriving, but I wondered if he'd even told Sal who'd be running the ship. My guess was no.

"Look at you all ready to go," said Lou as I returned from the walk-in refrigerator.

I set down the jug of milk and walked straight into his outstretched arms, inhaling his now familiar and comforting scent. It was the only time we'd get to touch, let alone talk.

"You okay?" he asked, smoothing my hair.

"I am now," I hummed into his chest. "The staff will be here soon. I wish we could stay like this forever, though."

"Me, too." Lou leaned down, placing a furtive kiss on my lips, but then pulled me back in for another that almost made my knees buckle. "But you have some cooking to do. It's a big party, but you're ready." He pushed back to look me in the eye. "You're going to knock it out of the park."

"Ah, so you do still like baseball," I joked, trying to catch my breath.

Within twenty minutes, the kitchen and dining room were humming with life. The line cooks crowded around my bench, waiting for their instructions and obligatory pep talk before getting to work. On the other side of the wall, the service staff set the tables with nice, rented linen and cutlery. It almost looked like one of those upscale restaurants down on Michigan Avenue.

"Thank you all for being here today. It's been a few months since we've hosted any special events, but it's like riding a horse. Back in the saddle we go. There's a lot to get right tonight, so let's stay on top of things," I said. "Now, I've posted a detailed schedule near the ovens. Please take a few minutes to get familiar with it."

I walked through each detail while they paid close attention. Soon the kitchen would be chaos, but for those few moments, I was in complete control.

Before finishing, I thanked them once again.

"If I don't get another chance to tell you, it means a lot that you've agreed to help today. The future of Cucina Bella is on the line. This is our chance to turn things around. Let's do it."

All seven cooks beamed back at me, looking ready to take on whatever I threw at them. I fluttered my wrists, shooing them to their stations. It was go-time.

It didn't take long for the small kitchen to fill with mouthwatering aromas, the sounds of bubbling pots, and chef's knives slicing away.

First on the schedule was the wide selection of antipasto that Sal had demanded be ready by the time the first guest arrived: whipped ricotta with bruschetta, smoked salmon crostini with capers and basil, fried stuffed olives, prosciutto wrapped-figs, arancini, and an array of fruits and Italian cheeses. Sal had even sent boxes of imported Italian wine from his private collection for Lou and Aldo to serve at the bar.

My back ached with all the hovering near the pass to ensure each platter looked and tasted like the fine dining experience I expected.

At one point, I heard Pa's booming voice float through the kitchen door as it swung open. Through the crack, I saw Sal's hand wrapped around Pa's back as he introduced him to a group of serious-looking men.

Jack, a line cook who'd worked at Bella years ago, shouted across the kitchen, "Rosa, the veal is ready for a check."

I'd tasked him with assembling and cooking the veal ossobuco, the most important dish of the evening, but I trusted him. He'd been making his way in the Chicago culinary scene for years now, jumping around several notable restaurants downtown.

Navigating through the busy kitchen, I lifted the lids of Dutch ovens containing the veal.

The meat had already fallen away from the bone, and the earthy, deep aroma filled the space. *Perfect*, I thought.

Next, I checked on a cook who'd been stirring five enormous pots of risotto for the lobster and saffron dish. Soon, we'd be plating. My heart rate picked up, sending ribbons of sweat rolling down my back.

"How did you do it?" Pa asked as I wiped down my station. "Everyone loved the food. They're gushing out there! I've never seen so much come out of our little kitchen. And the flavors, sorprendente!" *Astonishing*. He kissed the tips of his fingers in the air.

I looked over my shoulder. "What did Sal think?"

"He was very pleased, la mia ragazza." *My girl*. I hadn't been *his girl* in months, since before Sal tried to strangle the very life out of Cucina Bella.

"Does that mean he'll let us add to the menu?"

My father's face fell for long enough for me to notice. "We'll see. But either way, one day, your recipes will be celebrated across the city!" He leaned in to kiss me on the temple. "Thank you, Rosa."

As he slipped back through the swinging door, exhaustion settled over my shoulders. The cooks had already cleaned up most of the kitchen, so I let them go.

After taking one last look around, I turned off the lights in the cold-room, hoping I'd be able to slip out unnoticed. But before I could leave, I caught a glimpse of two men entering the office. For a second I thought it had been Pa and someone else, but as I inched closer to the door, still cracked open, I heard two distinct voices.

"This isn't the place to have this conversation," Lou's voice rang low.

I peeked through the gap to see Sal standing on one side of the desk, pointing his finger at Lou.

"Here is as good as anywhere."

Sucking in a sharp breath, I pressed my back against the wall behind me. Terrified Sal would do something to Lou, I stayed rooted in place. Did something happen at the bar tonight? It was the only thing that made any sense of why they were talking. Alone.

"What is *she* doing back here? Didn't I make myself clear? No lady chefs in my kitchens. They're a liability, clearly."

"She's a good chef—" Lou started to say before Sal cut him off.

"I don't care if she's the next Betty Crocker. Not in my restaurant. I want her gone; do you hear me?"

Either Lou didn't respond, or I missed it because Sal kept droning on. My heart sank. This made no sense. Lou couldn't fire me.

"But more importantly, we need to wrap this one up. Are you done with the books?"

"It's not that simple, Sal. I need more time."

I heard the mug of pens on the desk fall to the floor.

"More time? You've had months. Don't tell me you've gone soft for the Bianchis. Do I need to remind you what's at stake? You're thinking with the wrong brain, nephew."

I felt a punch to the gut. All the air left my lungs. *Nephew?*

"All you had to do was convince him it was hopeless. Cook the books, as they say.

"Why does this place even matter? It's a hole in the wall restaurant, a dime a dozen in these parts," said Lou.

Hearing Lou so callously dismissing Cucina Bella hurt the most. All these months, he'd been pretending to care. Tears welled, but I choked them back, refusing to let them fall. If they started, I didn't know if they'd ever stop.

"We need to start construction on the pool hall front *now*, before the new city administration takes over. They'll force us to go through the official channels for permits then."

The fog lifted then. Sal never intended to let my father work off his debt. He'd been planning to turn Cucina Bella into a pool hall as a front for one of his many business schemes all along.

And Lou was in on it. No, Lou was *family*.

Just as I'd heard enough, Sal slammed his fist on the desk, and I jumped.

"Get it done. Or I will make you pay back all the tuition for that fancy education I've fronted for you. Wouldn't your father be so disappointed if he found out I'd been paying your tuition?"

"He'd disown me if he knew I was working with you."

"Don't say things you'll regret. You have one more week to get them out."

The door swung wide, and Sal stepped out, catching my eye before I could turn away.

He scoffed and strode out of the kitchen. Trembling and unable to move, the whooshing in my ears grew louder. Slowly, I turned my head to see Lou's face go white with realization.

"Rosa, I'm so sorry—" he started.

"Don't."

I turned and hung up my apron, not stopping before I reached the back door.

Chapter 23

Lou

It took all my strength not to chase after Rosa. Or to not stomp into that dining room and cuss Sal out right then and there, in front of his entire crew. But the look on Rosa's face when I came out of that office rooted me to the ground.

What had I done?

For so long I'd kept my distance, knowing I'd only hurt her, and I'd been right. That was the hardest part—I knew better. Then I did it anyway.

That very first day, when she walked into the restaurant with those thick brown curls framing her face, I knew she would break me. I remembered every side glance, every accidental graze of her skin against mine. The way her forehead crinkled when she cooked, deep in concentration.

It woke something inside of me that wanted to claw its way out.

The only thing holding me back, in truth, was the fact that she was engaged. Although I knew he was no good for her, I'd never come between their relationship. And then it all changed when she called off the wedding. I lost all sense of myself, all control. A dam inside me broke, and I couldn't pretend I didn't want her anymore. Then I fell in love as easily as tumbling down a hill.

My uncle complicated things.

For years, I'd been trying to find a way out. Growing up, my father kept us away from him, only seeing him at Christmas. Sometimes he'd drop by for an unexpected dinner, and I'd be shooed into my room for the evening until he left.

My mother hated Sal. She crossed herself every time they were in the same room, and I never knew why. My father refused to discuss him, only stating there was a reason we didn't live in Chicago anymore. We'd moved to Wisconsin when I was a toddler and rarely ever made it back to the city. It didn't take much to figure it had something to do with Sal.

Then, when I turned eighteen, I received a letter from him asking to meet in the city for a celebratory dinner.

Being a curious and reckless teenager, I showed up, not sure of what to expect. Maybe a card with some money and a pat on the back. But he extended an offer. I'd been accepted to the University of Chicago on a partial scholarship, but I couldn't go. Even though the scholarship covered some costs, the rest would be up to me, and we didn't have that kind of money. I'd planned on working with my father, trying to get into the union instead.

Sal knew.

He offered to cover my portion of the tuition and some living expenses if I joined him in Chicago to help him with his "business." I'd asked what his business consisted of, but he laughed and said, "A little real estate. Nightlife. Distribution."

To a naïve kid, that sounded like an opportunity.

What I didn't know was that for the next four years, I'd be pulled into all kinds of shady, off-the-books deals. Especially when Sal learned I had a knack for numbers. It was the reason he'd forced me to go into forensic accounting. If you knew the rules, you could also break them.

I'd become detached from the work I did with Sal; the only way I could stay sane. My school life was separate from my work life. Compartmentalizing became my norm.

One night, I saw something I'd never be able to shove away in my mind. Sal had invited me to a poker game, a regular gathering of his close crew members in the back of a laundromat he ran.

Instead, it turned out to be an interrogation. And my initiation.

The night left me disoriented, drunk, and an accomplice to extreme violence. The next morning, I decided enough was enough. I had to get out. If they could make me do that, what else could they make me do? Where did it end? I couldn't stay around long enough to find out.

Not long after that, Sal put me up to following Marco to leverage his gambling habit so he could take over the space that his restaurant occupied. When Sal gave me the new mark, I told him it'd be my last job. After I graduated, I wanted to go legitimate and find a job, start my life.

Sal nodded along, saying, "We'll discuss it more after the job is done."

He knew I was stringing the job along. Buying time. That's where his anger came from tonight. And even though we shared blood, he'd only take so much from me before he retaliated.

He wasn't wrong. I *had* been stringing him along. At first, I tried to treat Cucina Bella like any other job. Get in, do what I needed, get out. But from day one, things were different.

Marco was not a dangerous man living a double life like many of the guys caught up in the Chicago underworld. He had had a string of bad luck, that's for sure, but he loved his family, his restaurant. He was a hard worker. Made a life out of nothing.

Taking over Marco's restaurant felt unnecessary, but Sal had targeted it a while ago. It was in the right part of town, an area he wanted to include in his expanded territory. And for now, many of the city council members were in his pocket.

I had a plan: finish the job and tell Sal I was out. He'd either accept it, or I'd leave and build a life somewhere else. Either way, I would be done. But now that I couldn't imagine a life without Rosa, that plan didn't work. If he found out about us, which he likely already knew, he'd use it as leverage.

The best thing for everyone would be to leave and never come back. Disappear.

But that meant leaving her, too.

Chapter 24

Rosa

Lou had lied. The entire time he'd been working for them. For Sal. He let me believe he cared about my family, about me. In reality, Lou wanted to push us out. We were nothing but a problem that needed sorting, not saving.

Another bubble of anger rose before it burst and left a rush of self-pity. No wonder Pa said nothing about my relationship with Lou. He was embarrassed for me. As he should have been. I'd been a fool.

But why didn't Pa tell me? The blade of betrayal ran so deep it grazed bone. Deeper than the wound Ant had inflicted. It had been staring me in the face the entire time, I just refused to see it. Even Camille had had her suspicions.

After the party, I snuck into the limestone basement we used as a small wine cellar and dusted off a bottle of red wine that looked decent enough to dull the pain so I could sleep. The house was silent except for the clock that struck midnight as Ma and Ivana slept upstairs.

I'd poured myself a second glass to the rim when Camille returned from the party, looking like she could fall asleep standing. She eased onto the bed beside me.

"What happened? I looked for you before I left, but someone said you'd snuck out early."

When I looked up, Camille clocked the hurt on my face. The wine had done nothing to soften the blow. She wrapped her arms around me and buried her face in my hair.

"Lou is Sal's nephew. They're working together to close Bella for good and turn it into a pool hall as a front for God knows what," I exhaled all at once. "Lou is supposed to be cooking the books, making it look like we have no way out."

She held my arms, pushing back to look at me. "He told you that?" Her eyes widened in shock, alive and alert.

"No. I overheard Sal talking to him in Pa's office at the party."

"Maybe you didn't hear right. It could be a misunderstanding."

"I wish it were." The look on Lou's face when he saw me confirmed everything. I took a long sip from my glass. "It's over. It's all over. The restaurant, my stupid dream, all of Pa's hard work. It's gone."

We sat together on my bed for a long time, not saying a word. The weight of our reality slapped down at our feet like a rotting slab of meat. After I'd finished the bottle, I slid into bed next to Camille. We held each other.

At least I had her.

The next morning my head felt like it could split in two. The clock on my nightstand read five past ten in the morning. I hadn't slept that late since middle school.

Camille was gone, but a note next to a full glass of water explained she'd be back before dinner. It wasn't until I read the note that I realized I hadn't told her about the apartment.

Before I could curl back up in the sheets, I stumbled my way to the shower. Lou might have blindsided me, but I wouldn't let it derail our plans. We'd find other jobs.

But first, I had to tell Pa about Lou's deception and Sal's plan. If he already knew, fine. But if not, I didn't want us wasting anymore of our time trying to save Bella. It wasn't worth it. Although Pa would never be the man we needed, I was still his daughter, and he deserved the truth.

Trudging downstairs, I found Pa already in his study, hunched over paperwork on his desk. A pencil stuck out of mouth.

"Morning," I croaked out.

"There she is. The prized chef. Where'd you go last night?"

I dragged a wooden armchair close to his desk and stared at the yellowing world-map hanging on the far wall behind him. Though I'd never been outside of Illinois, I now felt like I'd traveled to some of those countries by tasting their food.

A pang of something shot through my abdomen. Sadness? Guilt? Bittersweet remorse that it was now over?

"Papa, did you know Lou was working for Sal?"

He took the pencil out of his mouth and placed it in front of him with care.

"Not at first. He fooled me, too."

"When did you find out?" I asked, needing to know the details.

"I confronted him about it when I noticed you two getting close. He started to make me suspicious when he wouldn't let me see the books. I didn't want him to hurt you or Bella."

A small, sad laugh fell between us.

"Too late for that," I said. "So, you know there's no saving Bella?"

"There's nothing else we can do. It's gone." Pa looked out the front window at the leaves blowing into the small front yard. Then he turned back to me.

"But here's the thing, Rosa. Lou's looking for a way out. Has been for a while. He doesn't want to work for Sal anymore, and I believe him. We might not save Bella, but he gave us more time than we would have had otherwise. He tried."

My father's lips moved, but I didn't hear the words he said. Because that's all they were to me: words.

I thought back to all the times Pa wiped my tears as a child. The time I fell off my bike on the road in front of our house and skinned both knees. He ran outside and held me as Ma poured peroxide over the scrapes, and I screamed so loud that the birds flew out of the tree above us.

The time I sliced the tip of my pointer finger chopping parsley when I was twelve. He rushed over, wrapping my finger in a clean towel and bandaged it in his office with the first-aid kit he kept under his desk. He shushed my sobs away.

For all his faults, he loved us. Loved his girls in a way no one else ever would. And even though his betrayal shook our family, it didn't break it. We were still hanging on, if by only a thread. And I wanted to believe him. I wanted to lean into his hug and say, "Okay, Pa. You're right. I'll talk to Lou. It'll all work out."

But I wasn't a kid anymore. And he couldn't fix my problems. He was fallible, like the rest of us.

"It's over, Pa. And I'm tired of everyone's excuses."

I heard the phone ring several times that day, but told everyone I wouldn't be taking calls. I didn't want to talk to Lou or anyone else for that matter. There was nothing he could say.

By the evening, Camille still had not returned, so I busied myself packing our closet into the two old suitcases we never used that I found stuffed in the hallway linen closet. If Ma wanted them back, she could come visit us at our new apartment.

The realtor had called again and said we'd be able to move in next week, provided we could put down one month's rent plus the deposit. It would be a stretch, but I thought we could make it happen. It was the only thing I had. Without it, I might have sunk into a deep well of despair and self-pity.

Waiting for Camille to come home had turned into a sparring match between myself and my inner thoughts. To quell the tide of rising emotions, I cooked dinner for the family. Afterward, I'd take Camille out back, and we'd toast to our futures, to the new apartment. But as night fell with no sign or word from Camille, I worried.

Around seven, we ate, and I couldn't stop staring at the empty chair across the table.

"Where's Cammie?" Ivana asked. She'd called her Cammie since she could talk.

"Your guess is as good as anyone's, dear," said Ma, shaking her head.

"She'll be back. Probably got caught in traffic or delays on the train," Pa consoled.

It wasn't as if this was the first time she'd missed a family dinner.

After we ate in near silence, Ma and Pa retreated to the office, going over some paperwork for the insurance company since he'd told her that afternoon that they would lose the restaurant. Ma had only shrugged and patted him on the shoulder, saying, "We'll figure it all out."

A loud knock at the door jolted me out of a trance as I washed the last of the dishes in the soapy sink.

"Good evening, officers," I heard Ma say in a stiff, loud voice. "Everything all right?"

"Evenin' ma'am. May we come in?"

I dried my hands and stepped into the hallway. Two officers stood on the front porch, bugs swirling around their heads by the light fixture. Both clutched their navy-blue hats in their hands.

"What's going on?" I asked Pa, following the two officers into the small sitting room. Ma motioned for them to take a seat.

"We're sorry to drop in on you like this. Is Camille Bianchi your daughter?"

The floor tilted at my feet.

"Yes. What's happened?" Pa asked, voice breaking.

"I'm afraid she was in an accident this evening. She's at Mother Cabrini Hospital. We can take you there now, if you'd like us to escort you."

"Is she okay?" I blurted out. No one said anything. Ma continued to sit ramrod straight, hands folded in her lap, as if she were having a conversation over tea. Fury rose hot.

"What happened? What kind of accident?"

"Rosa! Lower your voice. The man said she's at the hospital. I'm sure she's fine. Go get your sister, and we'll leave."

"Ma'am, your daughter is undergoing emergency surgery. We don't know her condition, but the man who was driving didn't make it."

In that moment, Ma's face contorted with a dreadful realization. She wrung her hands together until her knuckles turned white. Pa was already out of his seat, slipping into his shoes and grabbing the car keys off the foyer table.

"Marissa! Let's go!" he shouted. She snapped up from her seat.

I took the stairs two at a time to grab my sister and we all piled into the station wagon. No one said a word.

Chapter 25

Nothing could be more excruciating than waiting.

We sat, tired and worried for hours in uncomfortable wooden chairs in the hospital waiting room, which smelled like old gym socks and disinfectant. To stretch our legs, we'd take turns walking to the small cafeteria, bringing back paper cups of lukewarm coffee. No one drank it. Half-full cups lined the small tables that dotted the rows of chairs in the waiting room.

A few weary-looking people sat alone in chairs near the nurses' station, also waiting for word on a friend or loved one. For so long, the door leading to the hallway remained still, and I had memorized every visible scuff and scratch.

When we arrived, a nurse told us she'd be back with more information when she could, but she only knew that Camille had suffered serious injuries to her legs, which the surgeons were trying to repair.

Then hours passed. Ma left to make a few phone calls, presumably to the church phone tree to start a prayer chain. Pa flipped open a magazine and kept re-reading the same page repeatedly. I stared at the clock on the wall while my sister played with the two dolls she'd brought, whispering to herself.

"This is ridiculous," Ma spat, looking down into her cup of tepid coffee.

"The coffee is awful," Pa said, not looking up from the magazine in his lap.

"Not what I meant, Marco. When will *someone* tell us what's going on?" She pushed herself upright and marched over to the desk where a bleary-eyed nurse sat under a single overhead light.

"Excuse me," said Ma, softening her tone. "It's been three hours. Do you know when the doctor will be out?"

"What's the patient's name?" the nurse asked without looking up from her folder of paperwork.

"Camille Bianchi. She was in a car wreck."

"She's still in surgery. That's all I can—" she said when the double doors swung open. Everyone in the waiting room whipped their heads around.

"Is the Bianchi family here?"

"Yes, we're here," Ma said, waving us over to join her.

He led us into a small room just inside the hallway for privacy.

Not only did the surgeon look young, but he also looked exhausted. I couldn't decide what that meant for Camille. My heart pounded against my rib cage. Whatever he told us, there was no going back. From this moment forward, our lives would be split in two.

The man who'd introduced himself as Dr. Waite removed his light blue surgery cap before we began.

"First, let me tell you, Camille is a fighter. She'll recover."

Ma let out a strangled cry and crossed herself while kissing the rosary she'd been clutching all night.

"Her right kneecap was crushed so she'll need physical therapy to walk properly again, but we repaired it for now. She also lost a lot of blood."

Ivana wove her fingers through mine. She hated blood. I stroked my thumb over hers.

"Thank you, Doctor. When can we see her?"

"In a few minutes. She's just left the surgical theater."

Pa shook his hand, thanking him in Italian.

"Oh, I almost forgot," Dr. Waite said, hand on the door. "The baby will be fine."

We all turned in unison to Ma, whose face contorted in confusion.

"What baby?" she asked, but the doctor had already left.

As soon as the door shut, she aimed her fury at me in a direct hit. "Tell me. Now."

I sucked in a long breath. "Camille should be the one to tell you."

"No. You'll tell me now. Marco, do something!"

Vanie slunk to the back of the room, leaving the three of us in a stare-down over the small folding table.

Pa tilted his head and said, "It's better this way. Tell her what you know."

I hesitated before inhaling to steady my nerves. "There's not much to tell. She's sixteen weeks along, and I'm going to help her through it. We found an apartment and will be moving out next week."

Ma tucked her rosary into the small pocketbook slung over her shoulder and then tapped her cheeks to bring back color.

Before turning to exit, she said, "What a shame. I thought it'd be you who'd ruin our family name. I was wrong. It'll be both of you."

Everyone left, but I stayed behind, unable to move, endless scenarios running through my head. It wouldn't surprise me if Ma tried to convince Camille to put the baby up for adoption or disown her altogether. Nothing could have prepared me for what was to come.

I heard a voice from the hallway, so I stuck my head out, wondering if the doctor had come back. Instead, Ant stood at the far end of the bright corridor. I didn't move, but he walked toward me like a man walking toward a chapel, every step deliberate. Then, he brushed a tear off my cheek that I hadn't realized had fallen.

I melted into his chest, heaving with sobs.

"It's okay. I'm here now."

"What happened to Jackson?" I asked, sniffling into the handkerchief he'd given me.

Ant's back stiffened.

I looked up at him, a question forming on my lips. Before I could get it out, he answered.

"He didn't make it."

My insides curdled and my heart felt ripped in two. Not for Jackson, but for Camille. For their unborn baby.

"No," I croaked. "I'd hoped they told us wrong."

"He was driving the car when it flipped and landed in the ditch. I don't know much else. It'll all be okay, though." Ant slipped his hand into mine. "We'll get through this together." I let him lead me back through the door to my family.

The next few hours went by in a haze. We saw Camille in her small recovery room, but she couldn't keep her eyes open for longer than a few minutes at a time. From the top half of the bed, she looked normal, as if she were only sleeping. One of her legs protruded out of the covers, elevated by a sling hanging from the ceiling and wrapped in thick white and tan gauze.

The medical staff informed us she'd be able to go home in a few days with crutches. They'd help her get comfortable using them. Then she'd go to therapy at least three times a week until her knee healed. It was possible she'd need another surgery, but they wanted to hold off until after she delivered the baby to avoid complications.

Every time someone mentioned the pregnancy in front of my mother, she looked away in disgust. The nurses ignored her, tending to my sister all the same.

Camille had a hard time staying conscious after the surgery, a small blessing because she needed her rest. The news about Jackson could wait.

Ant drove me home early the next morning before the sun rose to try to get some sleep. My parents had taken Ivana back a few hours earlier. On the doorstep, Ant kissed my temple and told me he'd pick me up around noon to take me back to the hospital. Without thinking, I wiped the kiss away and slipped through the front door.

Sleep came fast and deep.

For a few blissful seconds after I woke, I lay in bed looking at the dust specks floating in the bright sunrays shining through my bedroom window, the previous night's events still far away. Then it all came crashing back. I gripped the blanket hard, bringing it up to my mouth to muffle the cries. The relief of letting it all out soothed my tight shoulders, and I relaxed back down into the small bed.

Ant had been at the hospital, I remembered. He'd driven me home. Acted normally, like he belonged by my side as much as anyone else. He was picking me up in twenty minutes to take me back to the hospital. I needed to be there when our mother looked into her clear eyes and asked about the baby. When she broke Camille's heart with her callousness.

I heard the jingle of the rosary beads before I saw her.

"Is she awake?" I asked my mother, who was leaning against the window in Camille's hospital room. It was the first time I'd really looked at her in years. The wrinkles surrounding her brown eyes framed her face. She had her hair braided down her left shoulder to keep her curls from escaping like always, but now I saw how it had grayed to a muted brown.

"Yes, but she's hysterical. Frankly, it's embarrassing. Maybe you can talk to her," she said, moving closer to the bed.

"I'll try. Where's Pa?"

"He's gone to lunch with Ivana. I'm going to grab something from the cafeteria." She perked up when she saw Ant behind me. "Anthony, it's so kind of you to come. Thank you for taking care of Rosa last night. Would you like to join me for some tea?" The change in her tone made me grind my teeth together.

Ant, who'd followed a few paces behind me through the hospital, nodded at her invitation. I was grateful. Camille and I needed to talk. Alone.

When I swung the door open, a strong smell of antiseptic hit me like a wall, and I took half a step backward before recovering. I don't know what I expected to see, but it wasn't Camille sitting straight up in bed, reading a pamphlet.

"Ma said you were upset. What's going on?"

She looked up, and I saw the red rings around her eyes. The puffiness that swallowed her eyelashes. I eased myself into the reclining chair near her bed.

"Is he really gone, Rosa?" she asked. Closer now, I realized the pamphlet in her hand wasn't a pamphlet after all. It was a black-and-white photo of her and Jackson at the beach. "You'll tell me the truth, won't you? Everyone is being so evasive." She slammed her fist into her lap as she sniffled. "No one will tell me what happened."

"Jackson is gone." I reached for her hand. "I'm so sorry. Ant told me he was driving, and the car flipped into a ditch. That's all I know."

"I don't remember any of it," she said in a whisper. "But the baby is okay."

"The baby is okay," I repeated. "You're going to be okay."

Camille shook her head. "Everything is different now. Ma knows."

"She does, but nothing has to change. Our plan can still work. Look, I heard from the realtor. We got the apartment we wanted. The one in the small house, upstairs? If we pay the deposit, we can move in next week."

She shot her eyes up at me. "Look at me, Rosa. I'm not going anywhere. I'm a mess. You didn't sign up to take care of..." she looked at her leg, "this."

A flash of annoyance rippled through me. "Then what is your plan, then? You can't stay here forever. They said you'll be discharged in a few days. Where will you go then?"

"There's no point. I don't want to do this without Jackson. I can't. Before, I had hoped he'd come around eventually. Then we could be a proper family. Now there's nothing." She clutched the photo even tighter. "Ma says she can get me a spot at a home for women in my situation. She's made a few calls, and I can go there at the end of the week."

"What kind of home?" I asked, even though I knew.

We'd all heard of the *places* families sent young women if they fell pregnant out of wedlock. In high school, rumors would pop up when girls stopped coming to class, only to return months later, looking like shells of their former selves. No babies ever came back with them.

"What am I supposed to do? I can't do this alone."

"You're not alone. I'll help you. I want to help you. Please don't do this," I begged.

"Even if we were to move in together, raise this baby together, Rosa, we'd have no family. No one to help us. I don't want my child growing up without a family, knowing ours only lives blocks away. It would be too painful." Camille squeezed my hand, and my knuckles rubbed together. "And it would ruin your dreams."

"Who cares about dreams? You're my family. I care about you. I'll cook for us and help you take care of the baby," I said, knowing she'd already decided. Ma had worn her down in one morning. Shamed her into obedience, as she'd done our entire lives.

"What if we moved away? Started somewhere new? We could be whoever we wanted," I asked, one last attempt to get her to choose hope, even though I hadn't the faintest idea how to make it happen.

She laughed. "Where would we go? We have no money, and we've never been outside of Illinois. It's over, Rosa. And I want it to be. It'll only be a few months. When I get back, I can start over."

Chapter 26

The taxi line in front of the hospital crawled at a snail's speed. I kept glancing over my shoulder, ready for Ant to appear, whom I'd left behind.

Though he held me last night, tethered me to reality in a moment I thought I'd float away, it changed nothing between us. His embrace felt like a hug from a friend, not the burning fire I had experienced with Lou. My entire body longed for that heat.

And yet.

My mind raced through solutions, returning to the delusion that Ant's money and influence could be the answer. If I forgave him, maybe we could have a shot? We'd get back together, and I'd convince him to help me rescue Camille before she gave birth. Maybe then I could also get over Lou and learn to love Anthony as more than my childhood friend. Maybe, maybe, maybe.

When I returned home, a scattering of mail covered the floor behind our front door, greeting me. As I flipped through the envelopes, one-by-one, I stopped at a letter with my name scrawled across the front, blocky handwriting familiar.

My hands trembled as shuffled over to the small settee, ripping the seal open. A single piece of paper fluttered to the ground. I picked it up, hesitating before unfolding the letter.

My Dearest Rosa,

What can I say that will soothe the wounds I've caused you? My own selfishness led me here, and I have no one to blame but myself. For that, I am sorry. But I hope you'll let me explain. You are owed that, and I'd regret it if I didn't try.

To start, I never thought I'd meet someone like you. For years, I'd been plodding along, looking for a way out to start my life, but not once did that include another person. I am a fool.

What you saw the other night at Cucina Bella has been my existence for far too long. My life has become a series of small lies that have added up to something heavier than I ever meant to carry. If my father knew I was working for his brother, he'd die of disappointment, which is why I've kept it a secret, hoping I'd figure out a way to leave before I broke his heart.

Instead, I broke yours.

Years ago, after I'd graduated high school, I accepted an offer from my uncle that I thought would be temporary. It solved my biggest problem and allowed me to attend college. But it also took my freedom and made me do things that will forever haunt me. Sal turned me into a dishonorable man, and I let him. For what it's worth, Cucina Bella was supposed to be my last job. The plan was to graduate and leave the family behind for good. Find a job in a city far away and never look back. Then, I fell in love with you. The plan had to be changed.

Over the past two months, I've tried desperately to keep Sal at bay while working to salvage your father's business. As you know now, it's useless. There is no saving the restaurant, which is what I should have realized a lot sooner and told you. I'm sorry.

While your father has probably told you most of this already, what he doesn't know is that I'm leaving Chicago. I cannot continue to aid Sal and his "business" any longer, but the only way to do that without dire consequences is to leave. I cannot tell you where I am going for your own safety. But let's just say a certain fellow lover of the culinary arts has passed on and left me with an option.

In one last attempt to save what little might still be between us, I'm asking you to join me. I realize I am not the man you fell for, but I promise that man is in me somewhere, and I'd love nothing more than to spend the rest of my life trying to find him. It's a long shot, I know. The odds are stacked against me, but I have to try.

Bring Camille. Cook for us. Build a new life.

I'll be waiting at Central Station this Friday on platform three for the five o'clock train west. I'll have two extra tickets waiting. But if you don't come, I will understand. And I will love you. Always.

-Lou

For the second time in twenty-four hours, tears streamed down my face, leaving water droplets on the yellow piece of letter paper. Since the night of the party, I hadn't stopped to think about Lou's situation from his perspective. I'd been so caught up wallowing in my self-pity and punishing myself. But he'd been so young when Sal offered him a deal. Did he deserve to spend the rest of his life living with the consequences of one misjudgment? After reading his words again, I decided no. Lou deserved a fair shot at life, one that he had control over. But that didn't change how he'd made me feel. Like a real fool.

Yet, the life we could have together flashed in my mind. Although the details eluded me, the broad strokes painted a peaceful picture. I could see us somewhere together, happy. A simple life that included Camille and her child. We'd go on lazy evening walks after work together. I'd play with the baby while

Camille cleaned up after the dinner I cooked. Lou would mow the lawn. I'd find a job in a kitchen. We would build something out of nothing. A private yet fulfilling existence that we could call our own.

As soon as I saw it, the illusion shattered into tiny sharp shards. For all I knew, everything Lou wrote was a lie. The man I fell in love with was also a lie. There was no guarantee he'd ever be truthful again. The odds were indeed stacked against him.

If I couldn't forgive Ant, with whom I shared decades of history, how could I ever trust Lou again?

I forced myself to focus on the real things: a sister in the hospital. A broken family that couldn't be saved. A restaurant lost. A dream forgotten. A baby to be born.

My world felt too complicated. Too messy. Too hard. So, I did what I always did when life made no sense: I cooked.

By the time everyone had returned home for dinner, the house smelled as if I'd been cooking all day, which I had. Our butcher had delivered a quarter cow the day before, so we had plenty of meat in the freezer and some already thawed for the week. I had taken one look in the refrigerator and decided on ragu with homemade pasta. When the family filed in, I'd finished rolling out and cutting the dough into long noodles and started boiling them in a large pot of water in batches. No one said a word as they slid into their usual chairs at the table, with one noticeable absence, waiting for a meal that would feed their weary souls.

The ragu sauce, my father's family recipe, had been stewing on the stovetop for hours. Its aroma reminded me of the slow Sunday evenings we used to have as a family before the restaurant became popular when Pa still had time to cook for us. I spooned a small bite, tasting its sumptuous notes of red wine, sauteed onions and vegetables, and slowly rendered meat that balanced out its richness. Paired with the al dente noodles, it was the perfect comfort dish.

Even Ma relaxed, sitting back in her chair as she ate. There would always be a reason to argue, but for this perfect moment, none of it mattered. Food brought us together even on the worst of our days. From then on, that meal would be frozen in my memory as the last I'd have with my family.

For the next two nights, I agonized over what to do. Ma had all but shipped Camille off already, refusing to talk about alternatives. In her mind, Camille would go away for a few months and come back a woman who make better decisions. A daughter she could still claim as her own. As for me, I still had to be out of the house Sunday. I knew why my mother blamed me. Being the eldest daughter, my actions had a reverberating effect on my younger sisters. I had a responsibility to them that no one had to me. If only I hadn't been so ambitious, so delusional as to think I could be more than a housewife, I could have been a better influence on my sister. But there was no going back. Only moving on.

So, I continued to pack. For what, I was not sure. But each day, I stuffed more and more into mine and Camille's suitcases. I couldn't bring myself to think about what her life would be inside that home run by nuns, so I included everything.

On Thursday, Pa called me into his small office. He had something to tell me.

"Bella is still ours. We're paying Sal off."

The news stunned me into silence.

"Rosa, this is good. You can still cook. Our plans can still happen," he tried to explain, as if I didn't understand.

"But how?" I stammered. I'd heard Sal that night in the restaurant office. He wanted Bella for personal reasons. To let it go, Pa must have given him a lot of money. Money he didn't have.

"Always so nosy. I worked out a deal and Sal agreed to it." He shrugged as if he were telling me it wouldn't rain today.

I gave my father a weak smile and went back to my room to pack some more. Two weeks ago, this would have changed my life. Today, nothing mattered anymore. I didn't know what he did to make it happen, and honestly, I didn't want to. Nothing would be the same, anyway. We could never go back.

Sleeping alone in my room for several nights in a row unnerved me. I didn't want to get used to it, but I had no choice. Camille would be gone for months, and I'd be moving out. The realtor had negotiated a reduced rent since it would only be me in the apartment after all. The only thing left to do was drop the deposit check off the next day.

I woke up that night in a pool of sweat, which had become commonplace that week. Looking around for the glass of water I had kept by my bed, I realized I'd forgotten to refill it that night. Desperate for some ice to cool off, I crept down the stairs to the kitchen.

Before my foot hit the last step, I heard a faint voice coming from the living room. Someone was on the phone, but I couldn't imagine who'd be calling at midnight. Then I recognized my mother's hushed voice. I tiptoed forward, careful to stay out of sight behind the wall that separated the main living space and the hallway to the kitchen.

"Thank you for doing this, Father. I'm sorry it's so late. I wanted to wait until everyone was asleep to phone you," Ma said.

She was talking to Father Esposito from the church.

"Yes, Camille has agreed to leave tomorrow. She still has a lot of recovering ahead, but I'm sure the Sisters will take good care of her."

Ma listened.

"No, I haven't told her about our arrangement, and I'd like to keep it between us. Can you also assure me that the adoption will be closed? I don't want any chance of contact down the road from either side."

Another pause.

"Good, thank you. When can we expect to receive payment? I don't mean to be pushy, but Marco needs it soon." Her voice stiffened. "And I want this to be over with."

Payment? My mind whirled.

"Is it typical to wait until the baby is born to be paid? I'm afraid we don't have much time."

Silence.

"Yes, fine. Half of the ten thousand next week will work. I expect the second half upon delivery."

I pushed against the wall for support as blood rushed through my ears and the realization hit me like a lead pipe.

My mother had sold Camille's baby. She wasn't sending her away for her own good and reputation. She was solving the family's problems at Camille's expense. And Camille would never know.

I heard a click and rushed into the kitchen to fill my glass. Ma appeared in the doorway.

"What are you doing down here?"

"Getting some water." I held up the glass.

She eyed me up and down, then turned to go upstairs.

"Go to bed," she said, disappearing into the dark.

I did no such thing. Instead, I did the only thing left to do.

Visiting hours didn't start for another few hours when I arrived at the hospital, bags in tow, around six the next morning. A sliver of the sun peeked over the buildings, casting everything in an orange-red glow that reminded me of Camille's hair in the light as I walked up to the entrance. Last night, I pared everything down to two suitcases: one for each of us. We had to travel light.

We'd been told Camille could be discharged today. Ma arranged for a private driver to take her that morning to the Catholic women's home across the border in Indiana, so I had to hurry.

"I'm here to bring home Camille Bianchi," I said to the lady sitting at the nurses' station. She eyed my bags before responding.

"They're for my sister. She wanted options for what to wear, plus some of her makeup. Even leaving the hospital is an event for her," I explained, praying she'd buy it.

She shrugged and pulled out a manila folder with Camille's name on the top.

"Miss Bianchi should be ready to leave as soon as the doctor signs the discharge papers. Please take a seat."

"Is there any way I could go to her room to help her get ready?" I flashed her my most sarcastic grin as if saying, *I know, it's a lot. Some women these days.* "I don't want to be stuck here all morning waiting for her curlers to set."

Inside, I felt as if I could throw up. Every fiber of my being hummed with alertness, and the hole that had opened last night threatened to swallow me whole.

With a pinched expression on her wrinkled face, the nurse picked up the phone without breaking eye contact.

"Is the patient in room two sixteen awake?" She asked someone on the other line. "Great." She hung up the phone. "You can go see her now."

I thanked the enthusiastic nurse and trotted down the hallway. When I opened the heavy door, Camille was fumbling next to the other bed with the set of crutches she'd been practicing on.

"Need some help?" I asked, smiling at her wobbly attempts to secure them under her arms.

"Oh, thank the heavens you're here. I need to pee so badly it hurts!"

I set down the suitcases in the corner and helped her to the restroom. After, she hopped back to the bed, not bothering with the crutches this time.

"What are you doing here, though?" she asked. "And with suitcases? Did Ma ask you to take me today? I thought they'd say goodbye at least."

I held her gaze for a second. My plan had been to tell her everything, including the conversation I overheard last night, but the thought of breaking her heart again just about killed me.

"Rosa, what's going on?"

She needed to know. Otherwise, she'd never come with me.

"Ma arranged a paid adoption," I blurted out.

Camille's face crinkled. "What do you mean? I've been told the baby will go to a local family. I'll even be able to have visitations."

They flat out lied to her.

"I'm sorry, Camille. Whoever Ma is working with is paying her and Pa ten thousand dollars to put your baby up for a closed adoption. I overheard her talking to Father Esposito last night after everyone had gone to bed."

Camille looked as if she'd been sucker punched. All the breath left her broken body.

"How could they do that? Why?" she asked.

"To save Cucina Bella."

"Of course. The restaurant is worth more to them than we ever will be." Camille looked out the window. "What a weak, pathetic man."

"Who?" I asked, wondering if she was talking about Jackson.

"He let this happen. This is all his fault."

She didn't need to name him. Our father had done too much. Or not enough. I started to defend him, like I always did, but stopped. It'd all come to this. He'd laid down too many times and I couldn't help him now.

All I could say was, "They're both at fault."

"So, what do we do now?"

Chapter 27

Lou

I checked my wristwatch again for the tenth time since I'd entered the train station, a nervous tic I picked up from my father. Although I'd gotten to there early, I was paranoid I'd miss my train.

Glancing down the platform, I spotted the only wooden bench with an open seat and beelined forward. Before I sat down, I pulled the letter out of my back pocket to read it one more time because nothing felt real.

It had taken me over a week, but I finally opened the thick envelope from my aunt that Rosa had found. To my surprise, it didn't contain newspaper clippings of baseball game stats. Instead, the contents were wrapped in a handwritten letter from my aunt.

If you're reading this letter, I'm afraid I've finally croaked, she had written, and I could hear her voice plain as day as if she'd called me up to tell me the news.

Apparently, my aunt had been suffering from breast cancer for the past year but kept it a secret. The doctor had only given her a few months, and she didn't want to burden her family.

Plus, she needed time to get her affairs in order. Affairs that included me.

According to her letter, her estate was now mine.

The letter had been long, outlining many details, but mainly kept referring to her attorney I'd need to contact. Inside the envelope, she'd also included a copy of the deed to her house in Riverbend, Illinois, which she'd put in my name, and various bank statements I'd need to spend more time reviewing at some point. All I had to do was sign the papers, and everything would be mine.

That same day, I wrote a letter of my own.

I wasn't delusional. The chances of Rosa joining me to run away to claim my inheritance in a town she'd never been to were slim to none. But I had to try. If I didn't, I'd always wonder what could have been.

In the days after my conversation with Sal at Bella, I agonized over what to do. My options were thin, and I was running out of time. But how I wished I'd opened my aunt's letter sooner. If I had, things could have been so different. Rosa and I could have had a future together, one that did not include Sal.

Then I heard the news of Camille's accident. For two days, I parked around the block from their house, trying to glimpse Rosa coming or going. I guess I needed to see for myself that she was safe. It didn't do any good because the few times I watched her leave, I had to force myself to stay in the car. Her face looked hollow and pale. The crinkles around her eyes had slipped into unreadable pits of worry. She needed me more than ever, and I'd failed at the very basic task not being who I said I was.

I glanced down at my watch again as another train pulled into the platform behind me. Dozens of people shuffled forward, climbing the steps to wherever they'd go next. I'd be doing the same in twenty minutes. Time slowed down in train stations, but today it shot ahead like it wanted to leave me behind.

An elderly woman approached the bench, and I offered her my seat. More and more people filled the narrow platform, and I worried I'd miss Rosa if I didn't move closer to the entrance. Delusional.

The day before, I'd called my landlord and told them I'd be moving out, but that I'd leave all my furniture as payment for breaking the lease early. They seemed to accept this. That morning, I packed the only bag I had and nothing more. Where I was going, I'd have everything I needed. Except for the one thing I wanted.

Then, before I left, I made a phone call to my realtor friend. I told him I'd left an envelope of cash with the deli man downstairs to cover Rosa's deposit and a few months' rent. If she stayed, I wanted her to have a real chance at pursuing her dreams. It was the very least I could do for not saving the restaurant.

My chest tightened as the minute-hand continued to tick, creeping ever more quickly to the moment I'd be leaving everything behind. When the train pulled into the station, I gripped the three tickets in my hand, saying a silent prayer. I'd never prayed so hard in my life. Then, before I took my first step up onto the train, I looked one last time over my shoulder down the platform. At first, I only saw a short line of the stragglers behind me waiting to embark, but near the entrance a flash of red caught my eye. I saw it bobbing up and down, and I took a step up to see better.

It was Camille, slowly making her way through the throngs of people waiting for another train. Her crutches made her unsteady on her feet. My heart raced, then plummeted. What if Rosa had only sent Camille? What if she didn't come, too? Either way, I rationalized, I'd still be connected to her. There was still a chance.

"Camille!" I shouted over the heads of the other travelers, waving my hand frantically in the air and pulling myself up onto the train steps. "Over here!"

Her head shot up and her face broke out into a wide smile when she caught sight of me. The man behind me told me to move forward to get off the train. I was holding up the line.

"So sorry," I said, hopping down to weave through the suitcases and waiting people.

When I reached her, Camille's face was bright red, almost the same shade as her hair.

"Are you okay?" I asked, taking her arm.

"Dandy. Never been better," she joked, out of breath.

"Well, I'm sure glad to see you. You're a sight for sore eyes." I glanced around, looking for her luggage. "Do you have any bags?"

"We have everything we need."

I turned on my heel to see the face that had visited me in my dreams.

We didn't say anything for a long moment. Rosa was here, on this platform. She had come. I reached out to touch her face to make sure I hadn't hallucinated the whole thing, and she leaned into my hand for a second before the train's whistle jolted us back into our bodies.

"Let's get a move on. We're going to miss our train going to who-knows-where?" Camille said as she looped an arm through Rosa's, pulling us all forward.

Chapter 28

After

Riverbend was nothing I expected and everything we needed. At first, Camille and I found the place suffocatingly small. However, the community welcomed us with open arms.

Lou's aunt's house was large and well-maintained. When we pulled up to it in the taxicab after our train ride, Camille and I couldn't speak. The red brick and white columns seemed to expand forever.

"This is yours?" I managed to ask Lou, who'd explained the entire situation during the two-hour train ride.

"Ours," he replied.

I refused to call it ours until we'd tied the knot in a small civil service downtown a year later. Our relationship took a lot of twists and turns those first few months as I worked to forgive him—and trust him, again—but there was no denying our feelings. The fire still burned bright between us. Plus, we had the rest of our lives for him to make it up to me, which I had no doubt he'd do.

Although, for weeks after our escape, I had a hard time sleeping, worried that Sal would find us here, severing what little hope I'd clung to that first day. But after a few months, my worry faded, and I focused on making the house a home for us. Sal had wormed his way into Lou's life back in Chicago but now that he was gone, Lou could finally breathe again. We all could.

We wrote to Pa and our sister to let them know we were safe, but nothing more. This seemed to work for everyone.

The house's kitchen became my refuge, even though the cast-iron stove and oven combo was ancient. It ran on coal, which made cooking a chore. I missed the industrial ovens and stoves at Bella each time I lit the archaic beast. Nonetheless, it became my kitchen. I relished in it, cooking dinner for us each night. The local Italian Shoppe in the downtown district of Riverbend had fresh Italian ingredients, so I was even able to experiment.

On our six-month anniversary, Lou slid a slip of paper across the table to me at dinner.

"What's this?" I asked.

"I ordered it last week. It should be here in six days," he responded, a grin playing at the corners of his lips.

I flipped the paper over to see a picture of a state-of-the-art Frigidaire Flair stove and oven set up.

"How can we afford this?" I asked, knowing that Lou was still working on getting access to his aunt's full estate due to a handful of greedy distant cousins he had never met.

"Let's just say I had some money tied up in an apartment in Chicago. But the gamble went my way."

"Thank you. I mean it. But can you promise to never bet on anything ever again?" I asked, and Camille laughed.

"You got it," he said.

That stove changed my life. I filled my days cooking and learning to bake again, of all things, in that kitchen. While I didn't find a job at a restaurant like I had hoped, it didn't matter. When people found out that I could cook, I had no shortage of catering requests. The recipes that I worked on after meeting Lou, the ones that expanded my cooking beyond Italian fare, became town favorites. People even began to share their family recipes with me. At one point, I had so many recipes written on index cards that Camille bought me a tin box to keep them all in. I was determined to cook my way through them eventually.

Turns out I didn't need a restaurant to be a chef after all.

Between my catering and Lou's new job as an accountant for the city, we'd done all right. Camille found a job as a waitress and had a baby girl in the spring of 1962. She named her Jacqueline and called her Jackie after the father she'd never get to meet. Not long after, they moved back to the city so Camille could go to school. She became a delivery nurse, something she fell in love with after giving birth. Jackson's parents stepped in to support them where ours had failed.

We visited her and Jackie often. So did Pa and Ivana. Pa never got the restaurant back since we foiled their plan, but after a few years of cooking in various kitchens around the city, he saved enough to open a small food stand. He seemed happy to be serving people good food again. That's what it was always about for him: the food and the people.

Ma spent decades resenting the fact that Camille and I had "left the family." She never came around and her marriage to my father suffered from it, especially after he openly defied her wishes and maintained a relationship with all his daughters. Ivana ended up fulfilling Ma's dreams by marrying a boy from the neighborhood and going to secretarial school.

Unfortunately, Vanie never had any children, and Ma died not having met Jackie or my daughter, Barbara.

After all these years, I can now see how Ma gave me the greatest gift of all: a relentless focus on building the life—and family—I needed.

Because in the end, it's all we get to keep.

Acknowledgements

This book would not have been possible without the unwavering support of my husband, Thomas, and encouragement from my son, Theodore. Thank you both for continuing to put up with my "word count" anxiety.

I'd also like to thank my friends and family who read many drafts of the book, scenes, and gave feedback on my cover design. Your thoughtful messages and critiques helped in more ways than you will ever know. And a special thank you to Jan Walker who helped me edit it at the last minute!

And finally, thank you to the local independent bookstores in Fredericksburg, VA, for all of your support along the way.

About the author

Stephanie Nelson is a speechwriter, creative marketing consultant, and budding romance novelist. She holds a B.A. in Journalism and Political Science from the University of Iowa and is currently studying for her MFA in Creative Writing at Southern New Hampshire University. She resides in Fredericksburg, VA with her husband, son, and two dogs.

Connect with me

Follow me on Instagram @AuthorStephanieNelson &
@Stephlovessbooks

Also by Stephanie Nelson

A Recipe Called Home